STEALING HEARTS

USA TODAY BESTSELLING AUTHOR
LEX MARTIN

Stealing Hearts © 2025 Lex Martin

All rights reserved. No part of this book may be reproduced or transmitted in any form or by any electronic or mechanical means, including information storage and retrieval systems, without express written permission from the author, except for the use of brief quotations in a book review.

Without in any way limiting the author's exclusive rights under copyright, any use of this publication to "train" generative artificial intelligence (AI) technologies to generate text is expressly prohibited. The author reserves all rights to license uses of this work for generative AI training and development of machine learning language models.

This is a work of fiction. Names, characters, businesses, places, events and incidents are either the products of the author's imagination or used in a fictitious manner. Any resemblance to actual persons, living or dead, or actual events is purely coincidental.

www.lexmartinwrites.com

Copy Editing: RJ Locksley

Proofreading: Julia Griffis, The Romance Bibliophile

Cover Design: Najla Qamber Designs

Cover Photography: Lindee Robinson

Models: Nicole Moffatt & Tommy Spence

January 2025 Discreet Paperback Edition

ISBN: 978-1-950554-26-3

To the wildflower in all of us. You're stronger than you think.

FOREWORD

Dear Readers,

Welcome to the Wild at Heart series, a collection of companion standalones about the Walker brothers, gritty cowboys with rough edges, dirty mouths, and big hearts.

I've had so much fun crafting their town of Wild Heart, Texas. I was born and raised in San Antonio, and after many years away, my husband and I moved back home. Being able to reminisce about all the small towns I visited while growing up was one of the best parts of writing this book. (Next to visualizing the Walker brothers, of course!)

I hope you love the Wild at Heart series and my wild Walker brothers as much as I do!

PLAYLIST

Good Luck, Babe! | Chappell Roan
Way Down We Go | Kaleo
Where Is My Mind? | Pixies
Love Shack | The B-52's
Wildflower | Billie Eilish
Fuck It I Love You | Lana Del Rey
Stargazing | Myles Smith
Perfectly Broken | Banners
Drinkin' Problems | Midland
Need You Now | Lady Antebellum
Somewhere Only We Know | Keane
Sweet Home | SYML

PROLOGUE

FRESHMAN YEAR OF HIGH SCHOOL

PAIGE

W ITH A SHAKY HAND, I wipe the sweat from my forehead.

"Are you sure you want to do this?" my best friend Baylee Reyes asks as she eyes me from the other side of my small bedroom. "You look like you're gonna hurl."

"I'll never be able to live with myself if I don't tell him." I take a few deep breaths to calm down. "You think Amber's cheating, right?" Baylee has always had a sixth sense about things. "Because if this is all in my head—"

"I think she's a ho-bag who's sleeping around behind his back, yes."

Um. "Isn't that slut-shaming? I don't think you're supposed to say that."

Her eyebrow arches. "I can if she's cheating on Rhett Walker, the most stand-up guy in town."

That's the perfect way to describe my brother's best friend. Rhett is reliable and responsible... not to mention the most handsome man in Wild Heart, Texas. But that's beside the point. "What do I say? How do I tell him I think she's sleeping with

Kacey Miller?"

Baylee leans toward my mirror and reapplies her lip balm. "Tell him what you told me."

"What if my words get jumbled like they did when I gave my speech on the plague in history class?"

"Jot down notes this time."

My shoulders fall. "I had notes for that speech. It didn't help."

She smacks her lips together and turns to me. "My mother always tells me not to think about myself. Think about Rhett and how he's going to ruin his life if he marries that twatwaffle."

Baylee has a way with words.

Sighing, I pick at my chipped nail polish. Even though I've been secretly in love with Rhett for as long as I can remember, I think this would be easier to deal with if I hadn't seen what I did.

Amber and Rhett are high school sweethearts. Everyone says they're destined to get married.

And I have exactly two weeks to talk him out of it.

The thought of him being tied to that woman permanently almost makes my breakfast come up.

I've known Rhett my whole life. When I was little, he used to carry me on his shoulders and make me crowns from wildflowers. He'd push me in the swings and toss me into the lake. He never minded when I'd tag along with him and my brother. He even sat through my tea parties. Rhett was the one who told me I had a gift for tumbling and encouraged me to pursue gymnastics.

At first, he was just this beautiful boy with big feet and shadows behind his dark eyes, who'd clomp through our house with my older brother Danny.

Rhett was the boy who only ever seemed to smile at me and my brother, which made every laugh I wrung from him meaningful. I knew his home life was rough. That his mother took off when he was young, leaving him and his four younger brothers. I hated that anyone had caused him pain.

In first grade, our teacher was getting married, and I decided right then and there I was going to marry Rhett Walker someday. It didn't matter that I was six and he was almost sixteen. He was mine. He just didn't know it yet.

As I got older, and he started to get girlfriends, it dawned on me I was too young, and nothing I ever did would change that.

But when he met Amber, and I saw how he looked at her, I knew it was over. He was in love with her. It was obvious to the whole town.

Amber's beautiful. She has thick blonde hair, a great smile, and a perfect body. She was the most popular girl in school, which was fitting because Rhett was the captain of the football team. The only problem is she's nice to your face and a bitch behind your back, which makes me wonder if Rhett knows the real Amber.

The night I heard they got engaged, I locked myself in the bathroom and cried.

I'd finally come to terms with everything when I saw Amber nearly locking lips with Kacey behind the Shake Shack.

A car door slams outside, and my heart races like I'm sprinting the last leg of a marathon. My brother's laughter spills across the yard and through my open window.

"Oh, God. They're here." I press my hand to my stomach.

Baylee grabs my shoulders. "You can do this. Wait until your stepmonster leaves, and then sit his ass down and tell him."

I nod frantically as Baylee saunters across my room, slides open the window that faces the side yard, and hops out of it like she's a seasoned cat burglar. "Why don't you ever use the front door?" I call out.

She turns back to me with a laugh. "That's too predictable."

And then I'm alone.

My hands tremble as I grab a stack of notecards. At first, my writing is so wobbly, I can't even read them. So I crumple them up, toss them in the trash, and start again. By the time I'm done, I'm pretty sure I've developed a stomach ulcer.

Someone knocks on my door. "Wildflower, you hungry?" My eyes sting at Rhett's nickname for me. "Your brother and I ordered some hoagies. Want one?"

This is the perfect opportunity. "I'll be there in a sec!" I shove the notecards in the back pocket of my jeans and glance at myself in the mirror. My red hair is straggly, but it's too late to do anything about that now. I pull it into a high ponytail and smooth down my t-shirt.

I can do this. Rhett deserves to know.

Rhett, Danny, and our half-brother Tyson are hovering at our small kitchen table. At the sight of Rhett, my heart skips a beat like it always does. His shaggy dark hair hangs over his eyes, and when he sees me, his mouth tugs up in a half smile and he winks. Ugh, I love him so much. I hate that I can't get over him. He's freaking ten years older. I know he'll always think of me as Danny's kid sister, and it sucks.

Behind him, my stepmother Irma pours something in a Big Gulp container. If I had to guess, I'd say it's bourbon and Coke.

"Boys, I'll be at the church potluck this afternoon, but if y'all need anything, just text." She's so nice to my brothers. I'm sure my father had no idea she was Satan's twin sister when he married her. RIP, Dad. He passed away a few years ago after a construction accident at work, and now I'm stuck with bitchy Irma, who thinks this house belongs to her even though it's been in my mother's family for two generations.

When she sees me, she stops smiling. "Paige, did you vacuum the house like I told you to?" I nod, but she frowns. "Then make sure you do the dishes too."

I glance behind her at the huge pile of crap in the sink. "Why don't the boys ever have any chores? Danny and Tyson made that mess last night." They got a wild hair up their ass and decided to bake cookies, but they forgot the baking powder, and the cookies didn't rise correctly.

"Because Danny works all week, and Tyson has extra homework now that he's in the honors program." Tyson, the little shit, smirks at me. He's only twelve, and a huge pain in my ass, but I still love him. Irma juts out her hip. "Besides, it's a woman's job to keep house."

"Then why don't you do it?"

The table goes quiet. I'm digging my own grave here, but I'm so tired of doing all the chores. No one cares how much time I put in at the gym for cheerleading. No one cares how much time I spend cleaning the locker rooms and mats because we can't afford to pay. No one cares that I might be able to go to college on a cheer scholarship. The second I get home, I'm expected to clean up after everyone else.

"Watch your mouth, young lady. You're lucky you have someone to take care of you."

Meaning that my dad died, and I have no one else. *Thanks for that reminder, Irma. So kind of you.*

I look down at the ground. Besides Danny and Rhett, no one ever looks out for me. My nose stings.

"We'll help you," Rhett says as he elbows Danny.

My brother nods as he unwraps his sandwich. "We should've done the dishes last night, squirt. It's not fair to you."

Tyson's eyes bulge, and he jumps out of his seat with a sandwich that leaves a trail of lettuce in its wake. "Sorry, I'm going to the potluck with Mom."

See what I mean? Pain in my ass.

I can't even be mad at Danny. He hasn't been feeling well lately, which is why he moved back home after college.

As Irma heads for the garage, she calls out, "I want the dishes done by the time we're back."

The second the door closes, I give her the finger. Rhett's warm chuckle almost makes me smile.

Until I remember what I have to do.

"Cheer up, wildflower. Danny and I will get this place cleaned up in no time." Rhett's deep voice is so soothing, it makes me emotional.

Don't cry, Paige. "Thanks," I whisper. Needing a minute, I wander into the kitchen. "What can I get y'all to drink?"

I'm not sure why I ask because I know what they want. When Danny and Rhett both call out "root beer!" at the same time, I've already grabbed two glass bottles out of the fridge. After I pour myself some water, I return to the table.

Danny is sitting at the far end. My older brother has auburn hair like me, but instead of looking like a carrot, he's handsome. Rhett parks next to him, and I take the chair across from Rhett. Having a table between us is good. I need some space to say what I need to say.

Today, he's wearing a gray, long-sleeved Henley that's seen better days. There's a hole in the elbow I'd like to patch up for him. My high school offers a sewing class, so I'm taking it as an elective, which helps when I have to alter my clothes from the Goodwill.

I don't have to see the rest of Rhett to know he's wearing faded jeans and scuffed brown boots. He works on his family's ranch, so he's always looking like he just rolled in some hay. It's terribly sexy.

"You okay?" His deep voice sends chills up and down my arms.

I wish I could sit next to him so I could smell his cologne better. If I could drown in that woodsy scent, I would.

Clearing my throat, I nod. "I'll survive. I always do." I reach into the bag of sandwiches and pull out a roast beef. "Thanks for lunch. What do I owe y'all?"

Danny grabs me in a headlock and noogies my head. "It's on me, kid."

A beleaguered sigh leaves my lips. People say you shouldn't want to grow up too soon, but I'm tired of being fifteen. I'm expected to be responsible but don't have any freedom.

After a minute, the guys start talking about Rhett's bachelor party. "No strippers," he tells my brother. "Amber would shit a brick house if I get my face between tits that aren't hers."

Danny chuckles, and I want to crawl under the table and die. Rhett looks at me sheepishly. "Sorry, Paige. I shouldn't be saying that kind of stuff around you."

I shrug because what am I supposed to say?

Danny tosses a pickle at his best friend. "Well, if I was dating someone with a rack like Amber's, I wouldn't bother with strippers either."

I can't help but glance down at my flat chest. Will my boobs ever get bigger if I stick with gymnastics and cheer? That's the only downside to what I do. My body is muscular and lean, which I love, but bigger boobs would be great. I'm never going to find a boyfriend if I don't get a few curves.

Rhett reaches over and smacks Danny. "Stop talking about Amber's tits or I'll kick your ass."

They shit-talk each other for a while, and as I'm nibbling on a tomato, Rhett shakes his head. "I can't believe we're walking down the aisle in two weeks. I can't fucking wait. We went to taste the cake the other day, and she looked so happy. I love putting that smile on her face."

I'm going to be sick.

"Amber's cheating on you." When I realize what I've just said, I clamp a hand over my mouth.

My brother coughs, and Rhett's eyes cut to me. "What did you say?"

I swallow past a boulder-sized lump in my throat. "I, uh, I could be wrong, but I think she's cheating on you with... with Kacey Miller."

His eyes go glacial, and he stares at me like I'm a complete stranger. I lean back in my chair as he growls, "Why would you say that?"

Danny frowns. "Jesus, Paige, what the fuck?"

I look down at my lap and rush to spit it out. "I saw her with

Kacey a few weeks ago, and when she saw me, she jumped away from him like she was guilty of something. And then she was really nice to me afterward. Amber never talks to me, never, but after that, she was saccharine sweet."

Finally, I brave a look at Rhett, who frowns. "And?"

And? That's not enough? I scramble to think of what else to say. "Amber and Kacey are always talking when no one's around. Haven't you noticed that?"

He looks at me like I'm an idiot and rubs a hand over his face. "Paige, that's a shitty thing to say. You shouldn't make that kind of accusation without hard facts."

My eyes sting, but then my brother makes it worse.

Danny's voice gets soft, almost sympathetic. "Squirt, you're just a kid. You must've misunderstood what you saw. And based on how we all know you feel about Rhett, I think you're letting those feelings get in the way."

My breath catches in my throat, and I glare at him. "Danny!" When I glance at Rhett, he's staring at his meal like it personally offended him.

Danny shrugs. "Just calling it like I see it."

Everything I've said is bad enough, but I have to make things worse. "Amber doesn't appreciate you, Rhett. She always complains about how much you work and that you smell like cow shit. That you're too busy to take her on dates and that she wishes you'd get a life. But to your face, she's all smiles." It's so much like Irma and how fake she is, it's a small wonder they're not related.

If looks could kill, the one in Rhett's eyes would pulverize me. "How do you know she said those things?"

I swallow. There's no way I can tell him Baylee overheard Amber while working in her mom's salon. "This is a small town. People talk."

Danny winces. "Paige, you're embarrassing yourself."

I swipe at the tears that tumble down my face as I promise myself to never confront someone like this again. What was I thinking? "I'm sorry. You're right. I'm just a kid. What the fuck do I know?" I get up so fast my chair clatters to the ground, and I race to my room and slam the door.

Before my brother can find me to talk, I sneak out the window and sprint into the forest behind our house. If I could run away right now, to another city or state or planet, I would, but I have nowhere to go.

But one thing is sure. I'm going to have to avoid Rhett Walker and his new wife for the rest of my life.

Chapter One

RHETT

SEVEN YEARS LATER

CLEAN CUTS. I give my younger brother Beau a look. "A cow didn't do this."

He tosses me my gloves. "Who do you think did?"

As we run new razor wire between the fence posts to patch what someone obviously cut, I start to wonder if I'm in over my head. These days, it seems I'm drowning at every turn. We spent half the night chasing down cattle. "What are the odds it was those high school kids who got in trouble for tagging the grocery store?"

"Slim to none."

I was afraid he was gonna say that. "I'd hate to think it was Frank."

"He's pissed about the rent increase."

With the back of my arm, I wipe the sweat from my brow. "Dad gave the Fletchers that cottage for a steal. It's been ten years. We'd be fools to not increase the rent." Our father Augustus was an asshole, but if you drank or played poker with him, he'd do dumb shit like let you rent our cabin for a song. It makes me wonder if good ol' Gus gambled away the money he got from the second mortgage.

"I agree."

"And if he moves out, that's even better because then you could have the cabin." Beau's been living in a camper on our property, but he works his ass off on the ranch and at the firehouse. He deserves a place of his own. "I've never known Frank to be an asshole like this." Which leaves one other suspect. "What about the McAllisters?"

Beau's quiet a stretch. "Cash has a bone to pick with you, so I'd say he's a good bet."

That asshole. I grind my teeth as I think about the last time we got into it.

Once Beau and I finish inspecting the rest of the fence, we head back to the house. He lifts his chin. "Look on the bright side. At least we caught all of the cattle."

"This time. We were lucky."

After I wash up, I grab a loaf of bread and sandwich fixings, throw that on the table, and sit just as our younger brother Jace waltzes through the front door.

"Nice of you to join us," I grunt.

He flips the chair backwards and joins us. "Sorry I'm late. The traffic from Austin was a bitch."

"How'd your show go last night?" I ask as I toss him the bread. My brother's the lead singer for a band. Even though I need his help on the ranch, part of me hopes he'll hit it big and be able to contribute more financially. Plus, he's really fucking talented.

I remember what it was like to think I could do something other than herd cattle and shovel horse shit all day. If my brother can make a living doing something else, more power to him.

Jace slaps some ham on his bread. "Great. I slept with three groupies last night." I roll my eyes, and Jace chuckles. "Kidding. I only slept with two. But some A&R guys asked for our demo."

"Good luck. Hope something comes out of it." I don't mention how much gas his van guzzles when he drives it all over the state for those gigs.

Beau looks at his phone. "What time is that meeting?"

"Two o'clock. Can you still come?"

"Yeah, I don't need to get down to the fire station until six."

Jace downs half the sandwich and talks around his food. "What meeting?"

I scrub my face. "The one where I set aside my pride and beg Harlan Calhoun for a loan."

He stops chewing. "Are things that bad? I thought with Beau moonlighting as a firefighter, we were doing okay."

Leaning over, I grab the damn letter from the bank. "Between Dad's nursing home bill, that second mortgage no one knew about, and my alimony payments, I'm drowning. Shady Pines was gonna sue my ass if I didn't pay the rest of Dad's nursing home balance." It pains me to admit I can't even buy my boys clothes this summer. Hopefully Amber will use the money I give her for the kids and not her nails. "Dad's life insurance should've covered everything, but he canceled it." I unfold the paper I stared at half the night. "We have thirty days before the bank forecloses."

"Shit. Are you serious? You said things were bad, but you always come through." Jace reaches into his back pocket and pulls out a few hundred bucks. "It's all I have, but it's yours."

"Thanks, bro, but I need more than that. Keep your money. You earned it."

He slouches in his chair. "Guess this means no ranch rodeos this fall."

"Sorry. Can't afford it." Sure, we might be able to win, but ranch rodeos are more about bragging rights than payouts like the regular rodeo. And I can't justify the expense of entering.

"Damn. I was really looking forward to kicking the McAllisters' asses again."

That's always a highlight. "Maybe next year."

"What about Zey? Is he coming home now? Can he pitch in again?"

Meaning, is our brother Isaiah returning now that Dad has

passed? "I talked to him last week. He's in some hellhole in Ecuador doing God knows what. Probably teaching people how to BASE-jump off cliffs into a kiddie pool. But he's in the middle of some 'personal crisis' he was too cagey to explain and says he needs a little time to work through some red tape. Maybe he'll be back before Christmas. Except we need the money now."

I can't be pissed at Isaiah. He's pitched in financially more times than I care to remember. Considering our father disowned him, I'm just grateful he didn't disappear altogether.

Jace makes another sandwich. "Too bad Mav has one more year of college. If he could get drafted, we'd be set."

Our youngest brother Maverick is a hell of a football player. He'll be a senior at Lone Star State this fall. "I don't wanna take his money either, but yeah, a little liquidity wouldn't hurt. We could pay him back."

"Why didn't he go for the draft this year? I mean, the Broncos just won a national championship."

"He needs his degree." I take a swig of root beer that reminds me of my best friend Danny, and the thought of him only makes me feel worse. I don't let myself think about his little sister, who I haven't seen in years. I'm failing in all the ways that matter, and Paige is just a reflection of that. "No one is guaranteed shit in the NFL. At least with a degree, Mav will have options if the pros don't work out for him."

I went to college for a semester, but Dad was too drunk to watch my brothers and keep the ranch going without my help. Maybe I'd have more options too right now if I'd gotten that degree.

Jace grabs the letter from the bank and whistles. "Assuming we survive this, we're gonna put Zey back on the title of the ranch, right?"

"Damn straight." Fuck what my father wanted. He got us into this mess.

"So what's the plan?" Beau asks as he finishes his lunch and balls up his napkin.

I shrug. "What's that saying? Beg, borrow, or steal? I figure I'll try the first two before I become an outlaw."

Beau chuckles. "You mean you don't wanna add to the rich Wild Heart history of outlaws and bandits?"

Jace snickers as he chomps on his sandwich. "You know Rhett loves rules too much to take a walk on the wild side."

My rules kept my little brothers alive when they were growing up, but I don't bother pointing this out. "Before our bank appointment, we need to stop by the McAllister place."

Beau nods. "Hell yes, we do."

Jace shoves the rest of the sandwich in his mouth. "I'm game, but what's going on?"

Beau balls up his napkin. "You missed all the fun last night and this morning, little brother." He fills him in as we gear up to confront our asshole neighbors.

Twenty minutes later, I'm banging on the McAllisters' front door. Beau and Jace stand behind me with their shotguns. Can't be too careful in these parts. Wild Heart, Texas, has its roots in the lawlessness of the Wild West, and I'd be a fool to ignore that.

Cash's younger brother Trig opens the door with a yawn as he scratches his bare belly. He's clearly not expecting us because his eyes widen. "The fuck do y'all want?"

"Morning, Trig." I cross my arms. "Is Cash home? I need a word."

He slams the door in our face and yells for his brother, who's a few years younger than me. Cash and Trig also have a younger sister, Honey.

Our families have been feuding since Wild Heart came into existence. I'd been hoping we could forget that foolishness, but then Cash had to fall dick first on Amber.

The asshole finally emerges. "Don't recall inviting y'all over."

"Don't remember asking you to fuck my wife, but that didn't stop you."

Cash huffs out a breath. "I'm not blowing smoke up your ass when I say she told me you were splitting up."

I take a sick pleasure in that notch on his nose where I broke it. "Have you been messing with our fences? Someone cut them last night."

He smirks. "Can't say that was my work, but kudos to whoever did the honors."

Motherfucker. I lean closer to make sure he hears me. "I'm only gonna say this one time, McAllister. If I ever catch you messing with what's mine, I will end you. You hear me?" I don't really plan to shoot him dead, but you gotta act like you will around here or the vultures will descend. People have been trying to get their hands on my family's property for decades. "Stay the fuck away from my ranch, Cash."

"No one wants your shithole, Rhett." He holds open his arms. "In case you haven't noticed, I'm doing mighty fine here."

It pains me to admit his place is a helluva lot nicer than mine, but there's one thing I learned long ago—you can never trust a snake in the grass.

With a grunt, I tug at my collar that's cutting off the circulation to my brain. Been replaying that conversation with Cash all morning. If the McAllisters didn't cut my fences, and that's a big if, then who did?

Beau scratches his neck and then leans over to whisper, "Did we really need to wear suits?"

"Yes." We sit on the bench in front of Harlan's office at the Cornerstone Bank & Trust. I watch the president of the company, my father's old friend, through the giant glass windows of his office. He's on the phone, laughing, as he stretches out behind the executive desk. Harlan has to be in his sixties, but he doesn't seem to be slowing down and still commutes between here and the corporate office in Dallas. He and his brother Prescott have built a small banking empire in Texas.

We're in one of the alcoves that surrounds a large seating area in the middle. Across the reception area, I spot that little fuck Kacey Miller, who's chatting up his secretary. He's some low-level executive. He's reason enough not to come here, but I don't have family friends at any other banks.

Amber finally admitted she'd messed around with Kacey before we got married. Unfortunately, I never had the honor of breaking his nose, and now that I need this loan from his boss, I probably shouldn't be plotting to kick Kacey's ass.

I tap the manila folder against my leg and pray I can figure this out. I don't know what I'll do with myself if I let down my boys and my brothers.

Beau nudges me. "I have a good feeling about this."

I don't respond because, frankly, I think we're a bad bet.

Finally, Harlan's assistant waves us forward. "Mr. Calhoun can see you now."

I push through the giant glass door, and Harlan grins at us. "Good to see you, boys."

I'm thirty-two, but I guess I'll always be a boy in Harlan's mind. "Thank you, sir. Good to see you too. How's Mary Sue?"

"Great. She dropped off some homemade macaroni and cheese for lunch."

"She's always been a mighty fine cook." Must be nice. Amber hated doing anything domestic. Not sure why she thought marrying a rancher was a good idea. "Tell her hi for us."

My mood turns darker with thoughts of my ex. The best thing she ever did was sign our divorce papers three years ago. My boys are my pride and joy, but their mother is the worst thing to ever happen to me. After that experience, you'd have to hold me at gunpoint to even consider getting married. No, thank you. I'm done with marriage.

Harlan nods. "How have y'all been? Things must be rough after your daddy passed, rest his soul. Gus was a good man. He'll be missed."

I'm not sure Augustus Walker was a good man or that he'll be missed, but I hold my tongue. The town already knows he was a drunk. "Thank you. We're holding down the fort. Beau, Jace, and I have things covered." By covered, I mean we're barely making ends meet and working ourselves to death.

"That Maverick sure can play football. Hoo boy! That championship game had me yelling at the TV."

Beau nods. "We're mighty proud of him."

Harlan rubs his chin. "Did ya bring the financials I asked for?"

"Yes, sir." I hand him my folder. "It's all right there." Our profit and loss, which, unfortunately, is mostly loss at the moment.

He frowns as he flips through the paperwork. "Hmm. I see."

Shit.

After another agonizing minute, he closes the folder and sits back in his chair. "Fellas, I wish I had some good news for you, but you're mortgaged to the hilt."

"I know our financials don't look great, but it's mostly a cash flow issue. If we can gut it out until the fall when our cattle go to market, we'll have the funds we need."

He rubs his chin. "Why didn't you do it last month when you'd get the best price?"

I guess there's no way around that question. "The drought last year hit us hard, so the cattle weren't heavy enough." Not to mention I couldn't afford to get our trailer fixed to haul them. But taking them to auction in October or November is gonna suck too because the prices are usually low then.

He's quiet for a stretch, then leans forward with a sigh. "I sure wish I could help y'all. Rhett, you've done a fine job looking out for your brothers all these years." He means when my father was too drunk to get out of bed. "I sure do admire you, but the bank can't extend any more credit."

Fuck.

I nod slowly, wondering how much my life insurance would pay out. Maybe if I accidentally drive off Devil's Cliff, my brothers could pull through and save the ranch.

That's a dark thought.

Goddamn it. This can't be the end. What did I tell my brothers at lunch? That I'd set aside my pride and beg?

Resisting the urge to tug at my collar, I take a deep breath. "Would you consider a personal loan or a bridge loan?" I rush to talk before he turns me down. "Harlan, our families go way back. My grandfather taught you to drive a tractor. You went hunting with our father for years. Doesn't that count for something? I'll do anything to get the ranch back on track. If you could just see it in your heart to help us out, I would be forever in your debt."

He scratches his stubbled cheek. "What else do you have besides the ranch as collateral? The bank almost owns it outright at this point."

Beau sits forward. "We could put our horses, machinery, and trucks up as collateral."

Jesus Christ, we'd be ruined if we screw this up, but what choice do I have? "Beau's right. Those assets run well over two hundred grand, and we really only need a hundred K."

"Only need a hundred K?" Harlan says with a chuckle. "Do I look like I'm made of money?"

I ignore the impulse to stare at his Rolex. "No, sir. We're not trying to take advantage of you. We just need a break. Our father's nursing home bill knocked the wind out of us, but with this money, we'll set things right and get back on track."

I don't mention that my father took out a second mortgage and then blew the money on God knows what, but Harlan has our balance sheet, so he knows the big picture.

Harlan blows out a breath and taps his finger on his desk. "I'd be open to it—"

"Thank God," Beau says.

"Son, you didn't let me finish. I'd be open to it *if* Rhett here was a married man. Call me old-fashioned, but I have to listen to my gut. It's never let me down before. And my gut tells me that I should be wary of loaning that kind of money to a household of bachelors."

He gives me a look that makes me think he's heard the rumors of Jace carousing around town. Fucking hell.

I'm scrambling to think of something to turn this conversation around when Beau slaps me on the back. "You didn't hear? Rhett's been dating a nice girl for a while now. Things are getting serious, and he's gonna pop the question soon."

Harlan's eyebrows lift. "Really? Well, that's a whole different ballgame, son. I think I can work with that. Who's the lucky woman?"

That's a damn good question. "I... I don't think you know her, sir."

He stands and reaches over to shake my hand. "Congratulations." He stares at me long and hard. "I'm looking forward to getting that wedding invitation."

Son of a bitch.

Chapter Two
PAIGE

W**ITH MY ARMS** full of boxes, I limp by Marcus for the third time. I shouldn't be surprised he doesn't notice I'm moving out.

Because he doesn't care.

Back and forth I go. My ankle hurts like a bitch, but I can't carry these boxes and my crutches at the same time.

Finally, half an hour later, he finally looks up from his giant flatscreen. "What are you doing?"

"What does it look like?" When he doesn't say anything, I keep going.

"Paige."

I pause and turn to him. "I'm moving out."

"What? Why?"

He looks genuinely confused. Between the two of us, he's supposed to be the smart one. I roll my eyes and carry the last of my crap to my car. It's a sad reflection on my life that all of my belongings fit in my old Kia Rio hatchback.

"Paige," he calls out from behind me as I shove the box in my passenger seat. "What's wrong?"

I hate having confrontations, but I suppose there's no way

around this. I close my car door and turn around. "I heard what you said last night."

He follows me back into his apartment, where I grab my purse and my crutches. "I have no idea what you're talking about."

I'm tired, my ankle is throbbing, and I don't care about salvaging this relationship, which makes the words a little easier to say. "Do you remember what you told your friend when he asked if you were bringing me home for your parents' anniversary dinner?"

Marcus freezes. "You heard that?"

Yes, asshole. I heard that. But there's no sense in being antagonistic. "Thank you for letting me live with you last year when that tree bulldozed the house I was renting. I really appreciate you helping me then, but I've obviously overstayed my welcome. I left you the money I owed you for rent on the kitchen table."

He and I were never right together. I should've moved out months ago, like I told my friends I was going to, but I hate making waves. I knew I didn't love Marcus, and he didn't love me, but I guess I was hoping we'd break through that and level up.

All of my friends are falling in love and pairing off, and I want that too. I'm starting to worry something's wrong with me because I've never been in love. And when I say love, I mean adult love, not whatever idiotic thing I felt for Rhett Walker.

I hoped I could make it happen with Marcus if I stuck it out long enough.

Now I realize he's not the kind of man I want for my happily ever after.

"Baby, don't be like that." He tries to grab my hand, but I push him off. He follows me back outside. "It's just... my parents won't understand what you're doing with yourself after graduation."

I really don't need another person questioning my life goals. "Good luck finding the perfect trophy wife. I'm sure she's out there somewhere." I shove my crutches into the footwell of the passenger side. They barely fit.

"Look, you can come with me to their brunch if you want."

"Gee, thanks. Appreciate the invite," I say sarcastically as I drop into the driver's side with a groan.

When I try to close the door, he blocks it. "Paige, are you seriously going to walk away like this? I'm about to make junior vice president at the company."

"See, unlike you, I don't care one way or another if you're rich and climbing the corporate ladder."

"But we'll have more time to spend together once I get that raise."

I laugh darkly. "We have plenty of time together now, but you're too busy playing video games or hanging out with your bros to notice me. And that's fine. Live life the way you want to, only I'm tired of feeling like an afterthought."

"What if I took you on that vacation I know you want to go on?"

A sad smile graces my lips. "You can't buy my love, Marcus. It's not for sale."

With the windows down, I drive along the dusty road to my hometown. I avoid coming back to Wild Heart whenever possible because there are too many painful memories, but now I don't have a choice. It's too expensive to stay in Charming. All of my friends just graduated from college and moved away, so I'd have to get a place by myself, and I don't have the money for first and last months' rent.

When I spot a hill covered in wildflowers, I crank the steering wheel and pull off onto the side of the road. It takes me twenty minutes of limping around, but I manage to put together a pretty bouquet. Once I'm back in my car, I reach into my sewing bag and pull out a ribbon that I tie to the base of the flowers.

With a smile, I sniff the soft petals. Wildflowers are so pretty and cheerful. Most people would probably describe them as delicate, but I love that they often flourish in the toughest conditions.

It's been a while since I've visited Danny, and I think he could use something cheerful.

On the outskirts of town, I turn up the big driveway to the cemetery where he's buried. My sweet older brother died of leukemia a few years ago.

Danny and my mom are resting along the back. My dad's on the other side. Irma wouldn't let him be buried next to Mama.

When I reach Danny's plot, my eyes immediately go to the empty root beer bottles, and my heart pangs in my chest. "I guess you've had other visitors."

I've done an impressive job of avoiding Rhett over the years, but sometimes, the reminders of him and my brother hit me hard.

After I clean off the headstones, I place the bouquet between them. "Mama, I'm sorry I don't have flowers for you too. You and Danny can share. I know you're not supposed to cut bluebonnets, but I got a few for y'all. Daddy always said they were your favorite."

My mom died in childbirth with me, and my dad died in a construction accident at work when I was eleven, which left us with Irma.

I lean against Danny's headstone and stare at the empty cemetery. "I graduated from college last week. Irma and Ty didn't come. No surprise there." My ankle throbs, and I rub it. "I was supposed to start a new job this summer in Austin at this amazing cheer camp, but I got injured. The doctor says I'll need physical therapy, but I can't afford it." I can't afford anything right now. I shouldn't have given Marcus money for rent, but I hated the idea of owing him anything.

"I lost that job. Can't coach cheer if you can't spot the tumblers, you know?" I pick a blade of grass. "So now I need to eat some humble pie and ask Irma if I can stay in my old room for a while. I'd ask Baylee, but her sister is visiting with her kids, and they don't have the space.

"I worked so hard to eke my way through school, thinking I could coach, and then this happened. I got a degree in communications. That's probably ironic since I hate public speaking." That's one of the reasons I love cheer. When I step out on that field at halftime, I always know what to do or say. I wish real life was like that.

I blow out a breath. "Sorry I'm complaining. At least I'm not dead, right? Gotta look on the bright side." I know I should be grateful for what I have. My brother's life got cut short. My parents' did too. I need to make the most of what I have.

I just don't know how.

An hour later, I reluctantly get back in my car and head home.

Even though I get anxious when I come back here, I have to admit that Wild Heart is picturesque. Historic buildings built of limestone brick dot both sides of the main drag with boutique shops, many of which have been painstakingly renovated. Several shops surround the courthouse, where there's a grassy area and a pretty gazebo that townsfolk light up for the holidays with twinkle lights. And there's no shortage of cute restaurants, like the Honeybee Hideaway or the Blackbird Brew Coffee Shop.

There are trading outposts and Wild West memorabilia shops. If you want to learn how the outlaws of the 1800s stole cattle or robbed trains, the Wild Heart Museum highlights the most noteworthy ones and even hosts shootout reenactments on Saturdays for tourists at the Wild West Saloon.

My favorite part is the Eden River, which snakes through half the county and cuts through town. There's a mining kiosk next to all the food trucks that teaches people how to look for gemstones along the banks, but I suspect someone tosses out a few quartz every night so visitors have something to find.

If I didn't have the history that I do here, I'd think Wild Heart was adorable.

Unfortunately, when I reach my house, the fond thoughts flee.

Ghosts loom large here. That's the tree where Danny used to push me in the swing. His old Dodge is still parked in the gravel driveway. And that rusty bike he taught me to ride lies there in a heap.

After I wrestle my crutches out of the car, where they're jammed against moving boxes, I finally get them out and limp to the porch.

"Hey," I call out through the screen door. "It's me." I'm about to open it when the overwhelming stench of wet dog hits me. Gross.

Against my better judgment, I open the creaky screen door and hobble inside, where I find a half-empty bottle of rum on the weathered coffee table. Irma's still getting sauced. No surprise there.

When the door shuts behind me, a half-dozen dogs come tearing around the corner.

Oh, shit.

They pounce on me, and I crash into a wall with a scream. My ankle throbs, and I try to shove them off me.

A raspy chuckle makes me look up. "Looks like you met our Frenchies, huh?" Irma asks as she takes her time pulling them off me. "Tyson! Get in here and help me!"

My half-brother laughs when he sees me on the floor. "You should've warned us you were coming."

I haven't seen him in months, and this is how he greets me? "Nice to see you too, Ty."

He's not so little anymore. My brother is much taller than me. Still lanky, though. "Just here for a visit?" he asks as he helps me up.

I wobble and lean against the wall as he hands me my crutches. "I was hoping I could stay in my old room for a while. I got injured, so I can't start my cheer job." No sense in telling them I lost it. Irma's always putting me down, and I can't deal with any more negativity right now.

My stepmother makes a face. "Wish we had known you wanted your room. It's occupied right now."

"What does that mean?" And really, what the fuck? This was my *mother's* house. By all rights, it should be mine.

She shrugs. "Go look."

Struggling to stay upright as the dogs nudge against me, I finally make it to the hallway. When I open the door to my bedroom, the stench of dog shit almost makes me gag. "What the hell?" There are dogs in crates everywhere, in every space on the floor, and there are two dogs on the bed barking at me.

Irma walks up behind me. "Tyson had the best idea to breed French bulldogs. Do you have any idea how much these puppies bring in? I always knew my boy would make me rich."

I whip around and almost fall over. "You mean a puppy mill. Because that's what this is, right?"

"You're always so judgmental, Paige."

"Excuse me for being upset that my room is filled with dogs."

"Seeing that you rarely come home, how was I supposed to know you were going to stay here?"

"I left you messages."

She waves a hand. "I don't listen much to messages. You know how bad the reception is here. It's always spotty."

Irma keeps spouting her excuses as I hobble out to the living room. "So there's no room? Could I sleep on the couch out here in the living room?" I hate that I have to beg, but what options do I have?

"Ty sleeps here, since his room is full of pups too."

My jaw tightens. They're hoarding dogs in my mother's house, and now I have nowhere to go. Awesome.

Without another word, I head back out to my car where I struggle not to cry. I want to call Baylee, but she's at a hair convention in Dallas.

So I drive around town until I get to the park sometime around dusk. As the shadows fall, I wonder where I went wrong with my life. How did I get to the point where I'm sleeping in my car?

I finally pull out a few boxes of my stuff so I can lean my seat back and try to sleep. But it's so hot, I strip out of most of my clothes, only leaving on my sports bra and underwear. I glance down at myself and shrug. It's like wearing a bikini.

I roll down my windows a crack so I don't suffocate. I'd like to lower them all the way, but it's probably not smart to sleep like that.

As I settle for the night, I tell myself things will be better in the morning. They have to be. Once I've slept, I'll have a clear mind and will figure out what to do.

Several hours later, I have to pee. Half-asleep, I tiptoe to the bushes and do my business before I wobble back. It's almost daybreak. I should probably get going, but I'm exhausted.

I finally fall back asleep when some asshole bangs on my window and I jerk awake. With my heart pounding in my chest, I struggle to remember where I am.

"Paige Lewis," a cranky-ass voice yells. "Why the hell are you sleeping in your car?"

When I come face to face with a pissed-off Rhett Walker, I groan and shove my hair out of my face. "What do you care? Go away."

His coal-black eyes somehow darken, and for a brief moment, I let myself look at him. His hair is short on the sides and longer on top. He has scruff along his handsome face, and his lips look just as full as they always have. And oh, my God, the tattoos on his biceps are sexy as hell.

Never gonna happen, Paige. Give it up already.

I ignore the sparks of excitement that light me up at the sight of this asshole and roll over.

Except Rhett doesn't let up. "Either you get your cute little ass in my truck, or I'm gonna break in there and carry you out."

"Go ahead and try." When I hold up my middle finger, that just makes him growl.

A second later, I feel a cool breeze.

Shit. I forgot to lock my car!

And then I'm scooped out and go airborne.

Chapter Three

PAIGE

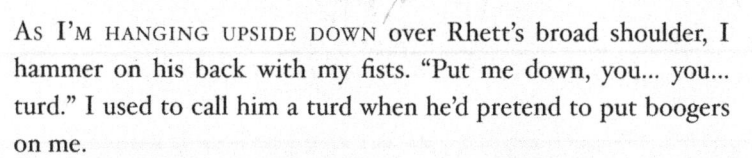

As I'm hanging upside down over Rhett's broad shoulder, I hammer on his back with my fists. "Put me down, you... you... turd." I used to call him a turd when he'd pretend to put boogers on me.

His shoulders shake. Is he laughing at me right now? I pound harder.

"Are those hits supposed to hurt? We need to get you into some self-defense classes."

He stops a few feet away in front of what I assume is his truck and lets me slide down his hard body.

Crap. Rhett still smells like that woodsy cologne, but now it's mixed with his own scent that's so... so masculine.

As soon as I'm free, I take a quick step away from him and almost fall over. He grabs my arms to steady me. But then he gets a good look at me and yanks his hands away. "Why the fuck aren't you wearing any clothes?" His eyes rake over me from top to bottom before he crosses his arms and stares at the horizon like the sight of me disgusts him.

"I'm wearing clothes. This is called a sports bra, and these..." I tug at the waistband of my boy shorts. "These are called underwear."

"Jesus Christ, Paige, I can see your nipples," he grits out.

I point at his chest that's wrapped in a snug white t-shirt. "If I look hard enough, I can see your nipples too. What's the big deal? All mammals have nipples. They really shouldn't scare a big, burly man like you."

A chuckle from the truck has me looking around him to find his younger brother hanging out the window. "Oh, hey, Jace. How's it going?"

"Hi, darling. Long time no see." He motions to his face. "Love the red hair. You look gorgeous."

I've been dyeing my hair brown for years, but Baylee said I needed to spruce myself up for graduation, and she thought red—really red—would be fun. I don't know if it's fun. I feel like a fire hydrant.

Jace's eyes skate over me, and Rhett growls for some reason. He jerks open the door to his truck and yanks his brother out of it. "Get in the back." Then he roots around for something. I do not check out his ass... for long. All I can say is it's muscular and perfectly encased by his faded jeans.

A second later, he turns around and wraps a long-sleeved flannel shirt around me. "What happened to your ankle?"

My feet are bare except for the wrap around my left foot. "Twisted it."

"Doing cheerleading?"

"No. Not this time, at least." I don't know why I'm answering his questions.

"You hurt it more than once?"

"What is this, an interrogation?" His jaw tightens, and I roll my eyes. "I fly off the tops of pyramids, Rhett, so sometimes I get injured. Of course I've twisted my ankle before. I've twisted my elbow, sprained my wrist, and gotten a concussion. I've had too many bruises to count, but I'm fine. I'm always fine."

"A concussion? What the fuck?" His big hands reach out for me, like he's going to cradle my head, and I recoil.

"Did I answer your questions satisfactorily? Can I go now?"

"Back to sleeping in your car?"

"Yes. It's barely dawn. I'd like to sleep a few more hours, Your Highness, if that's okay with you."

Jace chuckles again, and Rhett closes his eyes like he's praying for patience. He seems taller now than when I was younger for some reason. Maybe that's because he's probably gained thirty pounds of muscle. He picked me up earlier like I weighed nothing.

He hangs his hands on his hips and stares at the ground. His voice goes soft. "Paige, sister of my very best friend in the world, can I please escort you home or wherever you're going so I know you're not going to be kidnapped or murdered in the park by some psycho?"

At the mention of Danny, my throat closes up, and I fold my arms over my chest and look away. It pains me to admit this, but for some reason, I can't lie to him. "I... I don't have anywhere to go."

Rhett goes eerily still. "What does that mean?"

"It means that Irma is hoarding French bulldogs in my house, and there's no room for me. It means that I broke up with my boyfriend, so I can't go back to Charming. It means, because I hurt my ankle and need physical therapy, I lost my coaching job in Austin, so..." I shrug. "I don't know where to go."

My eyes sting, and I blink quickly so I don't start bawling.

"What about Baylee's place?"

"She's out of town, but her sister is staying over with her kids."

"Shit."

I motion behind me. "If you don't mind, I'm going to snooze for a few hours. I'm sure I'll figure out what to do once I'm rested." I start to turn, but his voice makes me freeze.

"I mind."

Our eyes connect, and that current of electricity I've always felt around him bolts through me. This man has always confused me. In a rush of anger, I hold out my hands. "What do you want from me, Rhett?"

His eyes rake over me again, and his jaw goes tight. "I want you to put on some fucking clothes. Then I want you to get your ass in my truck so I can feed you. How do you feel about breakfast tacos?"

"I'm not hungry." At that moment, my stomach grumbles.

He smirks. At the sight of his plump lips tugging up, my heart goes crazy, racing in my chest like I've just sprinted across town. "Don't lie to me, wildflower. I know what you need."

That's what I'm afraid of.

Chapter Four

RHETT

Jace smacks me on the back before he sits next to me at the kitchen table. "I got you."

That can't be good. "Don't do... anything. At all," I say under my breath as I watch Paige pour a glass of juice before sitting across from my brother.

I can't get over her red hair and how light blue her eyes are now.

Or how goddamn feisty she is.

Or those fucking curves she's never had before.

Thank God she put on some damn clothes. I mean, if you consider those short shorts clothes. The little brat buttoned two buttons on my flannel and tied it in front like she's a Dallas cheerleader.

It's fucking distracting.

I haven't seen Paige since she started college. I've asked Maverick about her over the years since they went to the same college, but his answers were always the same. *She's fine. She's good. She did some cool cheerleading shit at my last game.*

For some reason, having her here makes me consider my old house. My eyes catch on the mud tracks by the doorway and the pile of toys exploding out of the basket in the living room. The dirty dishes I need to wash.

I scrub my face. Not sure why I care that my house needs a good cleaning. I haven't wanted to impress a woman in years.

"So, Paige," Jace says as he bites into a chorizo and cheese taco, "what's the deal with your job? Will you be heading to Austin after your ankle gets better?"

Her shoulders droop. "Probably not. They're not holding the position for me. I need rehab, but I can't afford it because I don't have insurance. While I was a student, it was covered, but I got injured the night I graduated."

"What happened?"

She sighs. "I was out with my boyfriend, and his friends were drunk and acting like fools. One of them accidentally pushed me off the curb."

"What the fuck?" I slam down my glass. "Why didn't you call me to let me know you were hurt?"

Her eyebrows lift. "Why would I call you? We haven't spoken in years."

"Maybe if you'd picked up the phone when I called, that wouldn't have been an issue."

"*Maybe* if you'd *left a message* instead of hanging up like a damn stalker, I would have."

I grunt, and my brother chuckles.

Paige has avoided me at every turn since she told me Amber was cheating. It kinda broke my heart. At first, I thought she was seeing things that weren't there. She was young, just a freshman in high school. I knew she had a crush on me back then, but I thought it was harmless. I figured she'd grow out of it.

Yeah, I was pissed when we had that conversation. I got even angrier when she didn't come to my wedding. Not sure why I thought she'd come. Maybe because I loved her like a little sister and was hoping once she realized we were never gonna be an item, she'd get over it.

And then I was irate when I realized she was right—about everything. But I was too damn stupid to figure it out until years later.

Even now, I'm pissed at myself for not listening to her. Paige had the balls to tell me the truth about Amber, and I got upset with her. I'm a fucking dumbass.

I clear my throat. "I thought I'd see you at Danny's funeral."

She sucks in a breath, then blinks quickly. "I tried to go, but..." Her voice cracks, and every part of me wants to march to the other side of the table and pull her into my arms. Except that would probably only piss her off. "I got there at the end. After everyone left. I sat with Danny until the morning crew kicked me out. You know how much he hated the dark."

Jesus Christ. "You sat in the cemetery all night?"

She nods, her big blue eyes watery. "Danny would've done it for me."

Danny only got freaked out about the dark once he got sick. He said the long nights in the hospital gave him nightmares.

She sniffles, then whispers, "Thanks for the cookies. Cranberry and walnut have always been my favorite."

Of course I know that. And yes, I made her cookies and left them in Danny's hospital room. I had to get home to be with my boys, but Danny said I shouldn't feel guilty because Paige was staying with him almost every night. I don't know how this girl was juggling college and cheer and driving all those miles, but she pulled it off. Up to the very end.

That's why when he made me swear to look after her, I told him I would and meant it. But she's made that damn hard to do. Would it have killed her to pick up the phone even one time when I called?

After the funeral, I even drove to Charming and tried to track her down. I knew how close she and Danny were and figured she'd need the support. I wanted Paige to know I'd be there for her if she ever needed anything. But Mav didn't know where she was living, and her friends were reluctant to give a stranger her address. It was frustrating as hell. I started to feel like a goddamn stalker, so I finally gave up.

Jace whistles. "You two have some history."

Leave it to my brother to be dramatic. "This is a small town. Everyone has history. You have 'history' with more women than I can count."

He laughs, then winks at Paige, which pisses me off. "Paige, I have a proposition for you."

Good God, what's he gonna do?

She perks up. "Do you know of a job in town? I have a degree in communications. Not sure what it's good for, but maybe someone would care."

Damn, she's cute. Paige has always been adorable. Always been sweet and silly. But grown-up Paige? Fuck, I don't have words. She's beautiful in a way I can't even describe. I haven't laid eyes on her in years, and when I saw her sleeping in her damn car, I wanted to yank that vehicle apart, gear by gear.

When I carried her out, I didn't really get a good look at her. Not until I set her down on the ground and realized she was only wearing a bra and underwear. Fucking hell, this woman has a body. Beautiful, lean legs, a ripped stomach, high round tits, and a stunning face.

To my great shame, my dick responded instantly.

Jace smacks me on the back again. "Yeah, it's a job, in a sense."

She looks between me and my brother. I have no idea where he's going with this. Though… maybe I could use some help in the office.

But then he has to open his big, fat fucking mouth again. "Whatcha doing for the next six months or so? Because my brother here needs a wife."

Chapter Five
PAIGE

I CHOKE ON MY TACO. Frantically, I toss back a few sips of my juice until I swallow down that bite.

"What?" I ask, hoarse from coughing.

I must've misheard Jace because there's no way he asked what I think he just did.

He slings his arm around Rhett's broad shoulders. "You see, Paige, we've gotten ourselves in a pickle, but my brother can get us out of it if he's married."

"And you think he should marry me?" I ask dubiously.

Jace gives me a smile that I'm sure has charmed the panties off dozens of groupies. "You'd be perfect."

"Why? Because you think I'm desperate?" I shove my plate away from me. "Look, I know I'm not doing great at the moment, but that doesn't mean I want to marry some rando."

Rhett flinches. "I'm not some rando." But then he sighs. "For the record, I think this is a terrible idea too."

Jace clucks his tongue and sinks back in his chair. "Y'all, don't get your knickers in a twist." He points at me. "You need physical therapy and health insurance. Guess what? We have great insurance. Bet you could get your ankle all fixed up over the next few months, and then you can go back to your cheer camp right as rain." Then Jace turns to Rhett. "And you need a wife so Harlan loans you that money. Paige is perfect. She's not gonna rat you out and ruin this for us."

I wrap my arms around myself. "Why do you need a loan?"

Rhett rubs the back of his neck. "Our father's nursing home bill tapped us out. His life insurance should've covered it, but he canceled it without telling us. Between that, alimony, a second mortgage we didn't know about, and the regular operating expenses around here, we have a serious cash flow problem. We really just need to gut it out until this fall when we can take our cattle to market."

"I was sorry to hear that your dad passed."

"He was an asshole."

I chuckle. "Well, I didn't want to say that."

Rhett stares at me so intently, I look away. I can't believe this conversation. "So you need a wife. Don't you have a girlfriend you can ask?" It's been years, and I've spent all of that time fortifying myself against this man, but for some reason, I'm afraid of his answer.

"No girlfriend. Pretty much swore off dating when Amber and I got divorced."

"What about a friend with benefits?" My heart stops beating as I wait for him to answer.

Jace nudges Rhett. "You said Darlene's a good lay, and she seems like a nice person. What about her?"

Darlene must be a friend he sleeps with. My heart sinks, and internally, I shake my head at myself. I will not care what Rhett does with his free time or his dick.

Rhett closes his eyes. "Jesus Christ, Jace. Will you shut the fuck up?"

Jace snickers. "What? People are gonna see you and your 'wife' around town. This needs to be believable. Darlene always looks like she wants to maul you, so I don't think it'll be a stretch. Plus, she's hot." He holds his hands out to show us what her boobs look like.

My taco feels like it's going to surge back up.

Rhett smacks him over the back of the head. "You're not being helpful."

Jace just laughs. "Just to recap, we have Darlene, who might bang you through your headboard, or Paige..." Glancing at me, he hums. "Who looks like she might puke. You okay? My brother isn't that bad, I swear."

I stare out the window. "I don't want to be the laughingstock of town again."

Rhett stares at me hard. "What does that mean?"

I don't know why I'm being so honest with him, but I can't bring myself to lie. "On the afternoon I told you about Amber, I was really nervous I would forget what to say, so I wrote down some notes. They must've fallen out of my pocket when I jumped out my window. I think Irma found them because she told her friends. People made fun of me for it for years, all through high school. Until I left for college."

"Shit, I'm sorry."

I shrug. "Wasn't your fault I'm an idiot. I should've kept my mouth shut. It was none of my business. Trust me, I've learned my lesson."

His gruff voice gets soft. "For the record, you were right about everything."

Jace sing-songs, "We tried to tell you."

"Don't you have someplace to go?" Rhett asks.

He slaps Rhett on the back. "Love you, bro."

"Yeah, yeah."

Jace wanders down the hallway to one of the bedrooms, and then I'm alone with Rhett for the first time in seven years. He sighs. "My brothers never liked Amber, but I thought she'd grow on them."

I'm jittery, like I might jump out of my skin, but I force myself to sit still. "I wish I'd been wrong about her. I take no pleasure in being right."

He sighs again, and the weariness of it makes my heart hurt. "You tried to warn me, and I didn't take it well. I want to apologize for how I responded. I would've done this sooner if you'd picked up the phone when I called."

"I pretty much thought I might avoid you for the rest of my life." I finally have the courage to look at him. His soulful dark eyes pierce straight through me, and I tighten my arms around my waist. It pains me to admit this, but I want him to know. "You don't want to marry me. I, uh, I'd be a terrible wife. Maybe your friend Darlene is the better option."

He studies my face. "Why do you think you'd be a bad wife?"

I tug on the ties of his shirt and continue my truth vomit. "I can't connect to anyone. To men, I mean. I've had boyfriends, of course, but it's like there's a part of me that's locked away. Like I only have half a heart. You... you deserve someone who'll love you."

He swallows. "That's not what I want, Paige. I swore off relationships after I found Amber fucking another man in my bed. I don't want a real marriage or love, and certainly not more kids. I'm just looking for someone who can pull off this ruse for a few months, make my banker believe I'm a good bet, and get along with my family. That's it."

I consider what he's saying. "Are you sure you want to go this route? Won't a new marriage, however fake, be hard on your boys?" As much as I've tried to avoid news about Rhett, it was hard to miss that he had two kids with Amber. Baylee always gave me the highlights as gently as possible so I wouldn't be blindsided by them later.

Rhett rubs his scruffy jaw. "I've explored every other option to try to dig my way out of this financial pit. I'm not sure what else to do." I've never seen this desolate expression in his eyes.

"How bad is the money situation?"

He looks away. "We have less than thirty days before foreclosure."

Oh, God. "Are you serious?"

"Trust me, Paige, I'd never be entertaining marriage again if my family wasn't desperate. But Jace is right. We have pretty good health insurance. You could get the rehab you need, maybe save a little money if you'd like to help me out in the office. I'd pay you, of course—once I get that loan, I could afford to do that. And when the six months are up, you'd be ready to go back to your cheer camp."

When he says it like that, this is starting to sound more reasonable. "Where would I sleep? The couch?" I look at the living room where there's a roomy but worn sectional.

He winces. "Not sure that's a good idea. My brothers sometimes have overnight visitors, and I'm afraid word would spread that you're sleeping out here. Jace's bedroom gets more traffic than a Holiday Inn. I'd give you the trailer out back, but Beau stays there now. He and his friends sometimes trample through the house to raid my fridge on their way to his place, so there's not a lot of privacy."

"So where..."

"You can sleep in my bed, and I'll crash on the floor."

I laugh at the ridiculousness of that scenario. "Rhett, you're six foot three. You ride horses and bale hay and wrangle cattle all day long. You should get the bed."

He crosses his arms. "Does that mean you're considering this? If I can swing a shorter-term loan, I'll do that, but for the sake of my relationship with Harlan, I think we should stay together for six months. I don't want him to think I'm flakey."

I should tell him no, go back to my Kia Rio, and drive to the other side of Texas. That would be the smart thing to do, but no one ever said I'm smart. "Can I think about it? When would you need an answer?"

A look of defeat crosses his face, and he blows out a breath.

"Take all the time you need, Paige. This is probably a stupid idea. I don't wanna harangue you into doing something you're not comfortable with." He motions to my half-eaten taco. "Finish your breakfast. I'll drive you back to your car later today, and we'll go talk to Irma. See if we can figure something out."

Before I can respond, he pushes away from the table, grabs a bag of frozen peas from the refrigerator, and hands it to me. "Ice your ankle."

Then he heads out the back door, and I fight the stupid urge to run after him.

Chapter Six
PAIGE

"Baylee," I hiss. "We have to talk. This is an emergency."

"Why are you whispering?" she asks on the other end of my cell phone.

"Because I'm at Rhett's."

Silence. "What? Sorry, this convention is so loud. I almost thought you said you were at Rhett's, and we both know demon pigs would have to be flapping across the sky for that to happen."

I glance up at the bright blue sky that's full of wispy clouds. "There are no demon pigs as far as I can tell, but yes, you heard me right. I'm at Rhett's."

"What? Hold on. I need to go somewhere I can talk." A minute later, she returns. "I just locked myself in a utility closet. Tell me everything."

As I sit curled up on Rhett's comfy couch, staring out the window, I fill her in on the last twenty-four hours.

"Jesus, Mary, and Joseph. I leave for one week, and this happens? Why didn't you go to my house? You know my mother loves you."

"Isn't your sister staying with you now?"

"Damn, I forgot. Yeah, that would be a problem. I'd offer you my bed while I'm gone, but she's sleeping in it." She chuckles. "Did Rhett really get pissed off that you were in your underwear?"

My lips tug up. "So pissed. Like I had personally offended him. You know what we wear when we train. I'm constantly in sports bras and spandex shorts that barely cover my ass. If I wear more, it feels constraining. Anyway, he was acting like a big, growly bear. If I hadn't been so irritated at him, I would've laughed."

"What are you gonna do? Living with the Walker brothers won't be easy. They're messy, loud, and handsome as hell."

"They're definitely messy." There are toys everywhere, mud on the floor, crumbs on the island, and dishes in the sink. But if Rhett pays me to work in the office, I suppose I could help out in the house too. I can't judge him. Running this ranch is a lot, and between that, raising his kids, and dealing with his father's passing, I'm sure it's been overwhelming.

She gets quiet. "Is Maverick home yet?"

Baylee's always had a thing for the youngest Walker brother, who's our age. They call each other their best friends—other than me, that is—but they have crazy sexual tension. But Mav's not ready to settle down, and Baylee won't put up with him having extracurricular activities. Not that they've ever discussed it. They just dance around each other in this weird love-hate relationship.

"No, he's not back. Mav's probably still partying at school."

We both know what that's code for—hooking up.

"Whatever. I've decided to get on dating apps. I'm gonna get over that asshole once and for all."

"Good for you."

"Okay, enough about my sad love life. What are you going to do about your Walker brother problem?"

"I'm not sure it would be healthy to stay. I don't want to get wrapped up in Rhett again." I glance around the beautiful log house. It's old and worn down, but the bones are great. I've always loved the Walker Ranch. They have acres and acres of rolling hills that sit along the western part of the Eden River where we all used to go rafting on lazy Sunday afternoons.

When I was young, I used to fantasize about living here. Rhett and his brothers always made me feel so safe, and when I'd visit, I could envision a life free from Irma and her toxic ways.

Running through the pasture and riding horses felt like coming home. The memory of Rhett smiling at me when I learned to trot one of the horses was the image I'd conjure when Irma would go off on me in her drunken rants. In my mind, I'd escape to the Walker Ranch where I'd raise chickens or cook one of my mama's recipes I found hidden under the kitchen sink.

As I got older, that morphed into having a family and life here with Rhett.

Which was pure delusion.

Now it feels like some cruel joke. Do I even want that for myself anymore?

Those can't be the reasons I do this.

It's fake, Paige. Not real. You'll get a job and physical therapy while Rhett saves his ranch. It's what Danny would've wanted.

I rub the steady throb against my temple.

Baylee hums. "So... would this be a platonic situation, or would you fuck Rhett's brains out?"

"There would be no fucking of any kind. This is a business deal. He even spelled it out for me. Six months, we get his banker Harlan to buy into this, I rehab my ankle, and then we file for divorce."

"Harlan Calhoun? My mother went to him to get a loan for our salon, but he turned her down. So if he's willing to give Rhett a loan, he must believe in him."

I believe in him too. I'm not sure how their financial situation got so bad, but I do know how hard he and his brothers work. Rhett breaks his back every day to keep the ranch running. I knew that even as a child.

The thought of him losing this place chokes me up. What

would he do if he didn't have the ranch? Where would his brothers go? Could that jeopardize Rhett's custody of his boys?

Do I want to be responsible for letting that happen?

A door slams outside, and I lean up to see a shiny Audi parked next to Rhett's old truck. A beautiful blonde steps out of it. Amber.

"Hey, the Wicked Witch just got here. I need to go hide."

She chuckles. "Really? I'd pounce on Rhett, climb him like a koala bear, and give him an open-mouthed kiss that would set her hair on fire."

I shake my head. My best friend is crazy. "Go back to your convention. I'll call you later."

"Love you."

"Love you too. Be safe." I hang up and tuck my phone in my bra.

Another car door slams, and two little boys go bounding toward their father, who kneels down to hug them. When he stands, they're still clinging to him.

The look of pure joy on his face squeezes something in my chest. The front window is cracked open, and I can hear his sons' laughter.

But the smile on Rhett's face freezes when Amber sidles up to him. "I need to pick up the boys' sleeping bags." She toys with a long strand of hair. "What are you doing this week? Wanna come with us to the lake?"

I thought Rhett hated Amber. Why is she inviting him on her vacation?

"Amber, we talked about this," he says gruffly as he steps around her.

"Why can't we spend time together as a family? Why is that so bad?"

There's a pleading in her voice that surprises me. Why is she begging Rhett to hang out when she's the one who cheated?

I can hear his frustration when he grunts, "I'm not doing this with you again."

"You know what? Forget it. You never had time for me when we were married, so I don't know why I thought you'd have time now."

Ouch. As much as I dislike this woman, a part of me feels bad for her. Maybe she regrets cheating on Rhett.

They start walking toward the house, and I limp as fast as I can toward the powder room off the kitchen. I don't want to add kindling to that fire. I leave the light off and lean against the bathroom counter and pray Amber doesn't have to pee.

"Gabriel, Austin, don't y'all go anywhere," Amber calls out. "I'm going to grab those sleeping bags, and we're leaving. If you two disappear, you're gonna get it."

The vitriol in her voice makes the hair on my arms stand on end. I can understand her being angry at Rhett, but why is she such a bitch to her kids? Amber's heels echo down the hall.

"Dad, can you come with us to the lake? It's no fun without you," Gabriel, the older one, says. I've never met his boys, but Baylee says they're cute as hell.

"Daddy, I miss youuuuu," Austin says.

Rhett clears his throat. "I'm sure your mom has some cool things planned for you."

"You mean her babysitter," Gabriel grouses. "She's not going."

The click-clack of her heels returns. "Let's go."

"Boys, go sit on the stoop," Rhett says. "I wanna talk to your mother."

After a minute, the front door closes, and Amber huffs, "Make this quick. I'm late."

"So you're going to Canyon Lake?"

"I told you that already."

"No, I mean, are *you* going *with* the boys to the lake, or are you dumping them on someone else to look after?"

She lets out a long sigh. "I'm really tired of getting the third degree from you. Why do you care who looks after them?"

Rhett makes this growly sound that draws me closer to the cracked-open bathroom door. "Because the lake is dangerous, Amber. Do you know how many kids drown there because they don't have proper supervision?"

"Don't be so damn dramatic. I have to prep for a car commercial I just won. I can't look after them twenty-four seven."

"Then I'll keep them this week, and you can go do your thing."

"But I'm supposed to have them for two weeks for vacation!"

"Then spend some fucking time with them instead of handing them off to whatever loser friends you have who don't give a damn about my children." Her heels cross the house, and he yells her name. "Amber, wait." The clicks of her shoes pause. "Just... don't let them in the water if you're not with them. If you can promise me that, I'll stop being a pest. I know you want the best for them. I do too. I'm... I'm sorry I yelled."

"You're such an asshole. I don't know what I ever saw in you. The only thing you care about is this fucking ranch and your fucking cows."

"Yes, I'm an asshole. Can you promise me they won't get near the water if you're not with them?" He pauses. "Please?"

"Fine. Now leave me alone."

The door slams.

I'm so overwhelmed by what I just heard, my eyes sting and my throat closes up. Suddenly, the bathroom door swings open, and Rhett grunts, "You can come out now."

I stare at him, and to my horror, my bottom lip wobbles.

When he sees me, he freezes. "What's wrong?"

I cover my face. "I don't know." Then a sob breaks out of me. "I feel bad that you... you and the boys have to go through that." Hell, I even feel bad for Amber. Because she obviously still has feelings for her ex-husband.

"Oh, shit." He lets out a huff, and next thing I know, I'm in his arms. "Don't cry, wildflower. It's nothing I can't handle."

I shove my nose against his hard chest and breathe in his woodsy scent. He slowly strokes my back, and I try to calm down. Amber's rage and cruelty has me reverting back to the bullied little girl I once was when I lived with Irma, even though it wasn't directed at me. How messed up is that?

After a few minutes, he sets me down on the island counter in the kitchen and places his hands on either side of me. "Paige."

I can't bear to look at him. I've missed Rhett so much. There are so many things I want to tell him. Things I've done, places I've gone. Things I wanted to share with him over the last seven years, but I never got the chance.

I cover my face again and shake my head. "I'm sorry. I don't know why I'm crying."

He gently takes my wrist, and removes my hand. "Hey. I'm fine. The boys are tough. We'll get through this. You don't need to feel bad on our account."

Sniffling, I nod. "Okay."

He hands me a paper towel, and I wipe my nose.

His eyes soften. "Why don't you go take a shower and grab a nap? You can use the bathroom in my room and crash on my bed for a few hours. I need to shovel out the barn. Give me your keys, and Jace and I will drive your car over. Then we'll grab some lunch and make a plan to talk to Irma."

I sniffle again. "All... all right."

Rhett lowers me from the counter. "Guess I should give you a tour. A few things have changed since you were here last." He points to the hallway to the right of the living room. "Down here are Jace's room and my office, which used to be my bedroom when I was a kid. Mav bunks with Jace when he's in town, and Beau sleeps in the trailer out back, since he wanted more privacy." Then he walks me down the opposite hallway and points to the left. "This is still my father's old office, but it's a mess. Haven't gotten around to clearing it out yet. Hopefully this summer I'll get a chance. And here's the boys' bathroom and their bedroom."

He opens the door, and it's a bright room with two twin beds. The bedspreads are blue, and there are constellation stickers on the ceiling, which must glow in the dark. Their bookshelves are brimming with books and dinosaurs and trucks.

"It's a lovely bedroom." I clear my throat. "You must miss them when they're with their mom."

"I usually get them every other week, but since they just got outta school for the summer, Amber has them for two weeks."

"If you ever need me to help out with them, I'd be happy to."

"Thanks. I might take you up on that." He closes that door and opens the one behind us, which I know is the master bedroom. The moment I enter, I'm hit with the yummy scent of his cologne. It's a sparse room. Just a king-size bed, a small couch, a dresser, and a TV mounted across from the bed.

Rhett rubs the back of his neck. "This is nothing special, but you're welcome here. Make yourself at home. You can sleep on my bed or on the couch, though that's probably not comfortable. Off to the side here is my bathroom. If you'd like a shower, there are towels in the cabinet."

He looks so adorably awkward, I smile. "Thanks. This is great. Sorry I'm putting you out like this."

"It's no trouble at all. After all the times Danny saved my ass when we were growing up, it's the least I can do."

My smile withers. Of course he's only doing this because of my brother.

I'll definitely be napping on the couch.

Chapter Seven
RHETT

Sweat stings my eyes as I shovel out stall after stall, but there isn't enough work around here to purge the confusion brewing in my soul.

Seeing Paige cry because of me and Amber arguing hit me in a way I didn't expect. My natural instinct is to do what I've always done—comfort her. Only there's a helluva difference between picking up my best friend's pint-sized little sister versus the woman currently snoozing in my bedroom.

"Bro." Beau marches up to me with a scowl on his face. He sticks his thumb over his shoulder toward the house. "Is there something you wanna tell me?"

I shovel some fresh hay into the stall. "Like what?"

"Like why the hell Paige Lewis just stumbled out of your bedroom, wearing *your* clothes, looking freshly—"

"You'd better not say what I think you're gonna say."

"Looking like… she just tumbled out of bed." He scratches his chin. "*Your* bed."

"Where's she supposed to sleep? There's too much traffic in the living room. The girl needs to get some rest." I grumble to myself as I push a wheelbarrow full of horse shit to the next stall.

My brother trails behind me. "I feel like I'm missing something here. Because this is the same Paige Lewis who's been avoiding your calls for the last few years, right?"

"What's your point?"

He chuckles. "I love how evasive you get sometimes."

I lean the pitchfork against the stall. "Jace and I saw her car at the park this morning." I was with Danny when he bought it for her. I'd recognize that little Kia anywhere. "Sun was barely up. Thought maybe she'd been carjacked or high schoolers had taken her vehicle for a joy ride."

"Let me guess. That's not what happened."

"She was fucking sleeping in her shoebox of a car, if you can believe it. I nearly had a heart attack when I saw her all curled up in the front seat."

Leaning one arm against a post, he frowns. "So how did she end up wearing your flannel and pajama bottoms? Which were way too big for her, FYI."

"I gave her the flannel this morning, and the pajama bottoms?" I shrug. "She must've grabbed them when I told her to take a shower and a nap." I fight the urge to go see what she looks like wearing my clothes.

"And?"

I hold out my hands. "I don't fucking know, to tell you the truth. Jace said she should marry me so I could get that loan." I give him the Cliff's Notes version of our younger brother's plan.

"You're going to marry Paige?" The look of shock on his face tells me he thinks that's a stupid idea too.

I've been wrestling with that all morning. "I decided to find someone else. Paige isn't the right person." There's something fragile about her, and I don't wanna be the person who messes with that. I'm not a soft man, and I get the sense she needs someone who'll be tender and sweet. That's not me.

The real shocker is how much chemistry she and I have, and

that's just wrong. I'm ten fucking years older than she is. Danny would kill me if I messed with his baby sister.

I'm not going there with her. I made a promise to Danny on his deathbed to look out for her, and I aim to do just that.

Beau helps me shovel some hay and finally breaks the silence. "I wouldn't say it's a stupid idea. Paige might've been avoiding you, but deep down we all know you're special to her. I think she'd help you pull this off for Harlan's sake. Only..."

"Only?"

"Only I'd be afraid of her getting hurt."

"Which is exactly why I'll find someone else." I wipe the sweat from my eyes. Paige is too sweet. Too beautiful.

And too fucking tempting.

"I can appreciate you wanting to find the right person, but we're running out of time, Rhett."

Does he want me to do this or not? This conversation is starting to piss me off. "I know that, but I won't marry Paige. She deserves someone better. Someone who'll marry her for the right reasons. Someone who'll put her on a pedestal."

His eyebrows lift, and he whistles. "There's a lot there to untangle."

"I'll call up Darlene tomorrow. See if she's game." I get this weird pang in my chest the moment those words leave my mouth.

He snorts. "Don't get her pregnant. The last thing you need is to knock up someone you don't even want to date."

"This arrangement is for business. I'm not gonna fuck this person. It'll blur too many lines, make her think this is more than just a transaction. In six months, as soon as I'm done paying back Harlan, I'm gonna file for divorce. Sex will just confuse everyone."

"What are you gonna give Darlene to help you out?"

I shrug. "Probably expensive shoes and shit. Who the fuck knows?"

He smacks my back. "For once, I wish you didn't have to

worry about me and Jace and Mav and just do what makes you happy."

"I have no clue what would make me happy, but it would probably involve sending Amber to Canada."

Beau laughs. "Is that far enough?"

"Probably not."

I don't mention the shouting match I had with my ex-wife this morning or how I found Paige in tears afterward. It's all too much. I just wanna work until I'm too tired to think, and then kick back on the porch with a beer and pretend my ex-wife isn't going to crawl up my ass until our boys are eighteen.

Someone coughs from the other side of the barn, and Beau and I look up to find Paige, who's back in her short shorts.

I pinch the bridge of my nose. I don't have the strength to not admire her long, beautiful legs.

Beau pulls her into a bear hug that makes me clench my teeth. "So nice to have you back, Little Lewis."

"It's great to be back. I've always loved the ranch." When our eyes meet, I see the hesitancy in them.

I hate that I fucking put it there. "We're stoked to have you, Paige. You'll always be welcome here."

Beau looks between us and points behind him. "Gonna make some lunch. Y'all want some sandwiches?"

I nod, and my brother makes himself scarce.

Paige limps up to me, and I barely keep myself from growling. "Where are your crutches? Shouldn't you use them?"

"Yeah. I should." She shrugs. "I'm tired of hauling them around. I wish I could fling them off a cliff."

Her red hair's pulled up in one of those messy buns that makes her look effortlessly sexy.

I scrub my face. I will not think of Paige in that light.

A barn cat runs up to her and rubs his head against her leg. Lucky bastard.

Turning my back to her, I reach for the shovel so I can finish shoveling out the stalls. I listen to her coo at the cat.

It finally goes quiet.

"Rhett."

"Yeah?" I scoop up a pile of crap.

"I'll do it."

"Do what?"

"Marry you."

My heart damn near stops, and I turn to face her. "Paige, you don't have to—"

"I want to. For six months, that is. Like you said, it'll be mutually beneficial. I'll get the physical therapy I need and save some money, and you'll get the ranch back on track. Then we'll call it quits. Everyone wins."

I rub the back of my neck.

She must see something on my face because she takes a wobbly step back. "What?"

"Maybe you're not the best person to do this." This is awkward as fuck, but it needs to be said. "With our history... I don't want you to get hurt."

Her eyes go icy, and she lets out a hard laugh. "Are you afraid pathetic little Paige is going to fall in love with you and won't let you file for divorce? Think again. Here's some good news, Rhett. I don't fall in love. I never have, and I probably never will. That dumb crush I had on you when I was a kid was just that—a crush. Let me ask you this. Do you still have feelings for people you had crushes on when you were fifteen?"

"Well, no, but—"

"But nothing. This is no different. Guess what? Sometime in the last seven years, I grew up. And here's a shocker—I've even had full-fledged relationships with other men. But if you're squeamish about this, that's fine. Call up your friend with benefits. Let her do the honors."

She turns and starts to limp away.

Shit. She's pissed.

I drop the shovel and jog after her.

"Paige." I grab her arm and turn her to face me. "Don't be a delicate little flower. I was just being honest. If we do this, I don't wanna cross any lines. We're one hundred percent platonic unless we need to be affectionate around other people to pull this off. Otherwise, we're friends, that's it."

She finally turns those big blue eyes up to me. Glaciers in Antarctica are warmer. "We're not friends. We haven't been friends for a long time."

Ouch.

I don't know why, but this woman twists me up. "You're right, and that's my fault. Maybe… maybe we could work on that. We could learn to be friends again. I'll help you get back on your feet, and you'll save my ranch. I think that's a pretty good deal for both of us."

Some of that animosity melts away, and she nods. "It is."

This way, I'm keeping my promise to Danny. What better way to watch out for his sister than to move her in with me?

To be honest, I'm relieved Paige finally realized she didn't love me when she was younger. The fact that she doesn't think she's wired to fall in love makes me feel better about this. Because the last thing I wanna do is hurt her.

My reluctance is slowly fading. In fact, the more I think about how much this situation will help both of us, the more I like it.

I hold out my hand. "Deal?"

"On one condition."

"Name it."

"I want some chickens."

Did I hear her right? "Chickens?" I snort.

"Don't you laugh at me, Rhett Walker. I want some chickens, and you're going to get me some."

Chuckling, I nod. "Yes, ma'am."

When she places her small hand in mine, I smile.

I don't know why I've been so worked up about this. Paige and I are both gonna get what we need and then go our separate ways.

This will be a breeze.

Jace is a genius.

Chapter Eight
PAIGE

WHEN I SEE the price tag on the white slip dress, I cringe.

"Oh, I love that one," Baylee's mom Sylvia says. "Try it on."

"Aunt Syl, it's too expensive." She's not really my aunt, but I love her like she's family. I've missed her so much. She would've come to my graduation, but she was sick.

"Nonsense." She squeezes my hand. "It's not every day that my best friend's daughter gets married." Sylvia and my mom were besties back in the day. "If it fits and you love it, I want you to get it. I have some emergency savings set aside, so I can cover it. Your mama can't be here, and Lord knows Irma has done a shitty job of looking after you. Trust me, it would be my pleasure."

Behind her, Baylee tuts. "Haven't you learned you can't argue with my mother?"

Syl smirks. "Besides, you're marrying Rhett Walker, the biggest catch in town. I will not let you walk down that aisle in something you got secondhand. *Mija*, that white cotton dress you showed me is lovely, but you need something special. You're only getting married once."

Eesh. Guilt swirls in my stomach. "It's just the courthouse." We had to wait a few days so Rhett could make sure his brothers were here. Except for Isaiah because he never comes home. Plus, Texas has a seventy-two-hour waiting period after the marriage license is issued, which was fine because it gave me time to come to terms with this. Rhett also wanted to be sure Harlan could attend. At least now my limp isn't so bad.

The scary thing is even though this started out as a small ceremony, we've now added a reception at the ranch. One we probably can't afford, but Rhett told me not to worry about it.

"Try it on," Syl says and pushes me toward the dressing room of Texas Rose Bridal, a small boutique in downtown Wild Heart. "Go with her, Baylee. Make her see some sense."

As we head behind the curtain, my best friend is quiet.

The chill of the air conditioning pricks at my skin while I change. Baylee fusses with the hanger and wipes away imaginary creases in the beautiful silky dress. As I watch her, it hits me, how wrong this is.

We should be gushing with excitement that one of us is getting married. I should be thinking about how one of my brothers will proudly walk me down the aisle. I should be over the moon that I'm marrying the guy of my dreams.

Instead, I tug on the dress like I'm changing for a costume party. I'm not the blushing bride. I'm playing a role. By rote, I lift my arms, slide the gown over my head, and turn so she can zip me.

I'm getting married, but it's not for love. This isn't the fantasy I used to daydream about. This isn't about vows and commitment and building a family.

Sighing, I try to suck up my disappointment and accept that this is my life. At least for the next six months.

"You think this is a bad idea." It's not a question. I can tell by her body language and how awkward this moment is for both of us.

She shakes her head. "No. Not exactly. I just... I have a feeling."

"Oh, shit. Don't tell me." Baylee has a sixth sense. The women in the Reyes family all have it to some degree. I could list a dozen times Baylee's done this since we were kids, but the one that always comes to mind is how she knew Danny was sick before he ever shared he wasn't feeling well. She's the one who told me I needed to stay with him at night in the hospital.

I'm so grateful she urged me to do that. Otherwise, I wouldn't have been there when he passed. At least I got to hold his hand at the end and let him know he wasn't alone.

She fixes the strap on the dress and pushes my hair out of the way. Then her voice gets quiet. "I just don't want you to get hurt, and there's a lot of potential for things to go wrong."

I look her in the eye. "Tell me this. Will we save the ranch?"

She closes her eyes. Tilts her head. Hums. "Possibly, but… it's not a done deal. I see a lot of murkiness. Like, there could be danger."

Chills erupt on my skin, and I rub my arms. "What kind of danger? Rogue bobcats roaming the countryside kind of danger, or violent intruders?"

She lets out a frustrated groan. "That's just it. I can't tell. And that worries me. Maybe it's a metaphorical danger, like a danger to your heart."

"If we have a shot to save the Walker Ranch, I'm doing this. That property has been in the family for generations, Bay. I can't bail on them." Because this will affect Beau, Jace, and Mav, not just Rhett and his kids.

"You already told me the story, but I still can't wrap my head around how you went from not talking to Rhett for years to marrying him."

I shrug. "I saw him with his boys, and it hurt to watch how Amber dragged them around. It hurt to see her aim so much animosity at Rhett when she's the cheater." I run my hand over the soft material of my dress. "Look, I have no viable plans for my future if I don't get rehab. Can I eventually get a job with a gymnastics or cheer camp? Yes, but I'll make peanuts. If I'm at a hundred percent physically, maybe I'll get another shot at one of these elite training facilities and actually make a living. So even though I know this whole thing sounds wackadoodle, I'm willing to take the risk."

She hugs me. "Just guard your heart, okay? Don't give in to that Walker charm."

"Rhett barely looks at me, so I guarantee I'll be fine."

"What does that mean?"

I turn to the mirror. "Beau's at the firehouse this week, so I'm staying in his trailer. And whenever I see Rhett, he's kinda distant, which is weird because he said we'd use this time to become friends again."

"He probably has a lot on his mind. If you marry him, you're going to need to trust him on some level. Just don't fall in love with him again if you have sex."

"I was never in love with him. That was just too many fairytales and teenage lust."

She side-eyes me. "If you say so."

"I feel bad about your mom, though. She's really excited for me."

"Let her be happy." She looks me over. "And let her buy that dress for you. It looks incredible."

There's a funny little pucker of fabric at the waist, but nothing I couldn't fix with a needle and some thread. "Not too much for a court wedding?"

"It's your day. You deserve to look like a princess. You're going to let me do your hair, right?"

"I'd be honored."

She lifts it off my neck, and we stare at our reflection. "Girl, you might as well have fun doing this."

I smile at her. "You're right. Let's get the dress."

After Baylee's mom pays for my outfit, she drives us to the Cactus Bloom Diner. We sit at a booth and order lunch.

"Aunt Syl, you're going to need to let me reimburse you for everything when I have some cash."

"Nonsense. I don't want your money. I want grandbabies! You and Rhett are going to have gorgeous babies. I can't wait!"

My eyes widen at her loud declaration, and I glance around. Shit. Georgia Hightower is right there.

"Bay," I whisper. "Does Mrs. Hightower still publish the gossip column in the *Gazette*?"

"Yup."

I squint at my best friend. "Is she coming over here?"

She chuckles. "You know it."

Damn. Mrs. Hightower does it under the guise of wanting to announce weddings and graduations and baby showers, but locals sometimes use it as a way to air each other's dirty laundry.

Aunt Syl reaches over and squeezes my hand. "Honey, you are marrying the hottest man in town. He's too young for me, of course, but I have eyeballs in my head. If I were your age and marrying him this week, I'd be shouting it from the rooftops. It's okay to be proud."

Rhett did say he wants me to sell this.

If this was a real marriage, I'd be proud as hell to be marrying him. He's a great man. A hard worker and a good provider. Loyal as the day is long.

So when Georgia Hightower sashays over to say hi and asks what I'm doing in town, I tell her something close to the truth—I'm marrying my long-time crush and the man of my dreams.

And if a part of me enjoys playing pretend right now, well, that'll just be my little secret.

Chapter Nine
RHETT

Staring at the words on the website makes them all run together. I scroll through the post and read it again.

"I'm over the moon to be marrying Rhett Walker! He was my brother's best friend when I was growing up, and I've always looked up to him. We recently reconnected, and sparks flew! Who knew that we were written in the stars? I love him to pieces, and I can't wait to be his wife. I just wish my brother could be here."

Guilt, sharp and jagged, tears through me.

Marrying Paige is a terrible idea.

Because I remember the look in her eyes when Danny called her out all those years ago for letting her feelings for me confuse her.

I'm not all that sure it was a harmless crush, like she claims.

Maybe it was more.

I feel like Paige and I are a Pandora's box rigged with explosives, and one wrong move will make it blow up in my face.

Someone knocks on the bathroom door, and I shove my phone in my pocket as my brothers barge in.

Jace slings his arm over Beau's shoulders. "Look at Rhett. Our big bro is all grown up." He dabs at his eyes. "I'm getting choked up over here."

"Shut up, asshole." My brothers laugh. I try to adjust my tie, but it's tight, and I feel like I might choke. I glance at the toilet. There's a possibility I might hurl.

Beau frowns. "You okay?"

I nod, but the truth is I'm kinda shaken up from reading my "wedding announcement" in the *Gazette*. Paige warned me that Georgia Hightower cornered her at the diner, but nothing prepared me to read about her gushing over me.

I splash some water on my face. It's all bullshit. It has to be. But it makes me uncomfortable nonetheless.

Mav sticks his head in my bathroom. "We gotta go if you want to be on time for your wedding." He shakes his head. "Can't believe you're doing this. Talk about taking one for the team. At least Paige is awesome."

Mav would know this because he and Paige grew up together and went to the same college. Really, she's much more suited to be marrying someone Maverick's age. Not a divorced single father of two.

What the fuck am I doing?

And why did I think it was a good idea to get hitched without my boys? Since Paige won't be sticking around after those six months, I figured this transition might be easier for my kids if they didn't watch me tie the knot. Now, I don't know.

If people ask me about it, I'm just telling them Gabriel and Austin are on vacation with their mom and leaving it at that.

Maverick nudges me. "Just watch. I'm gonna get drafted, make a shitload of money, and pay you back for all of this crap."

After I dry my face, I grab Mav in a chokehold and scruff his head. "Don't worry 'bout us. You don't need that pressure. Just do your thing and focus on the game."

He breaks out of my hold and goes to tackle me, but Beau holds him off. "We don't have time for y'all to go wrestling around on the floor, and Mav, the last thing you need is to break something being an idiot. Come on."

I point to my little brother. "You think you're all big and tough, but I can still whoop your ass."

His chest puffs up, and he hops up and down. "Oh, yeah? I'd like to see you try."

I laugh and pat his back. I'm just talking shit. My little bro ain't so little anymore.

Jace drives Mav, and I let Beau drive me because I'm distracted and I need a minute to gather my thoughts.

As we head toward town, Beau lifts a finger off the steering wheel. "Just wanna give you a heads-up. Baylee's mom rented that cabin off the lake for y'all this weekend. She said you and Paige needed some 'special time away,' just the two of you. She said it's her wedding gift to you. She hasn't told Paige yet. It's supposed to be a surprise, so act surprised."

"Christ." I scrub my face. "I was hoping to relax with a few beers tonight after I set Paige up in the boys' room. Thought she could sleep there until they get back, but now we have this damn reception. I can't even think about that cabin."

"You can still have that beer, but now it's with the ultra-romantic backdrop of the cabin. So no one will hear you railing your little wife."

I growl. "Paige is not getting railed, okay? Get that through your head."

He chuckles. "Got it, chief."

After I roll down the window, I tug at my collar. "Is it hot? I'm hot."

"I have the air conditioning blasting in your face."

When we park, Beau starts to get out, but I grab his shoulder. "I need a minute."

"You gonna bolt?"

"I'd never do that to Paige. I just... I'm not sure this is a smart idea."

"Coulda told ya that, but it's kinda late now." He points to Harlan's Cadillac, which is pulling into a parking spot. He and his wife get out, and I watch them stroll to the courthouse.

I take a deep breath. "I don't want to hurt Paige."

Beau gives me a look. "Then don't hurt her."

"It's that easy?"

He nods. "Yeah. Don't be a dick. Treat her with respect, be kind, talk shit out, and you'll be okay."

I scratch the back of my head. "Where'd you learn all that?"

"I read it on a Hallmark card."

"A Hallmark card said don't be a dick?"

He chuckles. "It said don't be rude, but I put it in my own words, okay? Anyway, if you treat her like a friend, you should be cool."

"How'd you get to be so wise? And how come I don't know that shit, and I'm older?"

Beau shrugs. "Just don't forget your mutual goals and the timeline. You just gotta get through six months, and then you'll be as free as a bird again."

Six months. Right. Okay. I can do this. "Come on. I don't wanna be late to my own wedding."

I'm feeling better about things until Paige stands at the back of the room with her little white dress and a bouquet of white roses.

What the actual fuck? I thought we were doing casual? I'm wearing a suit, one of two I own—the black one, since I wore the brown one to my meeting with Harlan—while Paige looks ready to twirl around a ballroom. She stayed at Baylee's house last night because Sylvia wouldn't hear of her staying at my ranch the night before the wedding.

We agreed we'd only tell Baylee and my brothers the real reason we were doing this. That's too many people as it is, but I won't lie to my brothers. I need their support right now, so it's only fair she has someone in her corner too.

The downside to this arrangement is that Baylee's mom doesn't have a clue this is all for show, and now I have to figure out our sleeping situation at that cabin.

But first I have to get through our wedding.

The longer I stare at Paige, the harder my heart beats.

Her stunning red hair is piled high on her head with curls tumbling down her slender shoulders. She's decked out in a fitted, white, silky dress that hugs her gorgeous body to perfection. And she's wearing sparkling sandals that make her legs look amazing. Should she be wearing that with her hurt ankle? They've got a little heel. When she takes a step, I notice how gingerly she walks.

But then she smiles at everyone, and I forget my own goddamn name because she's so fucking gorgeous, I barely keep my mouth from falling open.

I glance at Harlan, and he gives me a thumbs-up.

Right. Play along, dumbass. Don't act so fucking out of it.

Baylee's mom walks Paige down the aisle and kisses her on the cheek before she hands her off to me. *"Que Dios te bendiga."*

She just blessed us.

I'm going to hell.

Paige beams up at me, and I feel like someone kicked me. Why am I dragging her into my mess? Danny would beat my ass if he was here.

Judge Tate smiles. "I just wanna say how happy I am to have this job today. I had Rhett and Paige in my Sunday school when they were yea tall. They were years apart, of course, but I'm still tickled about this."

I wanted a courthouse wedding because I figured it would be fast and impersonal. I didn't count on having Frannie Tate as our judge.

Frannie gives us another wide smile. "Can y'all turn to each other and hold hands?" We do as she asks.

As I stare down at my best friend's little sister, I catalogue how much she's changed over the years. There's no dirt on her face or knots in her hair. No cuts or bruises on her knees. No candy melted on her hands or undone shoelaces tripping her.

Gone is the little girl who trailed behind me and her brother. In her place is a glamorous, beautiful woman.

I hope she doesn't notice the dust on my boots, which I should've shined.

Frannie holds her arms open. "We're gathered today before these witnesses to join this man and woman in holy matrimony. May Rhett and Paige comfort each other in hard times, share one another's dreams, and be each other's biggest support. May they be the best of friends and love each other unconditionally, and may that love grow stronger every day."

Jesus. I don't remember my first wedding being this lovey-dovey, and that was held in a church.

"Rhett, will you have this woman to be your wedded wife, to live together in matrimony? Will you cherish her friendship? Honor and love her? Will you be by her side faithfully, today, tomorrow, and forever?"

Not six months.

Not until I get my loan and pay off shit.

Forever.

That's what this is supposed to be. These are vows, for fuck's sake. I always take my vows seriously. Promising to look after my brothers is what got me into this mess in the first place.

Maybe I just need to do what Beau suggested and be sure to treat Paige right, and we'll get through this.

I clear my throat. "I do."

When Paige is asked the same questions, she glances at me hesitantly, so I squeeze her hand and wink.

She takes a deep breath. Her lovely smile reemerges, and she says, "I do."

I wanna keep that smile on her face, so as I look into her breathtaking blue eyes, I try to reassure her. I know she doesn't have to help me and my brothers. She could've told me off and found some friends to stay with, but she's going through all this trouble to help me cover my ass. And I'll never forget it.

As I repeat after the judge, I make a promise to myself that I'll always do my best to protect this woman. "I, Rhett, take you, Paige, to be my wedded wife, to have and to hold, for better, for worse, for richer, for poorer, to love and to cherish, from this day forward."

Smiling, she repeats the same words, and I grin. She's so damn cute.

Frannie nods. "May the circles of your wedding bands remind you of this eternal promise. May these tokens of faithfulness remind you of your unending love for one another." Then she turns to me. "Please place the ring on her finger."

Reaching into my pocket, I pull out the thin band I bought from Walmart yesterday. It's a far cry from the diamond-encrusted ring I put on Amber's finger next to the sparkling diamond I saved up for a year to buy. Another twinge of guilt hits me, but I lock that shit away and try to focus on the beautiful woman in front of me I've known more than half my life.

It hits me. How selfless she's being. Yeah, she's gonna get her therapy, but I don't know a lot of people who would do this for my family.

Once again, I repeat after Frannie. "Paige, I give you this ring as a symbol of our vows. I honor you with all that I am and all that I have. With this ring, I thee wed." As I slide the band on her finger, my chest gets tight.

Paige pulls out a thick gold band that makes me do a double-take. Where the hell did she get that? After she drags it on my finger, she says her part. I swallow as her eyes get glassy, and that tightness in my chest grows.

When she's done, Frannie opens her arms again. "I now pronounce you husband and wife. Rhett Walker, you may kiss your bride!"

My brothers, who got the memo to go whole hog about this and act like this is the real deal, hoot and holler, and Baylee and her mother cheer. Harlan lets out a wolf whistle. Their exuberance catches me off guard.

It's the only reason I can think of that makes me take Paige into my arms, tilt her lithe body backwards, and kiss her like my life depends on it.

Chapter Ten
PAIGE

As I cling to Rhett for dear life, his mouth descends to mine in what I can only describe as the world's best first kiss.

His lips are firm but soft, and his breath is minty. And he's close enough that I can smell that amazing woodsy cologne I've always loved.

For those blissful ten seconds, the entire planet stops spinning, and I let out a quiet sigh.

If it wasn't for his arm pressed to my back when he straightens me, I would slump to the floor.

When he finally lets go, I wobble and grab onto his arm.

Rhett leans over and whispers, "Shoulda warned you. I'm a good kisser."

He looks so pleased with himself. "I should let you walk around for the rest of the day with lipstick on your face. Come here." Arrogant bastard.

When he leans down, I'm struck by how handsome he is. I've always thought that, obviously, but right now, with that shit-eating grin on his face, his good looks are downright sinful. I grab his scruffy face and wipe away my gloss. As my thumb slides over his bottom lip, he nips it.

I gasp and let out an embarrassing giggle. His grin deepens, and my whole body heats.

Baylee's flash yanks me out of his hypnotic gaze, almost blinding me, and I blink several times. Rhett and I agreed someone should take some pics to make this seem official, and my best friend offered.

Miss Frannie calls out, "May I present Mr. and Mrs. Rhett Walker."

Fifteen-year-old me is ecstatic. She's doing backflips down the aisle.

The real me knows that kiss was all for show. With Rhett's banker sitting in the second row, of course my "husband" was going to play this up.

Aunt Syl yells, "Who wants to bet we get a visit from the stork in nine months?"

Everyone laughs except me and Rhett.

Because that would certainly throw a wrench in our plans.

As we step away from the podium, Rhett places his hand on the small of my back and leads me to Harlan and his wife.

"Y'all sure do make a pretty couple," the older man says.

He looks vaguely familiar. I probably met him when I was a kid and don't remember. Wild Heart is a small town, and I'd be surprised if there were many people I don't know.

I shake his hand. "It's so nice to meet you. I heard you and the Walkers go way back."

"Sure do. I've known these boys my whole life, so you best be good to this one."

Laughing, I nod. "Yes, sir. I'll do my best."

"You know, we're gonna be neighbors. I just bought the property across the way from the Walker Ranch, so I'll be seeing y'all around."

Rhett's brows lift. "You bought the Gibson property?"

Harlan nods. "Just a few months ago. They needed the money, and I figured, what the hell, maybe we'll give this ranching thing a go. My son Jimmy thought we should diversify."

"Well, holler if y'all need anything." Rhett invites Harlan and his wife back to the ranch, and after a round of hugs from our friends, we head to his truck. I watch his brothers cram into Jace's vehicle.

I wish one of them would join us. It would be nice to have someone to break the silence.

Holy crap. I just married Rhett freaking Walker. I glance down at the thin band on my finger, and it gives me a strange sense of nostalgia. I remember pretending to marry Rhett when I was little, walking down the dirt path behind my house and holding my hair brush like a bouquet. My ratty old teddy bear did a poor job standing in for the groom.

"You okay?" His deep voice startles me.

"Yeah."

"Sorry about that kiss back there. Was it too much?"

"I don't know. I've never been married before. How did you kiss Amber?"

He thinks on that a moment. "Not like that. I just gave her a peck."

Huh. Interesting. "Well, I think Harlan bought it. That's all that matters, right?"

When he nods but doesn't say anything, I start to worry. "Was my fake wedding announcement okay?"

He clears his throat. "It was fine."

Fine? I thought he'd be excited about it. "Is there anything you need me to do at the reception besides moon over you and pretend I'm the happiest bride in town?"

"Just do what you're doing."

And then he's silent again.

Okay then.

If any part of me was hoping that kiss would magically make Rhett fall in love with me, his silence sets me straight.

By the time we reach the ranch, I'm itching to get some space, but there are cars parked everywhere and people spill out of the house.

"I thought you said this was going to be a small reception?"

After he parks, he turns to me. "Paige, you announced our wedding in the *Gazette*. I've been getting calls all day from people inviting themselves over this evening."

"What was I supposed to do? You told me to play up my part, so I did." When he doesn't say anything, I frown. "Did Irma or Ty call? Are they coming?"

I'd be lying if I said I wasn't hoping they would. After all the grief I got from Irma for having a crush on Rhett, I would relish this redemption, even if it won't last long. And Ty? He's still my brother, but I'm starting to think we'll never be close. Not with Irma always yapping in his ear.

Rhett looks down in his lap, and I don't even need him to open his mouth to hear that my family's not coming.

I don't know why I care. "Doesn't matter." I unlock my door and slide out.

"Wait," he calls out after me, but I'm already on my way to the house. Except the gravel on the driveway and my shoes don't like each other, so I have to slow down to keep my balance. My ankle is starting to hurt, but I love these sandals. They're so elegant. Plus, I don't have anything else to wear besides flip-flops or sneakers.

Rhett catches up to me with a grunt, then lifts me into his arms.

"What are you doing?"

He motions to the front door, which we're approaching. "Carrying you over the threshold. You know, one of those time-honored wedding traditions."

"Oh. Yeah. Okay." A thrill shoots through me at how easily he carries me. The man doesn't even break a sweat.

When we reach the house, he pauses. "Listen, in case I haven't told you yet, I'm really grateful for what you're doing. Thank you."

His gruff voice makes chills break out along my arms. I turn to look at him, which is a mistake because we're almost nose to nose. But I don't want to be that girl who loses her mind over him. I *can't* be that girl again. Going through that almost broke me the first time. So I give him a big, fake smile and ignore how easy it would be to maul him in this position. "No problem. Does this mean I get to eat now?"

He chuckles. "Come on, wife. Let's get you fed."

Wife?!

I let out a pathetic little sigh of delight. That sounded good. Too good.

When we open the door, everyone yells congratulations. I'm almost embarrassed by how many people came out. My third-grade teacher is here, my middle school librarian, the woman who owns my favorite coffee shop, and a few other locals who look familiar.

Rhett sets me down gently, but keeps his arm around my shoulders. I lean into him and smile at our guests.

He whispers, "By the way, you look gorgeous in that dress. If we were really getting married, I'd be a lucky man."

I swallow, hating that those words hurt, but I mask it with another fake smile and snark, "Too bad you can only look and not touch." I give him a saucy wink and make my way over to the beverage table, where I hope we have something stronger than beer because I'm going to need it.

After I pour a seven and seven, I make the rounds, saying hi to people I haven't seen in years. While I visited home a few times since I went to college, I hated all the gossip, so I mostly stayed at my house or with Baylee and didn't venture out much.

The patio doors open, and my eyes widen when I see picnic tables full of food and even a cake. Since Rhett is surrounded by well-wishers, I beeline it over to Jace and Beau, who are wolfing down hors d'oeuvres. "Where did y'all get the money for all of this?" I hiss. "I thought we were supposed to be frugal."

"Like that ring you bought our brother?" Beau asks with a smirk.

"I felt bad giving him something cheap." I shrug. "The jeweler gave me a line of credit." Beau closes his eyes like he thinks I'm an idiot. "It's not a big deal. I'll pay it off once I start working. It wasn't that much."

Actually, it cost way more than I wanted to spend, but seeing how I'll probably never get married again, I wanted to pretend for one day.

Aunt Syl waves me over, and she makes me and Rhett hug for a photo in front of some twinkle lights.

Who put up twinkle lights? It's so romantic with the sun setting along the hills in the background. The sky is awash with red and purple and orange. I could sit out here all night and stare at the incredible horizon. I eye the fire pit that's surrounded by old Adirondack chairs. I make a mental note to curl up there one night to read.

Someone grabs a glass and taps it with a fork, and suddenly everyone's doing it.

"Kiss her, stupid," old Mr. Valero yells at Rhett.

I laugh and turn to my new husband. Trying to delay the inevitable, I smooth my hands over his suit jacket. "I didn't know you owned a suit. I've only seen you in jeans and t-shirts. You clean up nicely, *husband*."

Rhett frowns, then leans down and pecks me on the mouth, and Mr. Valero groans. "Not like that, dumbass. Kiss her with some gumption."

I chuckle and put my hands up on Rhett's shoulders. "It's okay. Do your worst." Lowering my voice, I whisper, "You're good to go. I swear I won't fall madly in love with you."

That makes his frown deepen for some reason. I'm about to push up on my toes when he leans down to whisper, "Don't put weight on your ankle. I got you." Then cradles the back of my head and pulls me to his hard chest.

This time, he nips my bottom lip, making me gasp, and then uses that opening to slide his tongue across mine.

The kiss lasts a second. Barely a heartbeat of time.

And yet my whole body lights up like I'm a holiday display at Christmas time.

Our guests cheer, and I cling to his big, hard body.

Aunt Syl shouts, "Rhett Walker is officially off the market, ladies!" And everyone laughs.

"Hell, yes, he's off the market," I yell playfully, and the laughter grows. I wink at Rhett so he knows I'm just messing around. Though if I'm feeling possessive of him, I'll never admit it. When I spot the three-tier cake again, I point at it. "Can we smash the cake in each other's faces? I've always wanted to do that."

He chuckles. "Whatever you want, *wife*."

Baylee makes us pose for photos. We munch on pizza and wings, and I eventually reach for a beer because I don't want to hurl later. But the best part is when we cut the cake.

Rhett and I stand armed with vanilla cake that's filled with custard and smells amazing. "Don't get this on my dress, or I'll hurt you."

We both start to feed each other, and just as I'm about to take a bite out of his hand, he gets a glint in his eye, but I beat him to it and smash my slice in his face. Screaming with laughter, I turn around, but he wraps his arms around me, lifts me off the ground, holds me to his chest, and smears it across my cheek before he shoves a piece in my mouth.

I'm laughing so hard, I almost choke.

Especially when I slide down his body, and I'm greeted with something else that's really hard.

Good Lord, he's built like a bull. My eyes widen as I realize what's pressed up against my back.

"Shit," he grumbles. "Sorry." He pulls away, but keeps his hand on my shoulder, probably to buy himself a minute.

Why can't I ride Rhett later? I'm so bummed I won't get to enjoy his incredible body tonight, I could stomp. "Didn't know foot-longs were on the menu," I say under my breath.

After a few more photos, we wipe our faces.

As it starts to get dark, someone cranks a stereo through the open windows of the house. Mav hops up on a picnic table and yells, "Let's get the happy couple out here for a dance!" He jumps down and half-tackles Rhett, who laughs.

Ryan Hunt's newest hit, an enchanting love song about his wife, blares through the quiet night. I take a deep breath when Rhett grabs my hand and leads me across the backyard to the concrete patio.

When he pulls me into his arms, Mav starts barking like an idiot. Baylee elbows him in the gut, and I laugh. If anyone in our group of friends was going to get married, I always thought it would be them, but based on the sexy little blonde following him around, that's not happening anytime soon.

As Rhett and I sway, I try to keep from pressing against him, but it's difficult because I have to lean up to hold his shoulders.

He had a rock-hard erection earlier.

The intrusive thought makes my heart speed up, but I remind myself it was just his body reacting to having me rub against him, nothing more.

I finally brave a look at my husband.

He's already staring at me. "How's your ankle?"

His dark eyes have the thickest lashes. All the men in this family have beautiful eyes, and if this was real, I wouldn't feel so conflicted about losing myself in their depths.

"Hurts a little, but the alcohol helps."

"We'll get you off your feet after this. Get you a bag of ice."

"I'll be fine." As much as I'm enjoying being this close to him, I'm looking forward to getting away from him later tonight. Too much of Rhett is a bad thing. I need some solid boundaries if I'm going to survive the next few months with my heart intact.

Was I being honest with him about not being able to fall in love? To an extent. I've never come close to being in love with any of my boyfriends, and I've tried.

Do I think I could fall in love with Rhett? All too easily, which is why I'm hoping my heart can stay aloof like it always does.

When the song is over, Aunt Sylvia comes up to us, dangling something off her finger. "These are the keys to Love Bird cabin next to Firefly Lake. It's yours for the weekend. It's my wedding gift to you and Rhett. Y'all deserve a little honeymoon."

What the fresh hell? That cabin is where all the local couples go to "reconnect." It's supposed to be super romantic.

"That's so sweet of you, Syl. You shouldn't have." I hug her and try to mask my alarm. "You've already done so much."

"Nonsense." She smirks. "I have ulterior motives. I want those grandbabies."

What are the odds that cabin has two bedrooms?

Chapter Eleven
RHETT

My truck bumps along the dirt road as I drive Paige to the cabin. She's been quiet. She has the window rolled down, and she's half leaning out of it, staring up at the stars.

I'm usually good with quiet. Prefer it, really. Except, when she's pensive, it makes me nervous for some reason.

Didn't know foot-longs were on the menu.

I probably should be embarrassed about the way I got hard when we were cutting the cake. Is that what she's thinking about right now? Do I even care?

Change the subject, stupid. I glance at her again. "Are you hungry? I packed us some pizza in case you are."

"Thanks."

That's all she says. "Listen, I only found out about the cabin this afternoon. I meant to give you a heads-up, but never really had a chance."

"It's okay."

Paige is a lot of things, but quiet isn't usually one of them.

When we finally get there, I turn off my truck, and we sit in silence. The light of the moon reflects off the lake, making the still water glow.

The cabin is wrapped in vines and twinkle lights. Above the front door is a huge wooden heart with angel wings. I suppose if I was really looking to get away with my new wife, this ain't a bad place.

Finally, she turns to me. "I'm tired." Then she slides on her flip-flops and gets out.

I grab our overnight bags and follow her. She moves over to let me unlock the door, and I flip on the light, which turns on two floor lamps. There's a love seat, a small couch, a bookshelf, and a coffee table. That's it. There's no TV. Damn. Paige and I will actually have to... talk all weekend.

"This place is adorable," she says as she heads to the small kitchen. She opens the fridge and turns to me, wide-eyed. "It's full of food."

Frowning, I follow her in there where we find a note from Sylvia. *Congrats, guys! We love you! Aunt Syl and Baylee.*

"Ugh," Paige groans. "I feel so guilty that she went through all this trouble. She bought me this dress, those gorgeous sandals, took me to lunch, rented this place, and bought us all these supplies."

"I know what you mean. My brothers went all out, but they wanted to make sure Harlan didn't suspect anything."

"When this is all over, I'm going to find a way to pay her back."

Paige is really fucking sweet. I turn her to face me. "Sylvia loves you. It makes her happy to do this for you."

"She works really hard at the salon, and it's not like she's rolling in the dough. Aunt Syl can't afford this. What about when Baylee gets married someday? Shouldn't she use this money on her?"

I think about Paige's best friend. "She has a thing for Mav, right?" Baylee and Maverick have been "best buds" for years, and I sometimes think she looks at him a certain way, but then he does something dumb, and she won't talk to him for a while.

Paige stares at me. "If you think us being married means I'm going to share all of Baylee's secrets, you have another thing coming."

I hold my hands up. "I think they'd make a great couple. He won't talk about her, though, which I've always thought strange since he talks about..." She gives me a look, and I stop talking. "You're right. We won't talk about them."

She rolls her eyes as she pulls out her cell. "Do you have a signal? I have a crappy provider, and I only have one bar," she says as she walks around with her phone in the air. "I want to send Syl a text to thank her."

I check my phone. "Two bars. You can use my phone if you need to."

Her thumbs fly across the screen. "It went through." She glances around. "Think there's more than one bedroom?"

"This is the local love shack, so that's doubtful."

I follow her down the hallway, where there are two doors. One opens to a bedroom and the other to a bathroom. The bedroom has a queen wrought-iron bed with some frilly pillows.

I glance back to the living room. Shit. There's no way I'll fit on that couch. Hell, I'll barely fit on the bed.

"I brought a sleeping bag. I'll crash on the floor." I turn, but Paige grabs my arm.

"You sleep on the bed, big guy. I'll be fine on the couch."

She gives me one of those fake smiles she's been sporting all day, and that knot of guilt grows. "Thank you for the ring. You spent too much on it. At the end of our time together, we'll sell it and get your money back."

Paige swallows and looks away. "It's my gift to you. Something to remember me by when I move away to coach cheer camp. I'm thinking Boston might be nice. I applied for an assistant position there that starts in January."

Boston? Why the fuck does she wanna move to the East Coast?

Before I can say anything, she slides into the bathroom and shuts the door.

As I toss and turn in bed a few hours later, I think about all the crazy shit that happened today.

I married Danny's little sister.

I'm sorry, bro. I didn't know another way to save the ranch, but this will help me keep an eye on her.

At least, that's what I tell myself.

Sometime around two, it's so hot, I kick off the sheet and wander out into the living room to look for the thermostat. Instead, I find Paige sprawled on the couch in a cropped white tank top that barely covers her tits and a lacy white thong.

Fuck.

I pivot and head back to my room, where I throw open the window and pray for a breeze.

After I flop on the bed, I do my best to ignore my early morning wood. I will not jerk off to thoughts of Paige.

As I lie here, it's hard not to compare this wedding to my first one. I should've known my marriage to Amber was doomed. She was a total bridezilla. She snarked at the caterers, her bridesmaids, her family, and me. I spent a small fortune to give her the wedding she wanted, and she still complained.

In contrast, Paige got the discount courthouse penny-saver version, and all she did today was thank everyone. She was a gorgeous, gracious bride. If there was anyone who deserved her ideal wedding, it's the woman sleeping on the fucking couch.

I hate the idea of her moving so far away, but if that's what she wants, I'm going to do my damn best to make sure she has everything she needs when she goes.

The morning light shining through the window wakes me around nine. I don't remember the last time I slept this late. With a yawn, I use the bathroom and then head to the living room to look for Paige, but she's not there.

That's when I hear a splash.

I open the front door and see her swimming just off the dock. I wander down there, but she doesn't see me.

Which is how I come face to face with my very naked wife, who freezes halfway up the dock ladder.

Holy hell, she has a gorgeous body. Beautiful, round tits with nipples the color of peaches. A tiny waist and bare little pussy. Lean thighs I'd love to have wrapped around my neck.

As water drips off her hills and valleys, I lick my lips.

"Rhett!" She lets go and splashes back into the lake. "You scared me."

Shit. I turn around and hold up my hands. "Sorry. Didn't realize you were skinny-dipping."

"Sylvia packed my bag. She must've thought I didn't need a swimsuit."

Had this been a real honeymoon, she'd have been right. "Sorry 'bout that." It's gonna take some mental jujitsu to erase the image of Paige's naked body from my mind. "Do you want some breakfast? Thought I'd make us some omelets."

"That would be nice. Thanks."

When I get back to the cabin, I lock myself in the bathroom, wrap my hand around my aching dick, and let my mind wander back to that incredible view off the dock. I go off in an embarrassingly short amount of time.

After I clean myself up, I head for the kitchen and get to work.

She returns fifteen minutes later.

"Food's almost ready." I don't let myself look at her, but out of my peripheral vision I see that she's wrapped in a towel.

"I'm going to take a quick shower. Like, five minutes."

I give her a thumbs-up and return my focus to our omelets. When she emerges from the bathroom, her sweet floral scent follows her. It must be her soap because it's not an overpowering smell like Amber's arsenal of perfumes.

After I plate our food, I place everything on the small kitchen table. "Did ya have a nice swim?"

"Yeah. It was great. I was so hot last night."

"I'll mess with the AC. If we can't get it working, we should open all the windows. Maybe we'll get a breeze going tonight."

Now that we're alone without my brothers and neighbors, I'm struggling to think of what to say. I've missed out on so much of her life. I want to ask her if she enjoyed college. If she made friends. If she had fun cheerleading for the Broncos.

"Do you think Harlan bought the wedding?" she asks after she swallows a bite of the omelet.

"Yeah. You did a good job seeming into me." Paige had me fooled at times. I'd start to worry her real feelings were getting involved, but then she'd flash me one of those fake smiles, and I'd realize she was just acting.

She pushes food around her plate with her fork. "Are you meeting with him soon to get that loan?"

"First thing Monday morning."

"Great."

"We'll move your stuff into my bedroom when we get back. We can bunk together, but I'll take the couch. If that's okay with you."

She rolls her eyes. "Not this discussion again. I'll take the damn couch, Rhett."

I'm not letting her sleep on the couch for the next six months. I guess we'll figure it out when we get home.

Paige takes a sip of her water. "Is Amber going to be okay when she finds out about us?"

"I don't give a fuck how she takes it." Just the mention of my ex makes my blood pressure rise.

She stares down at her plate. "I just mean, if she doesn't take it well, won't that be hard on your boys?"

I grab my mug of coffee. "They'll get to know you, and it'll be fine." When she doesn't say anything else, I sigh. "I'm sorry I used that tone with you. Amber still pisses me off."

"I get it."

I don't know if this is the right time to share this with her, but she deserves to know. "You were right about her sleeping with Kacey Miller, but I didn't figure out she was sleeping around until I found her fucking Cash McAllister." It's like my ex went out of her way to find the worst person possible, the one she knew would piss me off the most.

Her eyes widen. "She didn't."

"Oh, yeah, she did. There's nothing more embarrassing than needing to take your kids to the doctor to get a paternity test."

She reaches across the table and grabs my hand. "Amber's an idiot. This is her loss. Most of the women in this town would give their left tit to be with you."

I bark out a laugh, and my eyes immediately drop to her chest. "Only the left one?"

Paige balls up her napkin and throws it in my face. "Shut up." But then she gets a playful expression on her face. "You've seen me naked."

"Both tits too. Not just the left one."

She snorts. "That's not really fair, is it?"

"What do you mean?"

"I mean, you've seen me naked, but I haven't seen you in the buff. So now you have the upper hand." She nibbles on the corner of her lip. "To make things equal, I should get to see you naked too."

Leaning back in my chair, I cross my arms over my chest. "Really?" I smirk. "Think you can handle it?"

She also crosses her arms. "You have no idea what I can handle, Rhett Walker."

Paige is a bona fide flirt. I kinda love it. "So... what? Like right here?"

"Be my guest." Paige holds out her hand. "Unless you're chicken."

I chuckle, unable to resist her challenge. "All right. Fair is fair." I stand, reach behind my neck, and scoop off my t-shirt. "Brace yourself. It's big."

She laughs. "Humble, aren't you?"

"Not really." I unbuckle my belt, flip open the button on my jeans, and hook my thumbs in the waistband of my boxer briefs. "You ready?"

"Scoot back. You're too close. I'm not gonna know where to look first."

"Oh, you'll know." She flushes, and I laugh. I'm mesmerized by her bright blue eyes. By the rosiness in her cheeks. By the way she's looking at me right now.

I'm playing with fire, but I'm so fucking tired of being responsible all the damn time, a part of me relishes letting loose.

I take a few steps back into the living room. Before I overthink this, I pull down my clothes and let her stare.

Yeah, I'm hard.

My cock gives her a full salute and springs up to my stomach.

Her eyes widen as she takes me in. "Is it difficult to walk with that rocket launcher in your pants?"

I chuckle and pull up my jeans. "It's only tough when my dick redirects the tides." Takes me a second to tuck myself away.

She laughs, and I join her back at the table. "Now we're even," she says, her voice husky.

I clear my throat. "Guess we don't need to be weird about nudity then."

"Nope. I've seen your goods, and you've seen mine." She takes another bite of her omelet. "Oh, Baylee said we need to take some pics while we're here."

"Just point me where you want me." That flush in her cheeks returns, and I smirk. "Why, Paige Lewis, is your mind in the gutter? Are you horny?"

She tuts. "It's Mrs. Paige *Walker*, thank you very much." Jesus, that sounds good. "It's nothing I can't handle. I brought my vibrator. I'll just rub one out later."

I choke on some bacon.

Maybe seeing each other naked was a bad idea.

Chapter Twelve

PAIGE

A%%%FTER WE PLAY%% a few rounds of Uno, we decide to switch things up.

"Wanna play chess?" Rhett asks as he studies the games tucked into the small bookcase.

"Sure, but I'm probably a little rusty. It's been a while."

He gives me a sad smile. "Your brother always kicked my ass at this game."

"Same." Danny taught me how to play during those long hospital nights.

We sit in companionable silence as we take turns. I finally get Rhett cornered. "Checkmate."

"What the fuck? No." He studies the board, then looks at me. "I don't think I've ever been whooped this fast before, not even by Danny."

I smile. "He taught me well, I guess."

When I realized we didn't have a TV set, I was worried about how we'd spend the weekend. My ex, Marcus, couldn't deal if he had to unplug from his PlayStation that long, but Rhett just rolls with it.

When he gets up off the couch to grab us drinks, I shamelessly ogle him. Clothes don't do him justice because his body is a work of freaking art. My breath catches in my chest as I remember him tugging off every stitch of clothing.

If all I get out of this marriage are those thirty seconds of Rhett stark naked, it was one hundred percent worth it.

He's freaking huge. Everywhere.

A minute later he returns with two glasses of champagne and some strawberries. I give him a look, and he shrugs. "Seems a shame to let this go to waste." He holds out his glass. "Here's to being married to a fine woman."

I smile and clink his glass with mine. "And here's to being married to a fine man." After I take a sip, I chuckle. "I didn't even have to give up my left tit."

He snorts. "I had no idea you were so funny."

Hell, I didn't know either, but now that I finally get to spend time with Rhett, I want to make him laugh all the time. I buff my nails. "It's part of my charm."

He chuckles and wraps his arm around my shoulders and hugs me. "I owe you big, Lewis."

It feels so good to be so close to him, but I pretend like I'm unaffected. "We're even. Beau said he'll make sure I get on your health insurance this week, and then I can book my therapy sessions."

"How's your ankle feeling?"

"It's a little achy, but that dip in the lake helped. I think I'm going to soak in the hot tub."

"There's a hot tub?"

I nod. "Out back."

He's quiet a minute. "Gonna skinny-dip again? Or can I join you?"

"You can join me. I'll wear my underwear. It'll be like a bathing suit."

We enjoy the strawberries and champagne, and by the time

I'm done, I'm feeling a little tipsy. The booze gives me extra courage.

"Come on. Let's go soak in the hot tub." I pull off my shirt, which leaves me in my bra, and head for the front door. He takes off after me.

Once I reach the hot tub deck, I tug off my shorts. A giddy shock of excitement surges over my skin as I feel his eyes travel over me. *Finally*, the little voice in the back of my head whispers. And since I have no shame, I bend slightly at my hips to jut my thong-clad ass back towards him.

When I turn around, Rhett's eyes dart up, and he clears his throat. "Here." He holds out his hand, and I take it to steady myself.

I groan as I sink into the warm water. "This is awesome. Get in."

Sitting, I watch him shrug out of his t-shirt. In the low light, his muscles stand out in stark relief. The sexy tattoos on his arms and shoulders make an ache start low in my belly. Damn, he's hot.

Then he slides down his jeans, which leaves him in black boxer briefs that strain against another erection. *Don't stare and make this weird, Paige.* I look away as he climbs into the hot tub.

The sun is starting to set, and I let myself get lost in the brilliance of the sky. "In high school, I couldn't wait to get out of Wild Heart, but now that I'm taking the time to appreciate how beautiful it is here, I'm starting to regret being away for so long."

"I'm sorry shit was so tough for you back then. I had no idea that people found out about our discussion, or that Irma was such a bitch about the whole thing."

I shrug. "It's my own fault for butting in. I had no business doing what I did. It's just..."

"Just what?"

My heart races as I carefully choose my words. "I know I was young, and I'm sure to you I was just Danny's kid sister, but I considered you one of my best friends. I cared about you, and I didn't want to see you get hurt."

When he doesn't say anything, I look over and find him studying me. "It took a lot of guts to do what you did, wildflower. If I'd had more sense at the time, I would've taken it more seriously. You were right about Amber all along, and I hate the idea that you've changed because of what happened back then. You're perfect. Don't let anyone tell you otherwise."

My throat gets tight, and I nod. "Thank you." If I'm so perfect, why is it so hard to find a good boyfriend? One who actually cares enough about me to introduce me to his family?

"And since you know all my dirty laundry, you gonna tell me what happened between you and that ex of yours? How long did you date?"

It's eerie how he nearly read my mind. "Ten months I'll never get back, though he did let me live with him after a tree destroyed my house."

"What happened?"

I pull my hair out of a ponytail and twist it into a messy bun. "We had a crazy storm that uprooted a tree, which slammed into the house I was renting. It actually pinned my roommate down."

"Holy shit."

"Abby was fine, but it scared the hell out of both of us. We couldn't stay in the house any longer, and Marcus invited me to stay with him. I had nowhere else to go, so I took him up on his offer. But he and I were a mistake."

His face goes hard. "Did he not treat you right?"

"He was always preoccupied. I always felt like an afterthought." I look down. "And then..."

"Then?"

I sigh. "I overheard him talking with his friends, and one asked if he was bringing me to his parents' anniversary dinner, and he said, 'Fuck, no. My parents won't like her. She doesn't have any real goals. They won't think she's marriage material.'"

"Are you serious? What an asshole."

"It would've been fine if he hadn't strung me along. If he'd just been honest that he was only into me for sex."

Rhett rubs a hand over his face. "Not sure I wanna hear this."

"Don't be so parochial. I lost my virginity when I was sixteen in Adam Olsen's backseat." I don't mention that I did it solely to get over Rhett. "Had a couple of boyfriends in college. Nothing noteworthy, though. What about you? Have you met any special ladies since you and Amber called it quits?"

"Nobody special."

"Just a few friends with benefits?"

"Just *one* friend, but we weren't serious."

"So she won't care that you tied the knot? Or..." I pause. "Do you still plan to hook up with her over the next few months? I just want to know what to expect."

He scowls. "Fuck, no. I'm not hooking up with anyone." He holds up his left hand. "I'm married, in case you didn't notice."

I glance away. "It's okay if you do. Six months is a long time to ask you to go without sex. I won't mind." A little piece of my soul dies when I utter those words. "Just don't tell me what you do or with whom. I don't want to know." This isn't a real marriage. I can't make any demands.

That gets me a growl, and the next thing I know, I'm in Rhett's lap. "Paige, listen closely. I'm not gonna fuck around behind your back. I hate cheaters, so I would never do that to you."

I stare up at his handsome face, at the scruff I want to rub against. "Okay."

He glares down at me. "Wouldn't it bother you if I fucked around? Because it sure as hell would bother me if you did."

I suck in a breath. Between the hot water and the champagne, I'm feeling extra brave.

Screw it.

I shift to straddle him and wrap my arms around his broad

shoulders. "Would it really bother you if I slept with someone else? I thought I was just your friend's little sister? Why would you care?"

His hands move to my hips, and he drags me closer until I'm pressing against that incredible erection. "Because I do, okay?"

"Did you really not mean our first kiss?" I whisper. "Because it felt real. It felt like it meant something."

His grip tightens. "It shouldn't have meant anything, but how can I kiss you and it be meaningless?"

My heart gallops in my chest.

Chapter Thirteen
PAIGE

Mustering up some courage, I snuggle closer until we're nose to nose. "Rhett, technically, we're married. No one's going to care if we have sex. In fact, half the town expects it."

He closes his eyes, like he's battling himself. When he opens them, he almost looks angry. "I don't wanna hurt you. I never wanted to remarry, and I have no plans to stay married. When this is over, and *it will end*, I want to have a clear conscience."

I try not to flinch when he declares that we have a deadline. Of course, I know this—he's been clear—but deep down, a part of me is hoping he'll want to stay together.

And that's just the stupid shit you see in romantic comedies. It's not real life.

My heart finally settles, finally slows down, and that aloof feeling I always get with men returns, thank God. I shrug. "So let's just have fun. We'll fuck this out of our systems, and in six months go our separate ways as friends."

He stares at my lips like he wants to devour me. "It's not that simple."

"Why not? I think we have chemistry. Why not explore that for the time we have together?"

He cups my face. "Paige, I'm ten years older than you. You and I were never meant to happen. This would be wrong."

"What's wrong about this?" I turn my face out of his grasp. "I'm almost twenty-three. I can choose what I want to do, and at the moment, I'd like to do you."

Rhett chuckles, leaning close enough that our lips are only a hair's breadth away. "Wildflower, you have no idea what you're signing up for."

Smirking, I rub against him. "I have a pretty good idea." He looks like he's waging an internal battle as his eyes shift between mine. I shrug. "Unless you're not into me. Maybe I'm not your type. You're really not my type. You're far too broody and big... and annoying."

He lets out a string of curses. "Let the record show I tried to be a good guy here." Then his hand slides into my hair, gripping it firmly, and tugs my mouth to his.

When his tongue slides against mine, I groan in delight. Holy hell, he feels amazing, so solid and strong. His other hand lands on my ass, and he pulls me closer. Knowing he wants me shoots a wave of excitement through my body. I take the hint and grind against him as I let my fingers drift over his incredible shoulders.

His mouth falls to my neck where he nips me. "You always smell so fucking good. It drives me crazy how good you smell." He lifts me up on my knees. "Take this off."

His gruff voice makes me shiver as he motions to my bra. I shift off his lap so I'm standing in the waist-deep water. Reaching between my boobs, I flick open my bra and slowly move it down my shoulders before I shove off my panties and fling them off to the side.

"Did you get a good enough look this morning?" I ask with a smirk. I can be cheeky and sarcastic because I know this won't mean anything to him. The time will come when Rhett will divorce me, and I want him to rue that day because every one of our encounters will be seared in his brain.

His eyes grow hot as they travel over me. "Come here."

I lift an eyebrow. "Or else...?"

"Or I'll throw you over my shoulder and spank your ass."

My nipples get tight at the threat in his voice. I chuckle. "You'd have to catch me first." I turn and try to race away, forgetting all about my ankle. I make it two steps before Rhett has me in his grip.

"Brat. I'm gonna make you pay for that." He sets me down, but only long enough to spin me around so he can put me over his shoulder.

The first smack of his hand over my ass cheek comes as a shock, and I gasp, but then my core clenches and I shudder. The second smack makes me groan as I cling to his strong back.

"Say you're sorry for running." His voice is a low growl that makes my pussy clench. He rubs that spot, easing the sting.

I laugh, pushing back into his palm, hoping he'll spank me again. "Not happening."

"If you say you're sorry, I'll let you come."

"Kinky," I chuckle, feeling the sides of his lips rise before he traces kisses up my thigh.

"Mmm. I tried to warn you." His teeth graze me. "You can always say no."

My pussy clenches again, and I relent. "I'm sorry. Please let me come."

"Good girl."

The praise quickens the pulse between my legs, and I realize I'll do whatever he wants if he'll put his hands on me again.

Leaning back, he lets me slide down his chest until his huge erection presses against my belly. He shifts me until my back is to his chest, then sits, pulling me into his lap.

The hot water swirls around us, amplifying every place on my body that touches his.

With my legs spread and my ass planted firmly against him, he ratchets my need another notch when his lips trace my neck. "Good girls get rewards."

My breath hitches. He's good at this. Too good.

His giant hands cup my breasts, and I suck in a breath, wild with lust for my husband. *Shit. My husband.*

His hands are gentle, almost reverent, as he molds and shapes me, but when his calloused fingers drag over my nipples, I moan.

Then his palm drifts down my stomach. "Wider, Paige." He helps me place my thighs over his until I'm wide open. I watch his hand stroke up my legs. He drags his fingers over the crease of my thighs before he pushes my pussy lips together.

"Oh, God." I arch backwards as he keeps toying with my nipple.

"If you wanna fuck, I have to stretch you out with my fingers first. You're a tiny thing, and I don't want to hurt you."

Spreading me apart, his thumb grazes my clit, and I groan. "Torture me all you want. Just remember that I get my turn next."

He chuckles. "That's not how this works, wildflower."

We'll see.

But then he presses his palm against me as he fills me with two fingers, and I gasp. Reaching back, I run my fingers through his thick hair.

He works me over, thrusting in and out of me as I writhe in his lap. Sucks on my neck. Pinches my nipple. The whole time pressing on my clit while he fucks me with his hand.

"Think you can take three fingers?"

"Try it."

It takes a hot minute to achieve this. I arch and moan and wiggle as he works himself into me. As I look down, the water is clear enough that I can see his hand moving between my thighs.

"You're so wet," he whispers in my ear. "I can't wait to fill you with my cock."

That's all it takes for me to detonate. I arch back with a

scream as fireworks ricochet through my body, leaving me panting and boneless in his lap.

I've never come this fast in my life, but I'll never admit that to Rhett.

Slowly, he removes his fingers.

I turn in his lap and throw my arms around his shoulders. Leaning up, I kiss him as I reach between us where his cock is poking through his boxer briefs. I lower the waistband, and it bobs up between us.

"Sit on the deck." I pat the area right behind him. When he doesn't budge, I bat my eyelashes. "Please." He smirks, then does as I ask. "Take these off." I tug on his underwear, and he stands to lower them before he sits again.

I let myself stare at his huge dick. It's beautiful and smooth. He's arrow-straight with a large, swollen head. I run my finger over the tip where it weeps.

Amber is a stupid, stupid woman.

After I wedge myself between his muscular thighs, I rake my nails down his chest before I kiss my way down his incredible body. I nibble his neck, nip his pecs, and lick his ridged abs. His breathing kicks up as I take a nice, slow swipe of my tongue across his swollen head. I glance up at him. He watches me through hooded eyes.

Rhett grips my hair again. Tight. "Open your mouth." I shiver at the command in his voice. Just to mess with him, I don't comply. Instead, I rub his dick against my lips, and he growls. "Paige."

I grab his length in one hand and his balls in the other and take him in my mouth. He grunts, and I'm pleased that I've reduced him to non-syllabic communication.

As I watch him watch me, I suck on his head, lick the tip, then take him to the back of my throat where I choke on him.

"Christ, you feel incredible." His grip on my hair tightens. "Smack my leg if this is too much."

I have no idea what he means until he uses my hair to drag me up and down his cock.

It's rough.

I love it.

I love that I make him lose control.

I bob up a few times before he holds me down. My nails dig into his thighs, but I don't let up, even when I choke. I'm totally getting off on the fact that I'm giving Rhett Walker head. I'm the one who's going to make him fall apart. I want this to be the best blow job he's ever had. And if I suffocate in the process, so be it.

When he lets me up, I gasp for breath.

"Too much?" he asks, concerned.

"Shut up." I take him in my mouth again and relish when he takes his thumb and rubs my lip that's stretched wide around him. I tug gently on his balls, and his dick jerks. He's close.

So I tongue that slit as I suck his head, then shove him down the back of my throat again.

He grunts, "I'm gonna come."

No shit. I almost laugh, but I can't because I'm holding myself down on him.

With a groan, he spurts his release. Pulse after pulse, I swallow him down.

In the distance, I hear a chime.

Focus, Paige.

But then he lets out a curse. "I need to get that."

Stunned, I watch him gently push me back. He gets up, roots around in his jeans, and pulls out his phone.

He did not just pull me off his dick to take a phone call.

"This better be important," he says as he's standing there with his hard dick that looks like it's ready to come again. After a few seconds, he curses again. "I'll be there in twenty. Tell her to calm her ass down."

Next thing I know, he's shoving on his clothes. "I'm sorry, Paige, but I need to run."

What? He's leaving?

Sinking into the water, I fight like hell not to show the disappointment crashing over me. "What's going on?"

"It's Amber. She heard we got married, and she's at the ranch, causing a scene and freaking out the kids."

I hate that woman. "Okay. Um. Hand me my clothes. I'll pack up our stuff, and—"

"No. I'll go. There's no reason you can't enjoy the cabin. I'll be back tomorrow to pick you up."

Just like that, our "honeymoon" is over.

My throat tightens as I watch him walk away. *This is why I have to guard my heart.*

But can I guard it for six more months?

Chapter Fourteen

RHETT

THE WHOLE DRIVE HOME, I debate turning my truck around to go get Paige, but then I remind myself that Amber will probably flip the fuck out when she sees us together, so I stay the course.

When I get home, I can hear the yelling from the driveway. Jesus, what the hell is her problem?

The second I cross the threshold, Amber's head swivels toward me like that girl in *The Exorcist*. "Please tell me it's not true! Did you really marry that trailer trash?"

She sleeps around with half the town behind my back, and she thinks she's entitled to call Paige names?

I bite my tongue and turn to my brother. Jace, who's holding Austin, shakes his head and mouths, "Sorry."

"Where's Gabriel?"

"Down the hall. I'll go check on him now."

As long as my boys are okay, I know I'll get through this. But then I see Austin's puffy eyes and red nose, and my anger spikes. I might not be an expert at this parenting thing, but I know it's not healthy for kids to hear their parents arguing.

Amber marches up to me, and I'm assaulted by her designer

perfume. "That bitch spread all those rumors about me before we got married, and you never stood up for me."

"They weren't rumors if they were true."

Her face gets red. "How could you? Paige Lewis, of all people. Do you know what people are saying about you? That you groomed her when she was little."

"People" are saying this? Or Amber? "I don't need to explain myself to you, but I will to set the record straight. All Paige and I ever shared when she was younger were hugs, the kind you give family. She had a harmless crush on me in high school, and after she told me you were fucking Kacey Miller—which you were—she and I went years without talking. So don't bullshit me with that grooming crap. Paige was an adult when we reconnected."

"When was that? Last week?" she asks sarcastically.

I can't respond because, yes, it was a week ago, but that's none of her fucking business. "Why are you crawling up my ass right now? Why do you care? We've been divorced three years."

"Because I have to live in this town too, and people talk." Her eyes narrow. "What's the real reason you got married again? Did you knock her up?"

Jesus, no. "Paige isn't pregnant. Maybe I married her because I love her. Did that ever cross your mind?"

She snorts. "You'll never love anyone more than your stupid ranch, and you've made no secret about how much you hated being married to me, so no, I don't buy it."

Who is this woman, and what the hell did I ever see in her? "This *stupid* ranch bought you all of your designer clothes and that car you love." We were doing okay before my dad got sick and I had to spend a fortune on that divorce attorney. Well enough to buy Amber all that useless crap. "But you know what? Maybe we need to reconsider the spousal support I pay you."

Technically, I don't owe her crap because we weren't married ten years, and in the state of Texas that's what would garner her alimony, but she's the mother of my children, and I wanted to make sure she had the money she needed for the boys.

Amber pales. "You said you'd always look after me."

"And you promised to be faithful. Apparently, we're both full of shit."

I need a drink. I head for the kitchen. I can't believe I left Paige naked in the hot tub for this.

I grab a beer and smack it on the edge of the counter to pop off the lid. After I take a pull, I turn back to my ex. "I'm assuming since you brought the boys back a week early, they're mine now?" Glancing at the calendar on the fridge, I note that we're supposed to go back to switching every other week after her vacation time. But fuck that. "You can pick them up on the twenty-first."

"But that's two weeks away. I still have one more week with them."

"Then maybe you shouldn't have marched into my house uninvited and dragged me away from my honeymoon."

She rolls her eyes. "What kind of honeymoon did you have if it took you half an hour to get here?"

Not the kind Paige deserves, but I don't have time to deal with that guilt right now. "If you have a problem with me keeping the boys, we can make an appointment with our attorneys this week, and I'll make sure we adjust the alimony so it reflects your complete disregard for our children's emotional well-being."

"What are you talking about? They're clothed and fed."

"You're not the one who has to deal with how sick they get when you drop them off." It's always worse if she yells. Their pediatrician said it's likely from stress.

"Whatever, Rhett. Just keep your wife away from me."

I chuckle. "I doubt she'll be inviting you over for coffee."

"Why are you such an asshole?" She stomps to the door, but pauses to look at me. "Mark my words. This won't last."

Tell me something I don't know.

Some part of me senses it's gonna suck when Paige leaves, but my life's a fucking mess. I don't wanna wrangle her into my crap any more than she already is.

Finally, the Grim Reaper leaves. I lock the door behind Amber and take another swig of beer before I go looking for my kids.

I find them with my brother in the boys' room. Gabriel is sitting on the bed, doing that rocking thing he does when he's stressed out, and Austin is curled up in Jace's lap.

"Hey, guys. Sorry about that." I kneel down in front of the bed. "Can I get some hugs? I haven't seen you two in ages."

Austin holds out his arms, and I hug him to my chest. "Missed you, bud." He sniffles, and I pat his back until his breathing calms. "Come here, Gabriel. Unless you're too big for hugs."

He shuffles down the bed, and I hold my other arm open to him. "Mama was mad."

"She's upset with me, not you. She might have a temper, but she loves you two to pieces." At least, I hope she does.

Gabriel leans back. "She said you got married. Was she lying? Sometimes Mama lies."

Fucking Amber. I blow out a breath. "Let's sit down for this."

My brother smacks me on the back. "I'm gonna take off, since you've got this under control."

"Thanks, Jace. I appreciate you holding down the fort. I owe you one."

"Anytime."

After I sit on the rocking chair, I grab both my kids and pull them onto my lap. "Did y'all have fun on your vacation? You went to the lake, right?"

Gabriel shrugs, and Austin doesn't say anything.

"Looks like you both got some sun. Did you go fishing?" Gabriel's been wanting to do that for a while.

When they don't say anything, I start to worry. "Were you with your mom or one of her friends?" Gabriel gives his brother a look, and my parental Spidey senses go off. "You can tell me, boys. I won't get mad." *At you.*

Gabriel looks down. "We were with one of Mama's friends, this guy Quentin. But he wasn't very nice. Mostly Austin and I just played outside by ourselves."

"Was an adult with you?"

They don't say anything, which tells me there was no adult.

I try to keep my voice soft so they don't know how pissed I am. "Must've been nice by the lake. How close were y'all to the water?"

"Super close, but Mama said we couldn't go in it. That was a bummer."

My children were unsupervised at the fucking lake. It's a small miracle they didn't jump in.

I kiss them on the tops of their heads, grateful they're home safe and sound. No thanks to Amber.

Gabriel starts to fidget. "Did you really get married?"

I was hoping he'd forget about that until morning, and we could all go to bed. "I did. She's a nice girl. You're gonna like her. Do you remember Danny? I have that picture of y'all on my desk that time we went to get ice cream when you were little." He nods. "Paige is Danny's younger sister. You'll meet her tomorrow."

"Mama doesn't like her. She called her a tramp."

"Well, that's not true. Besides, we don't call people names in my house."

"Yes, sir."

"But there's no need to worry. Paige is a sweetheart. She's not gonna change anything around here." My ex-wife is something else. I have never called her boyfriends names in front of our kids. "Your mom is just stressed out about her job. How did her commercial go?"

He shrugs again, and I'm starting to wonder if she had a gig at all. Amber models sometimes, but I think she uses it as an excuse to run off whenever she wants to.

"It's good to have you two back. I'm thinking maybe we need

to go fishing now that you're home. Since you didn't have a chance to do that on your vacation."

Gabriel's eyes light up, but Austin is too tired to do more than snuggle against me.

"Are you hungry or did you eat dinner?" It's late, but sometimes Amber loses track of time.

The boys want a snack, so I get them fed, clean them up, and tuck them into bed. An hour later, I'm ready to pass out, but I wanna check in with Paige. I feel bad I ditched her like that, but I didn't want to put her in front of Amber's firing squad.

But when I call, she doesn't pick up. No surprise there. The woman never answers when I call. "Paige, it's me. Just wanted to see how you're doing. I'll be back in the morning to pick you up. Hope you had a nice night."

A nice night? After I left her naked in the hot tub? I roll my eyes at myself. Messages aren't my strong suit, so I try to never leave them.

I flip on the baby monitor and crawl into bed. Gabriel's big enough to ask for help if he needs it, but Austin's barely out of nighttime pull-ups. If he has an accident, he'll start crying.

As I stare at the ceiling, my mind wanders to Paige. I've never been as turned on as I was in that hot tub with her insane body pressed against mine.

The memory of her hot mouth around my cock instantly makes me rock hard. She looked like a water nymph with all that red hair. I was in the middle of an existential experience when I got that damn phone call.

Reaching into my shorts, I'm ready to replay that incredible blow job, to imagine what it would feel like to sink my dick into her tight, warm heat, when Austin yells out through the monitor.

I leap out of bed. By the time I reach his room, he's vomiting.

But it gets worse.

A few hours later, I get a call that our fences have been cut again.

Fuck my life.

Chapter Fifteen
PAIGE

When I hear a truck pull up in front of the cabin, I let out a sigh of relief. We were supposed to be out of here hours ago. Rhett said he'd be back in the morning to get me, and it's almost three in the afternoon.

I'm trying really hard not to feel forgotten right now. I couldn't even call him because I barely have a signal.

Every bit of me wants to run and hide because I'm so mortified about last night, but I know I need to be a big girl and not avoid Rhett like I want to.

But seriously, who takes off and leaves their new wife alone in a cabin, naked as the day she was born, in a hot tub? Rhett Walker, that's who.

Yes, I realize this isn't a real marriage, but we were being intimate, for fuck's sake. Not bailing is just good manners.

I take a deep breath to steel myself. Except when I peek out the window, it's not Rhett.

"You asshole," I whisper. "Why do you always twist me up in knots?"

He fucking sent Beau to pick me up.

At the realization Rhett didn't come, my eyes sting and my

throat gets tight. I blink rapidly and wave at my face so it doesn't turn red. I don't want Beau to know I'd rather crawl into a bin of bees than return to the ranch.

"Knock, knock," he yells. "Hey, Paige. It's your favorite brother-in-law."

I glance at the rear of the cabin. Unfortunately, there's only one entrance, so I can't run out the back door. Though that window in the bedroom is starting to have more appeal.

"Paige! You there?"

Quickly, I back away from the door. "Yeah. Hold on!" I run to the bathroom and splash my face with water.

When I don't think I'll start bawling, I unlock the front door.

Beau's smile falls when he sees me. "You okay?"

"Yup. Great. Never better." I tuck my hands in the back pockets of my jeans. "Are you here to take me to the ranch?"

"Actually, Rhett asked me to pay for another few days here for you."

I'm going to kill him with my bare hands. "Really? Why's that?"

"We have a situation back at the ranch. The boys had a rough night, and someone cut our fences again. It's a mess. He thought you might be more comfortable here."

"You mean where I don't have a phone signal, a TV, or any transportation?" As I found this morning, I can send texts if I stand on my toes and hold my phone in the air, but my calls don't go through. "I could be murdered in my sleep, and no one would know for days. How thoughtful."

Beau winces. "I know this isn't ideal, but—"

"Are the kids okay now or are they sick?"

"They're, uh, they're doing better."

I can understand Rhett needing to be with the boys if they weren't feeling well, but the fact he wants to leave me in the middle of nowhere after ditching me last night is a step too far.

"Can you take me to Baylee's?" I'll sleep in her bathtub if I have to.

His head tilts. "I don't know. He really wanted to—"

"Beau Walker, I don't give a shit what Rhett wants. Tell him he can shove this cabin up his ass." I march back to the bedroom to get my bag. When I return, I cross my arms. "Take me to Baylee's or I'm calling Aunt Sylvia to get me, and she won't be as nice as I'm trying to be."

On the drive to Baylee's, it takes everything in me not to cry. How do I get involved with these kind of men? I thought Marcus was bad. Rhett has him beat by a country mile.

When we get there, Beau's barely put his truck into park before I fly out the door.

"Paige, wait."

Ignoring him, I head to Baylee's house. I knock, but no one answers. It's just my luck that no one's home right now. Beau watches me march around to the side, where I try to scale the fence. I'll just hang out on their back deck until they get home.

Behind me, he calls out, "Paige, let me take you to the ranch. Once you get there, you'll see what Rhett's up against. He's not doing this to be an asshole."

The knot in my throat is too much, and I give in to the tears. The truth is I feel left behind, like always. Why does everyone in my life do this? The only person who doesn't is Baylee. Oh, and my friend Abby, but she just moved to Houston.

With tears streaming down my face, I give up trying to scale the fence when my foot gets snagged and tweaks my ankle. *That's right, Paige, get more injured while you're at it.*

I lean against the fence to gather myself and then turn around. "Beau, please tell Rhett that I'm sorry, but I can't do this. If he needs me for a dinner with Harlan, he can text. Otherwise, I'll be here, okay?"

When he sees my face, he closes his eyes. "I'm sorry, Little Lewis. He didn't mean to hurt you."

I pull out my phone and text my best friend.

> Can I stay with you? I'm at your house.

She responds immediately.

> WHAT DID HE DO? I'll be there in five.

After I wipe my face, that detached feeling I'm used to finally descends, and I shrug. "I'm fine. I'll be by tomorrow to get my car and a few things from the house, okay?"

He watches me like I'm a wounded animal. "You're not gonna try to sleep in the park again, right? Because Rhett will have my ass if you do that."

"Let me remind you, Beau, that if I want to sleep in the park or cemetery or on a bench by the river, it's *none* of his business."

That's when Baylee screeches to a halt in front of her house. She's beside me a few seconds later. "Who do I need to kill?"

Beau holds up his hands. "I'm just the messenger."

She looks back and forth between us. "Where's Rhett?"

I shrug. "At the ranch, where he's been since last night when someone called him with an Amber-related emergency."

Baylee growls. "I'm going to strangle that man. My mother spent all that money on the cabin, and he ditched you to go talk to that ho-bag?"

"It sounds so much worse when you say it like that." I don't mention that he had just come down my throat. I hook my arm in my best friend's to make sure she doesn't charge at Beau. "It's fine. We all know this marriage is just for show. If Rhett wants to run off to talk to Amber, let him. Hey, let's go order a pizza. I have, like, twenty bucks left to my name, and I really want to spend it on something with carbs."

I'm dragging her back to the front porch when Beau joins us. "It wasn't really like that, you know."

I turn to look at him. "Actually, I wouldn't know, because he sent you to tell me to stay at that cabin by myself for who knows how long. Which tells me exactly where I stand with Rhett. And that's fine. I'm a placeholder, I get it. He literally could've married any girl in South Texas to do this job. But I have enough pride to not go where I'm not wanted."

Baylee yanks me through the front door and turns to my brother-in-law. "Fuck you, Beau Walker! And fuck your brothers too!" Then she slams it in his face.

I love my best friend.

Chapter Sixteen
RHETT

I'M PREPARING to track down our biggest bull when Sheriff Reynolds pulls up our drive.

"It's about damn time," our ranch hand Wayne grits out as we trudge across the yard.

"I got this. Can you get my horse saddled and tell Jace to be ready to ride in ten minutes?"

"You got it, boss."

Sheriff Reynolds is a grizzled old cowboy with a gray handlebar mustache and a kind smile. But one thing he's not is a hardass, and that's what I need right now.

He holds out his hand to me, and we shake. "Howdy, Rhett. Heard y'all are having problems again." I explain the situation, and he sighs. "Any suspects?"

"Just the obvious ones."

"The McAllisters?"

"I paid them a visit the first time this happened."

"What'd they say?"

"Cash denied it was them."

He twirls one end of his mustache. "Do you believe him?"

"Hard to say, but if it wasn't him, who's the asshole letting my cattle out?"

Crossing his arms, Reynolds stares across my fields. "Who else wants to mess with you?"

"You know as well as I do that my father was an asshole. I'm sure we're on a lot of people's shit lists." I lift my baseball cap and wipe my forehead. "The only other person I can think of is Mayor Gold. She wants half our acreage for that damn highway. But I can't really see her prowling around here at night in her designer heels, cutting our fences."

He chuckles. "She'll never get that approved. Eileen needs to drop that proposal. All she's doing is pissing off the ranchers."

Jace rides out of the barn, leading Apollo to me.

I turn to the sheriff. "I need to track down my best bull. But tell me, do I need to pay my neighbors another visit?"

He pats my back. "Son, you and I both know that's a bad idea. Let me do my job. I'll write up a police report and get statements from your ranch hands."

I level him with a stare because that's the same answer he gave me last time. "Then get me some answers and arrest the asshole who's doing this. I can't afford to lose any more steer."

As I head to Jace, Reynolds calls out, "Hey, before I forget, congratulations!"

"For what?" I grab my horse's reins from my brother.

Behind me, the sheriff laughs. "For getting married."

Son of a bitch. I forgot I got married.

When you come eye to eye with a pissed-off two-thousand-pound bull, it makes you reconsider your choices in life.

A series of questions run rapid-fire through my mind.

Like why did I think it was a good idea to approach this big fucker on foot?

Why didn't I tell the boys I loved them this morning?

And why didn't I fuck Paige last night when I had the chance?

If I die right now, it's my own dumbass fault. I blame my sleepless night and exhaustion for being stupid.

Out of my peripheral vision, I spot Jace circling us on his horse. At least one of us is smart enough to stay in the damn saddle, but I didn't want Apollo to get hurt on this outcropping. I can't afford another vet bill right now.

We've been trying to catch Diablo for two hours. We rode so far, I'm pretty sure we crossed county lines. Typically, we would surround him and redirect him, but he's done a good job living up to his name.

"On the count of three," my brother says, "I'm gonna lasso this asshole, and I want you to get the hell out of there."

I nod and hope the big guy doesn't bolt toward the ravine and drag Jace with him.

He counts down, and I leap out of the way just in time for Diablo to charge down the hill. Jace's horse slips but manages to stay upright, thank the good Lord.

I race back to Apollo, and a minute later, I'm hot on Jace's heels. I ride to his opposite side and lasso the bull. It's not tight. He'll be fine, but this way there's less of a chance he'll injure Jace or his horse.

By the time we make it back to the ranch, it's late. Yawning, I motion to the bunkhouse where our crew is waiting for us. "I want the guys to take turns doing patrols every two hours tonight. We need to catch the asshole who keeps cutting our fences."

Jace nods. "I already radioed Wayne. He's organizing the ranch hands."

"He'd make a great foreman. If we had the money, I'd give him the job tomorrow."

"Are you really ready to give up all that power?"

I chuckle and scrub a dirty hand across my face. "And all the prestige." When we reach the barn, I glance out at the pasture. "It's gotta be the McAllisters."

"I don't know who else would go through all this trouble. Plus, Cash hates you."

"Not sure why. He was the one fucking my wife, not the other way around."

He snickers. "Well, you did kick his ass when you found them together."

"Which he should've fully expected."

We get the horses unsaddled and brush them down before we hand them off to one of our guys, who'll get them settled for the night. Jace goes to the bunkhouse to make sure the patrols are set up.

That's my job, but since I was up all night, Jace does me a solid and fills in for me.

Exhausted, I drag myself into the house. Beau's sitting at the bar. "How are the boys?" I ask as I head to the kitchen to wash my hands.

"Fine. But..."

When he doesn't say anything, I turn to him with my hand on the faucet. "Is Austin still puking?"

"No. He's better. The kids are sound asleep. Just checked on them ten minutes ago."

"Great. I was so worried about him today. That fucking bull gave us a run for our money. We had to chase him down the damn highway. I wouldn't be surprised if we made the news."

"Glad you caught him, but listen. Paige didn't wanna stay at the cabin."

Shit. Paige. "What happened?"

"Well, after she chewed me out, she made me drop her off at Baylee's."

Christ. I'm never gonna hear the end of this from Sylvia. "Did you tell Paige that Austin was puking his guts out all night? That our fences got cut? That we had to chase down a dozen cattle?"

He winces. "Not in those words exactly."

"So let me guess, she's pissed I ditched her."

"Pretty much, yeah."

This is why I never wanted to get married again. No one understands how much responsibility I have here. Our entire livelihood is wrapped up in those cattle. The boys and this ranch have to come first if we want any hope of surviving. Maybe things will be different in a few years, but I don't have anything left to give a woman right now.

I rub the back of my neck. "I'll go get her tomorrow after my appointment with Harlan."

He clicks his tongue. "See, that might be a problem."

"Why's that?"

"She kinda said she didn't think she could do this, but that you could call her if you need her to meet up for appearances."

"When you say *this*, do you mean our marriage?"

"That's what I'm saying. I don't think you should wait to go talk to her."

I blow out a breath. "On a scale of one to ten, how pissed is she?"

He tilts his head. "That's just it. I wouldn't say she's pissed exactly, though she wasn't thrilled you left her at a cabin with no cell signal, TV, or car. But I think you hurt her feelings. I mean, you left her to go talk to Amber."

"When you frame it like that, I sound like an asshole."

Beau lifts his brows. "Not to be a dick, but it was your honeymoon."

I feel a vein throb in my neck. "It's a fake fucking marriage. We both agreed it wouldn't mean anything. Paige and I have mutually agreed upon goals and a deadline. It's not like I left my *real* wife behind after one night to talk to my ex."

He scratches the back of his head. "Can I ask you a question? You said you'd keep things platonic. Did you cross any lines this weekend? Because I don't really understand why she'd cry if you guys kept this strictly business."

I freeze, the guilt I've held at bay all day hitting me like a sledgehammer. "She cried?" Goddamn it. I knew this was a bad idea. I stalk over to the drawer where I keep my keys. "Text me if the boys have any problems. I'll be back."

"Gonna go get your wife?" He smirks.

"Fuck off." Of course I'm gonna go get my wife.

Chapter Seventeen
RHETT

MID-KNOCK, I stop to stare at my hands, which are still dirty. My boots are muddy, my shirt is torn, and I'm pretty sure there's blood—my blood—on my jeans. Damn, I never cleaned up. I just heard Paige was upset and raced over here like a jackass.

The door swings open, and Sylvia crosses her arms. "You gonna stand out here all night, or are you coming in?"

I take off my grimy baseball cap. "Thank you, but I'm pretty filthy. Maybe I should wait out here. Can I speak with Paige?" I don't know why I'm nervous, but with the way Sylvia's glaring at me right now, I should probably make sure she's not carrying any weapons.

She points behind her to the couch. "Sit." I do as she asks, expecting she'll get Paige. Instead, she perches on the coffee table across from me. "We need to get one thing straight. Paige might not be my daughter, but I love her like one. As her surrogate mother, I'm wondering why she was sleeping in my house two nights after she married you."

I knew Sylvia was gonna grill me.

"It's a long story." Her no-nonsense expression tells me she'll wait until I tell her everything, so I do. Minus the fact that I left Paige naked in the hot tub after one of the most explosive sexual encounters of my life.

"I see." She crosses her legs. "I'm going to be honest, Rhett. I know you and Paige are up to something. It's not every day the town's biggest bachelor up and marries someone no one has ever seen him date."

Shit. "Sylvia, I—"

"Stop talking." I clamp my mouth shut, and she points at me. "I went along with your shenanigans because I love Paige, and I didn't want her to be embarrassed by some half-assed wedding."

That explains a lot. "Yes, ma'am."

"I just wanted my girl to have one day where she felt like a princess. Because she is a great young woman with a huge heart, and she deserves all the good things this world has to offer. Irma treats her like shit and has for years, and if you add one ounce of pain to the burdens that girl carries, so help me God, you will regret it."

Shamed, I stare at my dirty boots. "I didn't mean to hurt her, I swear. I care about her, and I promised Danny I'd look after her."

"Maybe start by not ditching her at an isolated cabin."

I nod, hating that I disappointed Sylvia, but more disappointed in myself for hurting Paige. "I'd like to make it up to her if she'll let me."

"If you were wondering, the correct way to handle that situation was to bring your wife *with you* and let her face your ex *with you*. And, for the record, she didn't tell me those details. Like a good mother, I eavesdropped on her and Baylee." She studies me a moment. "You know I get feelings, right? That I can sense things?"

All the hair on the back of my neck stands on end. I nod because everyone knows Sylvia has a sixth sense. I don't usually go for that mumbo jumbo, but then again, I've never had Sylvia Reyes staring me down like this before.

Reaching out, she clasps my hand. "If you don't embrace this marriage and try to make it work, I don't see this ending well." She turns my hand over, looks at my palm, and mutters, "Stubborn as the day is long." After she studies it, she sits back. "Rhett, you can be happy in love, but not by doing what you're doing."

I promised Paige we wouldn't tell anyone what we were up to, so I can't explain to Sylvia that this marriage isn't about love. I let out a frustrated breath. "I'm doing my best."

She stands. "It's not your best. You just think it is."

Then she disappears down the hall.

Coming here was probably a mistake, but Sylvia is right about one thing. I need to treat Paige better.

"Hey." Paige shuffles into the room in a white t-shirt, shorts, and fuzzy socks. Her hair is pulled back in a long ponytail, and her face is free of makeup. Fuck, she's beautiful. "What are you doing here? Did you need me for something with Harlan?" Why is she confused to see me?

I stand, but when I take a step toward her, she steps back, and my heart sinks. I clear my throat. "I'm sorry about last night. I didn't mean to leave you like that." I explain what happened with Amber and how her freakout upset the boys to the point that Austin started vomiting.

"I'm sorry he was sick." She tugs at the hem of her t-shirt. "Did Beau give you my message?"

"That you don't want to be married to me? Yes."

Paige fights a smile and rolls her eyes. "I'm thinking maybe I should just come over if you need me for Harlan. That way, I won't be in your hair or upsetting your kids or your wife."

"My *ex*-wife. Pretty sure you're my current wife. Besides, I thought you needed a job. Don't you wanna work in my office?"

"We both know you don't need me for anything except appearances with your banker. I'll just help Sylvia at her salon. She needs someone to wash hair, do laundry, and clean up. So maybe I'll do that." She gives me a fake smile that's so removed from the carefree smiles she gave me in the hot tub, it makes me flinch. "I'm not your concern, Rhett. I can take care of myself."

I scrub a hand over my face. This is not going the way I hoped it would. But she's not getting rid of me that easily. "Can we sit, please? I haven't slept since our wedding night, and I'm about to fall over."

Her eyes grow concerned. "You didn't sleep last night?"

"I was up with Austin. Then some asshole cut our fences again, and we had to track down a dozen cattle, one of whom we chased for hours." I sit on the couch again, and she sits on the opposite end. Fuck this shit. I reach over and tug her into my lap.

"Rhett, what—"

"Shut up and listen." I angle her so I can look into her eyes. "I'm sorry I was an asshole. I'm not handling Amber or my kids or all the crap I need to deal with on the ranch very well. I'm especially not good at having a new wife." I cup her beautiful face. "But I don't want you to feel like I don't need you. I do. I..."

I debate what to say, but maybe Sylvia is right and I need to go about this differently. My instinct is to be the asshole I've always been. Except I don't wanna be that hardass with Paige. I stroke her soft cheek with my thumb. "I like being around you, Paige. We had fun at the cabin before everything went sideways, right?"

She reluctantly nods. "But you don't need me hanging around. I'd just be in your way, and I don't like to be where I'm not wanted."

I did this to her. I made her feel unwanted. If I could kick my own ass right now, I would.

"Wildflower, I always want you around. I realize our situation is unique, that you're leaving at the end of the year, but you've always been special to me, and it pains me to hear that I made you feel this way. Nothing could be farther from the truth."

When she doesn't say anything, I take her hand in mine. "Please come back to the ranch with me. Let me make it up to you. I promise we'll figure this out." I kiss her wrist. "Come help me organize my office. It'll be easier on your ankle than cleaning Sylvia's salon." And if I had to guess, Sylvia doesn't really need the help.

Her eyes get glassy, and she whispers, "I don't want to get attached to you. We agreed this isn't forever."

I don't know why, but it hurts to hear that. I try to save face by cracking a joke. "So what you're saying is you need me to be a little bit of an asshole." She laughs, and I kiss her forehead. "Let's try to be friends like we said we would. Once you're healed up, you'll go to Boston or to whatever cheer camp is lucky enough to have you." I feel the need to underscore this point. "Paige, I can't stay married, and that's all about me and my issues. But it would make me really happy to have you around in the meanwhile. To make sure you get back on your feet again. Let me take care of you until you leave, sweetheart."

A long silence stretches, and I hate that I brought up divorce. Except I was a terrible husband, and I don't wanna make the same mistakes again. Especially with my best friend's little sister, who deserves someone who will make her the center of his universe.

"Okay, but..." She sniffles, and the regret in her eyes kills me. "You were right about the other stuff. I don't think we should sleep together."

That's fucking tragic. But she's right. "Then we won't sleep together. We'll pretend we never saw each other naked." Fat chance.

Paige nibbles her delectable bottom lip. "All right, husband."

"All right, wife."

Damn, I shouldn't love how that sounds.

Feet stomp down the hall, and Baylee, who looks angrier than that bull I chased this afternoon, storms in. "Rhett Walker, please tell me you're gonna stop being a giant dick."

"I am, I swear." From the bottom of my cold, black heart.

She looks at Paige, and they have some kind of silent conversation before she turns back to me. Baylee holds up two fingers to her eyes and then points them at me. "I'm watching you."

"Wouldn't expect anything less."

Chapter Eighteen
PAIGE

"Here's another blanket," Rhett says as he slips his thumb through his belt loop on his jeans.

I now have four. "This is great. Thanks."

He scans my side of his bedroom like it pisses him off. "When I get that loan, I'll buy you a better couch. This one's crap."

"It's really okay."

He motions to the bathroom. "Wanna use the facilities first?"

"Sure." Ugh, this is so weird. We're married. We've seen each other totally naked. We've gotten each other off. But we're acting like two people on a blind date.

One thing is clear. I don't understand Rhett Walker at all.

As I go to brush my teeth and wash my face, I'm still not sure what to make of tonight. Rhett had every opportunity to go live his best married life—as a single man. I tried to give him space. I offered to only come over if he needed me to meet with him and Harlan. I kept my emotions at bay so he wouldn't feel bad or guilty.

And he still wanted me to return home with him.

I consider the man in the other room. He's covered in mud, hasn't slept in forty-eight hours, and he spent the last fifteen minutes fussing over me and my sleeping situation. My heart melts a little.

Awkward Rhett is adorable, but I definitely prefer asshole Rhett. Because that version of him will be easier to leave in six months.

When I'm done, I head back to our bedroom.

I find him passed out, muddy boots and all, on his bed. He's leaning against the oak headboard with his arms crossed over his chest, like he was so tired he needed to sit down while he waited for me and fell asleep.

His thick hair looks like he raked his dirty fingers through it more than once today. He has sexy scruff on his chin like he hasn't shaved in a few days. He's wearing an open long-sleeved button-down over a t-shirt I suspect might've started out white.

Does he really want to sleep like this? He's going to get mud everywhere.

"Rhett." I gently shake him, and he doesn't budge. "Rhett," I say a little louder.

Nothing.

Poor guy. He's exhausted.

Now that I know what he was up against last night and today, I feel bad I wasn't more understanding. I still think he was wrong to leave me at the cabin by myself, and I was humiliated he sent his brother this afternoon, but I get it. The Amber situation was really bad, and the boys were so upset, her yelling made Austin physically ill. Or at least that's what their pediatrician explained to Rhett when it happened before.

I'd been stewing all night and morning, and when I saw Beau at the cabin, something in me snapped. I don't do well with humiliation. I suppose no one does, but after what happened in high school where the whole town made fun of me, it's definitely one of my buttons that's easily pushed.

I let my eyes wander over Rhett. Even when he's asleep, he's sexy. His arms are roped with muscle. His waist is lean, and underneath his clothes, I know it's stacked with ridges. His thighs are perfectly encased in those worn jeans.

Let's not forget about that loaded weapon in his denim.

Why does he have to have a perfect body? Now that I've seen every square inch of it, keeping some distance will be harder. Heaven help me, I can't be lusting over this man for the next several months, or I'll go crazy.

I head to the foot of the bed and tug off his boots before I fold the comforter over him and turn off the lights. Then I sit on the couch a few feet away.

"Goodnight, husband. Sleep tight."

Bright sunlight pouring through the window wakes me close to ten. Yawning, I look for Rhett, but the bed is made. Maybe he's in the kitchen. After I use the bathroom, I grab one of his long-sleeved flannels from his closet and throw it on. Then I wander down the hall. I find him and his brothers speaking in somber tones at the kitchen table.

"Morning. Can I make y'all some breakfast?" Might as well make myself useful.

Rhett gives me a soft smile, then shoots Jace a dirty look when he laughs and says, "Breakfast was hours ago."

I tuck my hands deeper into the sleeves of Rhett's flannel. "What time did you get up?"

Beau sips his coffee. "Around five."

My eyes widen. "Oh, wow. Okay. I'm sorry. I'll set my alarm clock early tomorrow."

Rhett heads to the kitchen, and I follow him. "No sense in that, wildflower. You might as well get your beauty sleep. You don't need to rush to the office. I can't get in there till about noon anyway. Want some coffee?"

"Yes, please."

"You still take it with extra cream and two sugars?"

He remembers how I took my coffee when I was fifteen. Why can't this man be mine? It takes me a second to catch my breath. "No sugar, just the cream, please." He stills for a moment, and I chuckle. "Ignore the innuendo. I didn't mean it like that."

"I know, honey." He winks.

Actually, I would love to mean those words, but we promised we'd be platonic. And that's a solid, adult decision because I don't think my heart can take getting naked with Rhett again and leaving him in a few months.

Which it looks like I'll have to do because the man does not want to stay married, and no amount of wishing will change him.

Jace and Beau shoot each other a look. I suppose I should get used to that. I'm the interloper here.

Rhett hands me my cup. "Thanks for taking off my boots," he says.

"I felt bad you fell asleep like that after chasing all those cattle."

Reaching out, he tucks a lock of hair behind my ear. "A long day in the saddle is good for a man's constitution."

Ugh, I could get lost in his beautiful dark brown eyes.

Beau coughs. "I hate to interrupt, but we need to discuss those contract terms."

"What's there to discuss?" Rhett heads back to the table and sits in front of a stack of paper. "I'm gonna sign it. Where else are we gonna get the money?"

"It's twenty percent interest."

My eyes widen. "How much is the loan?" I ask the question before I can think better of it. Really, it's none of my business.

"Hundred grand." Beau waves at the stack in front of his brother. "We need the cash, but that's a steep price to pay."

I grab a seat next to Rhett and turn to him. "That's a lot of interest, right?"

"We don't have a choice. We have a major cash flow problem.

And because of that drought last year, our cattle weren't heavy enough for market last month."

Jace chugs his water. "Our trailer broke down and needs work, so even if we wanted to sell a few heads to get by, we couldn't swing it."

Rhett taps on the table. "Yeah, the interest sucks, but the bridge loan allows us to hold off on making any payments until the due date. That'll help me get caught up on the mortgage, make payroll, fix the trailer, get extra bales of hay—the list goes on and on. The only downside besides the interest is the collateral."

I lean forward. "Which is what?"

"Our horses, our trucks, and all our machinery." His voice gets quiet. "And if we lose that, I'm not sure how we keep the ranch."

My eyes widen. "And if you don't take this loan?" There has to be another way.

"We lose the ranch later this month, thanks to a second mortgage we didn't know about." He explains that his father took it out while at the nursing home. "I only found out about it a few weeks ago when I went to pay the final bill at Shady Pines and they finally gave me our father's belongings. That's how we missed the notice of default and the bank's other warnings."

"So if you hadn't gotten those items, the bank could have foreclosed, and you wouldn't have known until it was repossessing the ranch?"

"Pretty much. Because all of the invoices were being mailed to the nursing home." He lets out a weary sigh. "Dad signed a power of sale clause that means the bank has a preauthorization to sell the property without taking us to court. It expedites the process."

"Is there any way to contest the loan itself? Your dad was in a freaking nursing home. Did he have the mental capability to know what he was signing?"

"That asshole was playing poker with his old buddies every week," Jace says. "He seemed sharp to me."

This whole situation is so messed up. "I thought Harlan was a family friend. Why's the interest on your loan so high? Why did he make you jump through hoops just to hit you with twenty percent?"

Rhett leans forward and presses his face into his hands, then shrugs. "Had I known that was the price, I wouldn't have dragged you into my mess. But that's what I get for not asking the terms. I just figured it would be fair, and I suppose it is. Some banks are charging twenty-five percent interest for a personal loan right now. I got twenty percent because this is a four-month loan. Besides, it's not like we have great credit."

I feel like I'm not seeing the whole picture. "Did Harlan's bank give your father the second mortgage too?"

He shakes his head. "Different bank. Harlan would've given us a heads-up."

Rhett looks so tired, like he's just hanging on. I cover his big, rough hand with mine. "Are we going to be able to repay the loan and all that interest?"

He squeezes my palm. "Gonna try my damnedest. I'll go through the books this week and see what we can cut back on, but we gotta stop losing cattle."

"How many have we lost?" I let go of his hand and grab my coffee.

Beau sighs. "One wandered into a field with moldy sweet clover, and we didn't get to him in time. And we never found two, though where those fuckers went, I'll never know. It's like they disappeared off the planet. If we wanna cover our nut this fall, we're gonna need every one of those beautiful beasts."

"Do we know who's cutting the fences?"

All three brothers say the name at the same time. "Cash McAllister."

Damn. "Cash is behind this mess? Are you serious?"

The McAllisters and Walkers have had a long-standing feud

for decades. I can't imagine how hard this must be for Rhett, especially after Amber cheated with Cash.

Rhett rakes his hands through his hair. "It's either the McAllisters or the mayor. You know how Eileen Gold wants to run a highway through town? She offered to buy up half our property. Where the hell am I supposed to graze our cattle?"

I didn't know about the highway. Wild Heart has changed a lot since I graduated high school. Locals used to want to keep this place off the map. "I'm guessing you turned down her offer."

He scowls. "I told her to shove it up her chimney. That woman offered us a quarter of what it's worth."

As I sip my coffee, I think about Mayor Gold. I went to school with her sister. The Golds are one of those founding Wild Heart families who always think they're entitled to make decisions for the entire community. "So you think she hired some guys to do it?"

"It's possible." He crosses his arms. "My money's still on the McAllisters, though. They're the most likely assholes. I'm thinking it's time to visit those fuckers again."

Beau nods. "I'll get the shotguns."

What the hell? "Y'all are not going to show up on their porch with shotguns."

Rhett stands. "This is Texas cattle land. Of course we are."

Alarmed, I grab his arm. "Please don't do this now. Wait a few days and see if the sheriff gets any leads. A few head of cattle are not worth dying over."

"Paige, if we let this go, this could escalate, and we can't afford to lose more steer."

"Just... It's not worth getting shot." Because the McAllisters have shotguns too. "Please. Let's see if the sheriff gets any leads."

He stares at me long and hard before he blows out a breath. "We'll see. I can't make any promises."

At least he's not charging over to Cash's house.

The back door slams, and the boys race in. Rhett's eyes immediately light up, and he sits back down and holds out his arms. "How're my favorite cowboys?"

"Good!" the older one shouts.

They crawl up into his lap, and he turns them to face me.

My heart thumps hard in my chest. I can't believe this is the first time I'm meeting his children.

Oh, my God. I hope they like me.

Chapter Nineteen
RHETT

THE EXPRESSION on Paige's face when she sees my boys is adorable. "Hi, guys, I'm Paige. It's so nice to meet you."

I bounce the big one on my knee. "This is Gabriel. He's six. He loves fishing and Hot Wheels." Then I bounce my little one. "And this tough guy is Austin. And he loves food. Of any kind."

Austin buries his head in my chest while Gabriel looks away. Damn, I was hoping they'd love her.

I squeeze my boys a little. "What do we say, fellas?"

Gabriel mumbles hi, and Austin shakes his head no.

My brothers give me a sympathetic smile, and Beau points toward the barn. "We're gonna give y'all some space."

Let's try this again. "Do y'all remember those incredible cheerleaders at Uncle Mav's games? Paige is one of them."

My sons love the cheerleaders. I admit I always look for Paige when we're watching Mav's games.

When the boys don't say anything, Paige's smile slowly falls.

But then Gabriel lets out a huff. "Are you our new mom? Because we have one already."

Shit.

I jiggle my leg again. "Buddy, I know this is a lot, but let's try to be welcoming."

I hate the rejection in Paige's eyes, but she pastes on that fake smile and leans forward. "I know y'all have a great mom. I'm not trying to take her place. I just want to be your friend."

Amber, a great mom? That's a stretch, but Paige is just trying to be nice.

When Gabriel doesn't say anything, she tries again. "Would that be okay? Can we be friends?"

It takes effort to bite my tongue. I wanna be encouraging without pushing the boys too hard.

Finally, my older son nods. "Yeah. I guess."

Austin finally looks at Paige. "You're pretty."

She gives him a glorious smile that makes him bury his head in my chest again. "Thanks, handsome. I'm kind of a mess today, but I appreciate the compliment."

Her red hair is in one of those haphazard buns that looks sexy as hell. And I fucking love that she grabbed one of my flannels. It makes me wonder what she would look like in just that shirt and nothing else.

I squeeze my kids. "Boys, I was thinking we should go fishing this weekend like we talked about. Would it be okay if we asked Paige to tag along?"

"Aww, Dad," Gabriel grouses. "I thought it would just be us. Girls are no fun."

I sigh. This is gonna be tougher than I thought, but Paige rolls with it.

"It's totally okay if y'all go without me. I don't want to scare your fish. Would it be okay if I made you some sandwiches and cookies for your trip?"

Gabriel looks at his brother, then Paige. "Can you make some chocolate chip?"

"Sure can. Any other requests?"

"I like grilled cheese and pickle sandwiches."

"Can't say I've ever had that before, but it sounds tasty. I'm not sure that would be good for a fishing trip, though, because they'd get cold. What if I made them tonight for dinner? Would that be okay?"

Damn, she's sweet.

Gabriel nods. "Yeah. Can you add extra pickles in mine?"

"Of course."

I wink at her. "Thanks, wildflower."

The smile she gives me is genuine, and I love that I put it on her face.

I bounce the boys on my knees. "Okay, my tiny terrors, who wants some ice cream? I need to drop off a contract at the bank, and then I was thinking the four of us should head into town for a scoop of pralines and cream. Paige is gonna help me organize my office, and I need to butter her up so she doesn't quit on the first day. Think we can trick her into thinking she'll have fun figuring out Daddy's messy office?"

Gabriel giggles. "No one wants that job."

"You stinker." I tickle him until he squeals. I set the boys on the ground. "Go potty. We'll leave in ten minutes. Gabriel, help Austin use the bathroom, okay? And y'all wash your hands afterward."

The boys race away, and I watch Paige watch them.

She has a wistful smile on her face. "They're beautiful, Rhett. They look so much like you."

I take her hand in mine. "Thanks for being so patient with them. They'll warm up to you."

"Don't worry about me. They've been through so much. I just want to make this easy for them. Who watches them during the day? They can stay with me if you need them to."

"Wayne's wife Pauline babysits while I'm working, but she might like a break once in a while."

"I'd love that." She gives me a smile that reaches her eyes. "I should get dressed."

As she walks away, my eyes linger on her legs that I've been fantasizing about for the last week.

Although I'm grateful we didn't fuck at the cabin, because that would've made things more complicated than they already are, I can't stop thinking about the what ifs. What if I hadn't had my phone with me and we'd continued things back in the cabin? What if I'd pulled her on my cock and fucked her till she screamed my name?

What if we'd simply carried on like a normal married couple once we got home?

Guess I'll never know.

I've got Austin in my arms while Gabriel walks on one side of me with his finger hooked in my belt loop. Paige, who's at least two feet away, strolls next to me.

Main Street isn't all that busy at this time of the afternoon, but a few people look at us funny.

"Darling, come here." I hold open my free arm, and she realizes what I need and scoots closer.

"Sorry," she whispers. "I don't want to intrude on your time with the boys."

Stopping, I turn to her. "Wildflower, no matter what happens, you're family. You and Danny have always been family, you hear me?" Because I hope she realizes that just because we get divorced in a few months doesn't mean I won't be there for her.

She bites her bottom lip and nods.

I grab her hand and tug her closer. "This okay?"

"Yes." Her lips twitch in what I think might be a smile.

When we reach Scoops, I catch our reflection in the window. Me and the boys and sweet, lovely Paige. It makes me think about what Sylvia said. That I could be happy in love if I do shit differently.

But what does that mean? I've been in this grind on the ranch for years. If I let up, everything's gonna fall apart. Even before my father got sick and retired, the responsibility to keep our family afloat fell on me, especially after he disowned Isaiah.

I guess I need to be grateful. My brother has had a worse time of things than I have.

"Rhett, are you okay?" Paige asks softly.

"Yeah. Sorry, just got a lot going on."

She's such a good woman. And damn, I swear she somehow gets more beautiful every day. My little wife's wearing a white floral dress and some sneakers. No one should look that sexy in sneakers.

An image of us at the cabin flashes in my mind. Paige naked and wet and writhing in my lap in the hot tub lives rent free in my head.

Not the time or place, dumbass.

I open the door. "After you." Once she enters, the boys and I follow. I yell out a greeting to the woman behind the counter. "Hey, Mabel!"

"Howdy, Rhett," she says. She sees Paige and grins. "Hey, stranger. It's been a while."

"Hi, Mabel. It's so nice to see you."

I think they went to high school together.

Mabel leans over the counter to wave to the boys. "What can I get y'all?"

Once we order our cones, we sit in the corner. I set Austin on my knee because he's not quite himself yet. Gabriel and Paige sit on either side of me.

She takes a lick of her dessert, and suddenly, I'm thinking of other things she's licked.

I clear my throat. "Paige, you should have your insurance soon. Let's get your physical therapy scheduled."

"Thank you. I'm really grateful to have that."

"We'll get you whatever you need to get back in top form. I

should have that loan deposited by the end of the week, so it shouldn't be a problem." I dropped off the signed contract to Harlan on the way here.

The bell over the door rings, and I look up to find Paige's stepmother, Irma. I'm instantly pissed off knowing she put Paige on the street.

"Incoming," I mutter. "Boys, here's some money. Go get a pint of something for your uncles."

They hop out of their chairs and race to the counter as Irma approaches our table.

She barely glances at Paige. "Why, Rhett Walker, it's been an age."

I saw her two weeks ago at the grocery store. "How's it going, Irma?"

"I was just wondering when you and the boys were gonna come over for dinner. Ty would love to see you."

Most notably absent from that invitation is my wife.

Paige looks like she wants to curl in on herself. After I scoot my chair back, I grab her hand and tug her into my lap. "Irma, did you hear I got hitched?" I kiss my wife's temple, and Paige turns a beguiling shade of pink.

"I mean, I heard, but I figured it had to be a rumor." She looks like she just sucked on a lemon. "I never figured you'd be dating someone so young."

I scratch my chin. "Wasn't Paige's father ten years older than you?"

Paige snorts. "Fifteen years older."

Irma rolls her eyes. "That was a different time."

"You still hoarding all those dogs?" I ask because it's time to cut the crap.

Her mouth drops open. "We're not *hoarding* them. We're breeding them."

"Do you have a license to do that? Because as far as I know, you're only allowed five animals unless your property is zoned for agriculture." She huffs, but I cut her off before she spouts more nonsense. "I'm just thinking you should be nicer to my wife, seeing as how she's trying to get her bearings in Wild Heart. I'd hate for people to give her a hard time again like they did when she was in high school when some asshole shared my private business with the whole town."

She pales. "Why... why... I'd never do such a thing."

"Good to hear it."

Irma starts to shuffle backwards. "Well, I'd better go. I saw you in the window and just wanted to say hi."

"Wait. Don't you want to congratulate my wife on our marriage before you take off?" I ask, just to be a dick.

Her expression goes flat. "Congratulations, Paige. Looks like you got what you always wanted."

Paige flings her arms around my neck and kisses me. With a huge grin, she looks at her stepmother. "Damn straight I did."

Fuck, I like this woman.

Chapter Twenty
RHETT

As I shove another bite of the grilled cheese and pickle sandwich in my mouth, Paige rushes back to the stove. "Who wants another one?"

It's the second time this week we've had grilled cheese, but everyone's hands pop in the air, including mine, because these are fucking delicious.

She chuckles when she sees that every Walker man at the table wants one. Jace, Beau, Mav, and my boys all seem to be on a quest to down as many as possible.

I watch as she flips them on the grill. Her face is flushed, and a tendril of hair hangs down from her messy bun.

Beau nudges me. "Careful, or you're gonna fall for your wife."

No shit.

I ignore my brother's questioning look. "Paige organized those files you were bitching about."

Knowing that she has to wade through my mess is sobering. To be fair, my father was not organized, and I never took it upon myself to do things differently. I had a pile system. It worked until it didn't.

Beau shouts, "Paige, whatever we're paying you to deal with our office isn't enough."

My wife chuckles as she heads over with another platter of sandwiches that are neatly cut in half. "It's not so bad."

She scoops gooey slices and places them on my boys' plates. They start to shove them in their mouths, but I grunt, "What do we say to Paige for making your favorite dinner?"

"Thank you!" they yell.

"I'm lucky y'all like easy meals." She scruffs Austin's head, and he smacks his lips and smiles up at her.

Even Gabriel grins at her today.

Life should always be this easy.

I turn to my youngest brother. "Maverick, how long will you be staying with us? Just asking so I can get enough groceries. You eat like a damn horse." He came for the wedding, but I've barely seen him since.

"Just a few more days," he says around a mouthful of food. "I have a summer school class, so I need to get back to Charming. I'll train there with the guys."

"Take it easy on the partying."

"Okay, Dad," he says sarcastically, the little shit.

He's joking, but he's not. I spent more time with him than our father ever did. "Hey, when you're a hotshot NFL player, don't forget who threw you a thousand passes in the backyard."

"I did," Beau says.

I reach over Paige's empty chair and shove Beau. "You know I threw more balls than you did." Beau laughs and rolls his eyes.

After Paige makes another round, I grab the platter out of her hand, set it on the table, and pull her onto my lap. "Have you eaten yet?" I ask her while my brothers shit-talk each other.

"I snacked while I cooked."

Unacceptable. "Stop worrying about us. Eat some dinner. The guys and I will clean up since you made the meal."

She bats her eyes playfully. "Thank you, husband."

"You're welcome, wife."

I don't ever remember being this enchanted with that term when I was married to my ex.

I start to tuck that loose strand of hair behind Paige's ear, but pause to run it between my fingers. It's silky soft. Realizing what I'm doing, I let go. "Scoot. Go eat." I pat her ass because it's right there and too enticing to resist.

I'd happily let her stay on my lap, but my brothers are giving me looks, and I don't feel like dealing with them.

Once everyone's done, Paige tells me she's gonna go take a shower. I try not to think about that visual as we get an assembly line going at the sink while Gabriel and Austin help Mav dry the dishes.

Beau nudges me as he washes a plate. "She's pretty awesome. No one would flinch if you tried to make it work."

Could I do that? Could I stay married? What about Paige's plans to move to Boston? I glance at our old farmhouse that needs a new paint job. I look at the chipped cabinets and dirty windows. I think about our mountain of bills. Sure, the loan will get us through this year, but what happens if there's another drought? What happens if one of us gets hurt? What happens if the price of cattle drops again?

I seriously question why Paige would want to stay here with me. The woman loves coaching cheerleaders. She wants to move to Boston, an exciting, cosmopolitan city. I'd be asking her to give that up so she can look after my dumb ass and live in Wild Heart.

"It's complicated," I mumble.

When we're done, I toss my boys in the bathtub 'cause they stink.

"Wash as high as possible." I raise my hand to my head. "Wash as low as possible." I point to my feet. "Then wash possible." I motion to my groin. They laugh as they scrub themselves.

I sit on the closed toilet and wonder how many towels I'm gonna have to use to dry the floor when they're done.

By the time I get them in their pajamas and tucked into bed, I'm ready to pass out myself.

"Daddy, I wanna story," Austin says.

"A story, huh?" I grab Gabriel and carry him over my shoulder to Austin's bed. We all squish on the twin mattress. When we're situated, I scramble to think of something. "Once upon a time, there was a little dog named Poo Splat."

They giggle.

"Poo Splat was an industrious fella. He had a good nose for solving crimes. One Christmas, all the holiday gifts went missing."

"I'd be so sad." Gabriel leans his head on my shoulder.

"Son, no one would steal your lump of coal," I tease, and he giggles again.

By the time I finish the story, they're both yawning. I carry Gabriel back to his bed and tuck him in. "Love you, kiddo."

"Love you too, Dad." I start to get up, but he tugs on my shirt. "Just..." He shrugs. "Paige ain't so bad."

I chuckle. "She likes you too, bud."

I cross the room to Austin. His eyes are already closed. I smile at my sweet boy and pull the covers over him. Before I leave, I flip on their dinosaur night light. "Night, boys," I whisper.

Stepping into the hallway, I leave their door cracked open behind me. I have another week before their mother gets them, but the closer we get to that date circled on the calendar, the more dread builds in me. I fucking hate that I can't see my children every day.

When I reach my bedroom, I knock to make sure Paige is decent.

"Come in."

She's curled up on the couch. Her damp hair is pulled up in a ponytail. She's wearing a little t-shirt and a pair of sleep shorts. And she has one of my flannels in her hands.

"Whatcha doing?"

"Sewing your shirt," she says as she pulls a needle through the fabric. "Did you know that almost all of your long-sleeved shirts and flannels have holes or tears?"

Paige is mending my clothes. Fuck, that's... I don't have words. "Baby, you don't need to do that."

She smiles. "I don't mind. I love to sew."

"Thank you. In case I haven't said it lately, you're fucking awesome." I motion toward the bathroom. "Gonna go get cleaned up. Do you wanna watch a movie with me? I'll probably fall asleep, but maybe we can watch half tonight and half tomorrow."

"I'd love that." It's early by most people's standards, barely eight in the evening, but since I get up so early, I can't stay up late or I'll be dead on my feet in the morning.

I toss her the remote. "Pick something. I'll be back in a sec." I take a lightning-fast shower. I ignore the erection I sprang when I saw Paige's nipples poking through the thin fabric of her shirt. I'm tempted to jerk off, but then I'll crash as soon as my head hits my pillow, and I'd like to spend some time with her.

I'm out in less than ten minutes. I'm scrubbing a towel over my head when I return to the bedroom.

"What are you in the mood for..." Her voice fades away as her eyes trail over me.

I'm wearing pajama bottoms, which is what I always wear to bed, but since we're hanging out, maybe it's not appropriate. "That's a loaded question, wildflower." I chuckle as I reach into my dresser for a shirt.

"Don't feel the need to get dressed on my account," she teases as she eyes my chest.

Well then. Forgoing the shirt, I head for the bed. She's sitting on the edge, perched like a little bird about to take flight. "Make yourself comfortable. Should I turn off the lights for the movie?"

"Yes, please."

I flip off the light switch and cross the room. I pull down the top sheet and comforter because, chances are, I'll knock out in a bit. After I flop on the side closest to me, I adjust my pillows and then pat the space next to me.

She lies down and turns to me. "Can we watch a chick flick?"

"Whatever you want."

"Really?"

"Why do you look so shocked? I'm sure I'll enjoy whatever you pick. After that great dinner and dealing with my office all day, you deserve it."

"It's just..." Her pretty brow crinkles. "Marcus hated chick flicks and anything with a hint of romance."

"Which is probably why you dumped him." Douchebag.

She stares at the ceiling. "He wasn't terrible, but I needed more than he was able to give."

"You deserve someone who'll treat you right."

Her voice gets so soft, it's barely a whisper. "It's funny that you treat me better than he did, and you and I aren't even together."

Why does everything feel so fucking tragic when she says shit like that? "Come here." I hold out my hand, and she immediately scoots closer and settles in the crook of my arm. I turn my head to kiss her temple. "You just haven't met the right man yet, sweetheart."

It kills me to say those words.

Because someday she's gonna meet someone who's smart enough to snatch up this sweet beauty.

She snuggles into me, and I reach down and pull the covers over us because she has goosebumps. "Cold?" Paige shivers as she nods, and I pull her closer. Her arm wraps around my chest. Having her in my bed feels so right, I close my eyes. "I might not be able to stay awake. I'm too comfortable, and you feel too good like this."

She lets out a relaxed sigh. "Can I stay here for a bit? You're so warm."

"Stay as long as you want."

Even if that's past December.

Chapter Twenty-One

PAIGE

I don't bother with the movie because Rhett is asleep within minutes. His deep breathing is soothing, and it makes me sleepy too.

It feels so good to be held, it chokes me up for some reason. I don't remember the last time someone held me like this. Marcus never did it. Neither did any of my previous boyfriends.

Rhett isn't even doing this for sex. He's out for the count.

I never got hugs growing up except from Danny. My dad wasn't very affectionate, and Irma always hated me. Not sure why. I never did anything to her except breathe. My dad always said I looked like my mama, so maybe Irma was jealous? But that's a weird thing to be upset about. Unless she just didn't like sharing his attention with another female, even his daughter.

My lips tug up when I think of how Rhett held Irma's feet to the fire when we were at the ice cream shop earlier this week, and my heart swells with affection for this man.

Rhett is such a sturdy, safe presence next to me that I finally start to relax. With my nose pressed to his chest, I revel in his woodsy, masculine scent.

Soon, I'm drifting off too.

I wake with a start a few hours later with his big body spooning me. His thick thigh is tucked between mine, his arm is thrown over my waist, and his face is buried in the back of my neck.

I should go. I should get up and march to the couch. Rhett has no plans to stay married, and if I go down this road, I'm only going to get more attached.

But then he groans and pulls me tighter to him, and I'm greeted with his thick erection against my ass.

My breath catches in my chest.

Images from our night at the cabin run through my mind. The way he held my legs open and fingered me to the best orgasm of my life. How he could do that with just his hand is crazy. And then that blow job. Dear God, that blow job. I was throbbing all over again when I went down on him.

I shiver and try to block that out. I told him sex was a bad idea.

Why does my husband have to be so damn tempting?

From deep within my soul, I know this is one of those huge crossroads in my life. If I get up and sleep on the couch, this dream ends. I'll keep my distance and know better than to get under the covers with him to watch movies.

But if I stay...

If I stay, maybe we don't have to split up in a few months. Maybe I can convince him that he wants more. Maybe I can convince him that we have something special. Maybe I can convince him to love me.

Like I've always loved him.

I see that now, how I never stopped loving him. In high school and college, I masked the pain of his rejection with indifference, but the feelings were always there beneath that facade.

How can I not love Rhett? He works himself to the bone for

his boys and his brothers and this incredible ranch. He starts before dawn and doesn't stop until his kids are tucked away in bed. His dedication to those he loves is awe-inspiring.

I swallow, terrified of his rejection. Sure, I can coax him into having sex with me—we already came close to it at the cabin—but that doesn't mean he'll ever love me.

Through the moonlight streaming through the window, I stare at the bare couch.

That's a lonely spot. That's a one-way ticket to Boston where I don't know anyone. That requires leaving the only people who care about me to coach strangers' children instead of loving up on the kids who are already in my life.

That's probably a series of relationships where I don't let myself feel anything.

It would be so easy to go back to that place. To block myself off and amble through life with a painted smile on my face, which is probably a bad look for a cheerleader.

Closing my eyes, I decide to take a chance.

Before I can stop myself, I reach back and rake my fingers through his thick hair. He groans again, and I arch my back.

My panties are wet by the time he starts thrusting against me.

But then his breathing changes, and he stops.

His mouth moves to my ear. "Paige, baby, we shouldn't do this."

He could fuck me ten ways to Sunday right now, but I know he'd never take advantage of me.

This is the moment. Do I scurry off to the couch? Or do I take a leap of faith? As much as I want to avoid this confrontation, I know I can't live like that anymore. It'll eat me alive if I don't say something.

Please don't reject me, Rhett.

Slowly, I turn in his arms so we're nose to nose. "What if I don't want to stop?"

When he doesn't say anything, I close my eyes and rush to tell him what's in my heart. "I'm tired of being with you but still having to keep my distance. Of being your partner halfway. Of wanting you but never having you." I suck in a breath and finally have the guts to look at him. "Unless... unless you don't want me."

His hand grasps my face, and his gaze studies mine. "You know I want you. I've wanted you from the moment I dragged your cute little ass out of your car. But darling, I don't wanna steal your dream of coaching. There's nothing here for you in Wild Heart except dust, dirt, and filthy cowboys."

But what if I want a filthy cowboy? I bite back the words because he's obviously trying to let me down easy. He doesn't want to do this. "I see." I start to pull away. I need to get to the couch before I start crying.

But then he pulls me back and leans up over me. "I'm not done." My eyes widen at the gruffness in his voice. He drags a rough finger over my bottom lip. "If we do this, you have to promise me one thing."

Is he really considering it?

"What's that?" I'll promise him anything. I hate that I'm so eager. That he holds all the cards right now. But then, he always has.

"You don't make any decisions about staying here until you're healed up. I want you to keep your options open. You're young, just outta college, and you've had a tough few weeks. I'd hate for you to make a rash decision and regret it later."

Why is he talking to me like I'm twelve instead of twenty-two? I push him back. "Rhett, I've lived a whole life away from you. I've had boyfriends and shitty jobs and crappy landlords and won fucking national championships. I've traveled across the country with friends and seen so many things I wanted to share with you but couldn't. I've also lost my parents and my brother along the way. I don't have anyone left." The part of me that used to be numb feels everything right now, and my eyes sting. "So don't tell me what I'll regret. If you don't want me, if you don't want to do this, just say that instead of—"

He slams his mouth against mine. "Of course I fucking want you." In between kisses, he mumbles, "What sane man wouldn't?" But then he stops. His chest heaves as he pulls away. "I won't be the one to steal your dream, wildflower. We can be together for now, but hold off making any big decisions until you're rehabbed. That's my offer."

This infuriating man. "Fine, but—"

His mouth is on me again, and any further discussion is lost to the heat ricocheting between us.

A million emotions race through me. Elation that he's finally giving in. Lust because I want him so badly. Frustration that he's put another condition on our relationship.

And fear that we might burn bright before we burn out.

But then he tucks me beneath his big body, and all rational thought evaporates. His weight feels so good, I groan.

He kisses me long and deep as he wedges himself between my legs. Everything about him is rough. The scruff on his chin. The pads of his fingers. His dry palms.

I want to kiss all those places.

"You're so beautiful, Paige." He stares down at me. "Do you know that? Do you know you're a gorgeous woman?"

The reverence in his voice undoes me. "Thank you." I know I'm a decent-looking girl, but right now, with the way he's looking at me, I feel like the most beautiful woman in Texas.

"May I?" He tugs on the hem of my tank, and I nod.

It flies off, leaving me in a sheer bra.

His hands bracket my chest as he thumbs my hard nipples, and then he ducks down to suck on them. First one, then the other. My head thrashes as he nibbles me through the fabric.

Reaching between us, I unsnap the clasp, and he groans when he sees me bare. He squeezes my flesh, molding and shaping me as he sucks my nipple.

When he stops, I'm afraid he's going to tell me this is a mistake. That we shouldn't do this.

But then he pinches me playfully. "One sec. Gotta grab some condoms."

I'm so relieved I almost laugh. I watch him duck into the bathroom. When he returns a minute later, I shove off my bra and wiggle out of my shorts, which leaves me in a sheer pair of panties. "I'm on the pill." I have a big, stupid smile on my face.

He sits next to me and nods slowly as he looks down. "Maybe that's something we should talk about before we go any further. Because I don't want more children."

That smile freezes as my heart plummets to the ground. He told me that already, but I hoped he'd change his mind if we really became an item. Because I've always wanted kids. A big rowdy house of children who can have the happy childhood I never had. "You mean, ever? Or just in the immediate future?"

Leaning forward, he scrubs his face. "The ranch and the boys are about all I can handle. Plus, Amber had a real tough time of it." I don't know what that means, and he doesn't elaborate. "And, well, I'm not all that good at marriage. I'm afraid I'll stir up another mess. I know that's not fair to you, but that's another reason I think you need to wait and see what you want. Most people figure out this shit when they're dating. Unfortunately, we didn't have that option."

If I stay with Rhett, he doesn't want children with me.

I hate Amber so much. He wanted lots of kids with her. That bitch got everything with him, and she threw it all away.

My throat gets tight, but I breathe through it. Part of me wants to scurry over to the couch and forget we ever did this. Except... I want to know what it's like to be with Rhett. At least once, I want to scratch that itch.

I force a nonchalance I don't feel. "You're right. We'll just play it by ear for the next few months. No sense in making any big decisions now."

When he doesn't say anything, I sit up and slip my arms around him. At first, he doesn't move. Doesn't say anything. Then he clears his throat. "I don't deserve you, Paige. I know that."

I kiss his shoulder. I'd give him my heart and soul on a platter if he asked for them, but I don't think he wants them. That's okay. I haven't had a lot of love in my life, but I'll take what he can give for now. "You're a good man, Rhett. I've always known that. And I'm honored to be your wife, even if it's just for a little while."

Sliding out of bed, I come to stand in front of his spread legs.

We might only have this summer and fall. We might burn bright and then burn out. We might be happy for now and then go our separate ways.

But I'll be damned if I don't make this the hottest sexual experience of his life. I hope I can burn myself into his memory. Into his heart and soul. Into every one of his dreams.

So when we come to an end, because it sounds like we will, he'll never forget me.

When our eyes connect, I let down my long hair and shake it out before I shimmy out of my underwear. His hands grip my hips. "Christ. You're incredible."

"Take off your pajama bottoms."

He stands, and I move back while he shoves them down and kicks them off. My gaze tracks down his tight abs, catching on his proud erection.

That's because of me, and damn if it doesn't make me feel powerful.

Licking my lips, I kneel between his legs and grab his thick length. As his hands tangle in my hair, holding it away from my face, I drag my tongue along his swollen crown.

The groan that rumbles in his chest spurs me on, tightening my nipples as his eyes hood. I stare up at him as I slowly work him over, sucking his cock like it's the sweetest lollipop I've ever tasted. When I take him to the back of my throat, that hand in my hair tightens, and he holds me there.

I know all I have to do is nudge him and he'll let me go, but I don't want that. I swallow him, and he lets out another groan. Finally, I come up with a gasp. My eyes tear up and I'm slobbery, but his hot gaze on me spurs me on. I do it again and again until he pulls me off.

"Not this way. Wanna come in your hot little cunt."

I shiver. I love a dirty-talking Rhett Walker.

With my elbow, I wipe my mouth. He helps me up, and I stand there as he rips open a gold packet and rolls on a condom over his swollen flesh. I expect him to pull me onto his lap.

Instead, he tosses me on the bed, and I land with a laugh. And then his head is between my thighs.

He nibbles my pussy lips before he spreads me apart and takes a long lick up my core, pausing right before he reaches my clit. I push his head down, but he chuckles and licks around the spot where I need him. Then he sinks two thick fingers into me, and I squeal.

His eyes are riveted to where he sinks in and out of me. I can hear my arousal, slick on his hand. After a few moments, this brilliant man curls those fingers and he finally sucks on my clit.

I thrash underneath him. "Yes! There!"

"Shh."

I cover my mouth with one hand and grip his hair with my other. I hold him to me as he licks and sucks.

Our eyes meet. His are dark as pitch. Fevered. A reflection of my own.

My legs drop open, and that dirty man pauses to lick his other finger and then drop it down to my asshole where he slowly pushes into me.

Two sucks later, I fly apart with a scream that I barely manage to muffle.

Panting, I lie there boneless. He slides up the bed, somehow keeping that finger in my ass. He gives it a wiggle, and I laugh. "Found something there you like, huh?" I ask sleepily.

"You have no fucking idea," he grunts as he crawls over me.

One breath later, he sinks his thick cock into me. It's a slow slide because he's so thick, but the fullness is magical with the pressure of his finger in the back. "Oh, my God, Rhett."

His other arm comes around me, and he kisses me deep as he bottoms out.

I draw my legs around his waist, which makes him sink deeper, and we both groan. Slowly, he pulls back, almost all the way out, before he slams back in, and that incredible pressure builds again. Our slick bodies slap together, and he wiggles that finger, and I detonate again.

I shove my face into his neck as I come with a scream. He thickens between my thighs and a second later releases with hard pulses. I feel each and every one as I quiver and shake in his arms.

Panting, he rests his forehead on my chest. When he lifts it, his hair is going every which way, and the concern in his eyes puts me on alert. "Are you okay, baby? I didn't..." He frowns. "I didn't mean to get carried away. That was kinda rough. I should've—"

I put my finger over his swollen lips. "That was perfect. I like it rough." Apparently. Who knew?

"You do?"

He sounds so shocked, I laugh. "I came twice, which is a personal record. So please don't apologize." My throat is hoarse from all that screaming.

"You tell me immediately if anything we ever do is too much."

"Yes, sir." His dick kicks once more in my body, and I chuckle.

Now I really am boneless, and when he slides out of me, I groan and flop on the bed. He returns from the bathroom a moment later with a warm washcloth and cleans me up. I'm so impressed with his manners. "I'm going to leave a review for you on Yelp. It'll say, 'Fabulous curb-to-curb sex service.'"

He smirks, turns me on my side, and smacks my butt. "Smartass."

When he slides into bed, he pulls me to his warm body, and I throw my leg over his and curl into his hard chest.

"Mmm. You feel so good," I mumble.

Rhett kisses my forehead. "So do you, wildflower. Too good."

I want to ask him what that means, how something could feel too good, but I fall asleep.

Chapter Twenty-Two
RHETT

I WHISTLE as I shovel out the stall, and Beau gives me a look. "Someone's in a good mood."

"It's a lovely day." I've been replaying last night in my mind all morning. Paige is... well, she's spectacular. Waking up with that woman is about the best thing I've experienced in years.

He chuckles. "If I had to bet, I'd say you got laid."

My smile evaporates. "If you say one word about my wife, we're gonna have a problem, brother."

He laughs harder and holds up his hand. "I would never say anything about sweet, beautiful Paige Lewis."

"That's right. Let's keep it that way. And it's Paige *Walker* now, in case you didn't get the memo."

I exit the stall with the wheelbarrow, and he closes it behind me. "Does this mean she'll be sticking around after those six months?"

I shrug. "Not sure."

"Why's that? Y'all obviously get along well, and anyone with two eyes can see how well she fits in with the family. Even the boys are warming up to her."

I pause to take off my work gloves and get a drink of water. "I told her I want her to be fully rehabbed before she makes any decisions. That girl's been doing gymnastics and cheer since she was little. Where's she gonna use those skills in Wild Heart? She's an elite athlete, Beau. I can't ask her to stay so she can be a rancher's wife."

His expression goes flat. "Are you serious?"

"I just want what's best for her. Danny would want me to push her to go after what she really wants and not... not settle."

He frowns. "Why is the best option not you? She'd have a good life here. We'll get our financial situation all figured out this year, and then y'all could have a few rugrats, and we'd—"

"I'm not having more kids. That's off the table. I already told her."

His brows lift. "You just *told* her? And she was okay with that?"

I shrug. "She didn't argue. Then she agreed to hold off making any decisions about us for now."

Beau shakes his head. "I love you, brother, but sometimes you're a dumbass."

He doesn't understand. That's fine. But I need to do right by Paige. I scrub a hand over my face. "Are you coming fishing with me and the boys tomorrow?"

"My shift starts in the morning, so I need a raincheck."

"I hate that you have to take on so much." Beau works his ass off as a fireman and then puts in a shitload of time here at the ranch.

"It's no more than you do."

What was I supposed to do when my father was too drunk to get out of bed? Let this place fall apart? Thank God I have my brothers. I'd never be able to handle this place by myself.

I put my gloves back on, and he follows me out of the barn. I dump the manure several yards away. "Did you test the pH balance of that field we discussed?"

"It's ready to be fertilized."

"Can you get the guys on that? Make sure the manure is laid down in a thin layer?"

He nods. "I'm on it."

"Also..." I wipe my forehead with the back of my arm. "Would you mind making a run to the lumber yard later this week? I have a list of things I need for a project."

"Sure. What are we making?"

"A coop." I squint into the bright sun. "How do you feel about chickens?"

I get through my to-do list in record time before I book it back to the house. As I'm stomping my feet on the welcome mat, I open the back door. "Paige. Baby, you ready?"

I promised I'd take her to her first physical therapy appointment. It's just an assessment, but she seemed nervous, so I offered to drive her.

"Um. Rhett? I have a visitor. Can you give me a sec?"

Why does she sound funny? I stomp into the house and find her talking to some dude in a suit. I'm momentarily distracted by the sweet little sundress Paige is wearing. It's yellow and shows off a fetching amount of leg.

I turn to the guy. "You from the bank?" I ask as I wipe my hands on my jeans. "Did Harlan send you?"

His brow puckers as he looks at Paige, then back to me. "You know my uncle?"

I frown. "You're related to Harlan?"

"Harlan Calhoun?" he says slowly. "I'm his nephew."

Paige's eyes widen, but before I can say anything, she puts her hand on my chest and coughs. Then waves at the suit. "This is my ex, Marcus. Marcus, this is..."

She pauses like she isn't sure what to say.

"Her husband," I add as I put my arm around her petite shoulders.

It's dipshit's turn to eyeball us. He stares at us for at least thirty seconds. Then the idiot bursts out laughing. He laughs so hard, he has to wipe his eyes. Then he smiles at Paige like she's a tasty treat. "You almost had me there." He chuckles. "I brought your mail. Your stepmother said you were here." He glances at me, then turns to Paige. "Listen, I feel bad about how we ended things. Let me take you to lunch and make it up to you. I miss you, gorgeous. I'm getting a bigger apartment, so you can move back in with me if you want."

"The fuck she's moving back in with you," I growl.

Still sporting that stupid smile, he has the balls to pull her to the side. "Whatever, man." He turns to her and lowers his voice as though I can't hear him from three feet away. "Paige, I know I wasn't very attentive these last few months, but I was busy at work. You know how demanding my job is. I just don't have the energy to hang out like you want sometimes. When I get home, I just want to chill. Watch TV. Kill a few zombies on my PlayStation. Have dinner. Maybe fuck."

I'm gonna kill him.

I'm not sure how it happens, but next thing I know, I have his pretty white shirt balled up in my fist and his neck pressed to the door. "Listen, motherfucker, Paige ain't interested in your half-assed attempts at being a good boyfriend."

"Rhett, let him go." She tugs on my arm and gives me a pointed look. "He's Harlan's nephew," she hisses.

Shit. She's right. It takes everything in me to unclench my fist, but not before I grit out, "She's not gonna fuck you anymore, Marcus, because *she's my wife*."

When I let go, he staggers. "What, you're serious?" His gaze shifts between me and Paige.

"Do I look like I'm fucking joking?" I could kill this little weasel and bury him in the backyard. Doubtful anyone would miss him.

His shit-eating smile finally disappears, and now he genuinely looks upset. "Paige? We broke up a week ago."

I pin him back to the wall. "She broke up with you *two* weeks ago. Now get the fuck out of my house."

When I shove him loose, Paige's eyes are saucers. Shit. I hope I'm not scaring her. I'm not usually a violent guy. But when a stranger waltzes into my house and talks to my wife like she's his personal sex toy, I feel at liberty to let him know he crossed a goddamn line.

He wobbles to one side, then the other. When he regains his equilibrium, he reaches into his man bag and tosses a bunch of envelopes on the floor. "Fuck y'all. She's not worth this shit." Then he scurries off like a rat back to the sewer.

When the door slams behind him, I expect Paige to read me the riot act. Instead, she grabs my hand. "Are you okay? I'm sorry. I swear I didn't know he was coming here. I would've warned you."

The concern in her eyes makes me frown. "Sweetheart, you don't owe me any apologies. You can have anyone over at any time. This is your house now. But I would definitely appreciate a heads-up about any ex-boyfriends so I don't blow my top when they look like they want to slurp you up like a tasty treat."

She shakes her head. "I can't believe you almost beat up Harlan's nephew."

"Who almost beat up Harlan's nephew?" Beau appears in the back door.

Paige points at me. "The Hulk here."

I smirk. "Let the record show that I held back."

She rolls her eyes as she crosses the room. I follow her and lean against the kitchen counter and tug her to my chest. "Sorry, wildflower. Didn't mean to rough up your ex."

She sighs. "I didn't know Harlan was his uncle. They have

different last names. And I thought Marcus's family lived in Dallas."

"Harlan spends a lot of time up there."

"It makes me realize how little effort Marcus put into our relationship. I remember telling him where I grew up, but he was playing a video game at the time, so I guess it went in one ear and out the other. Because wouldn't he have said, hey, I have family there too?"

I tuck her hair behind her ear. "He's a dumbass."

Beau reaches into the fridge. "What if he says something to Harlan? Do we need to be worried?"

I should be more concerned about that, but the moment I saw Marcus get up in Paige's business, I wanted to rip his head off his scrawny shoulders. Fuck. I don't know why I get so wound up about this woman.

My wife considers his question. "He didn't want to introduce me to his parents because I wasn't the right caliber of girl, so hopefully he's too embarrassed about the whole thing to mention this to anyone."

Tugging her closer, I growl. "I should've kicked his ass. What a moron." My brother has the good sense to make himself scarce.

Paige tilts her head up, her lips tugged up in amusement. "I appreciate you trying to stand up for my honor, but maybe we don't put our hands on anyone next time."

Leaning down, I kiss her forehead. "Yes, ma'am."

Maybe this should concern me, but I'm finding it's easier and easier to promise Paige whatever she wants.

Chapter Twenty-Three

PAIGE

Baylee takes the towel off my head. "You've been strangely radio silent about what all's been going on at the ranch."

We're at her mom's salon, but it's early, and I'm the first customer. I swivel my chair away from her so I can face the mirror. "Actually, something really funny happened the other night. I walked into the kitchen to get a glass of water, and Jace and one of his groupies fell out of the pantry half naked." I snort. "I left a container of Clorox wipes outside his bedroom door with instructions to sanitize any area that his bare ass might've touched. I woke up the next morning, and the whole house smelled like bleach."

She laughs and shakes her head.

I tug on my hair, debating whether I should try bangs. "Oh, and Rhett built me a henhouse. He and Beau painted it red with white trim. They even made a sign over the doorway that says 'Paige's Little Cluckers.' It's freaking adorable. Then we went to the tractor supply store and got some Rhode Island Reds, and soon we're going to have farm-fresh eggs." I clap like a little nerd. "I've always wanted chickens. The ranch dogs get a little crazy around them, but Rhett says they'll get used to my cluckers soon enough. Let me show you some pics."

After I scroll through twenty-three photos of my chickens, Baylee chuckles. "Look at you, farm girl."

"I know. I love the ranch so much. Last night, I sat out by the fire pit and read a book on my Kindle. There were a million stars out. It felt like a slice of heaven. I even forgot about the Marcus situation for a bit."

She grabs a comb. "I'm kinda sad Rhett didn't at least punch him."

"I don't want Rhett to get in trouble. What if Marcus tells Harlan we dated? That I broke up with Marcus days before I married Rhett? Then he'll know Rhett just got hitched so he could get that loan. But we saw Harlan last weekend at the grocery store, and he just waved. Still, I'm paranoid."

She combs out my wet hair. "It's crazy that Marcus is related to Harlan."

"It is, but it isn't. Marcus is an investment banker or something, and Harlan owns banks. Or maybe his family does? I'm not really sure."

"Are we doing the same shade of red?" she asks as she studies my roots, which aren't too bad since my real hair is auburn.

"Yeah. Rhett loves it." The fiery color has grown on me. I want to be the kind of woman who can pull off bold hair.

"I'm sure the Harlan stuff is stressful, but that's not what I'm talking about."

I wrinkle my nose. "Do you mean the sabotage? I talked Rhett into waiting to hear back from the sheriff before he storms the McAllister compound. But it's been weeks, and I'm starting to worry we'll never find out who's been cutting our fences. But isn't Cash smarter than that? Would he really mess with Rhett? I don't think he has a death wish."

"I'm not talking about the sabotage." My best friend rolls her eyes. "I'm talking about the hot monkey sex you're obviously having."

I laugh and cover my mouth. "Baylee."

"What? You've wanted to bed Rhett Walker since we figured out what sex is, and now you're not gonna tell me anything?"

"He's my husband, not some hookup."

She makes a face. "It's that good, huh?"

I grin. "It's ah-maze-ing. It's so good, I'm sore."

"Bitch. I wanna have Animal Planet sex." She pouts. "I'm definitely getting on dating apps. I'm gonna hop on some hot guy's dick and forget all about Maverick Walker once and for all."

I reach behind me for her hand. "It's his loss."

"Will you help me do my profile? I'm terrible at this stuff."

"Absolutely. It'll be fun."

Her phone rings with a video call, and she peeks at the screen. "It's Abby!"

"Answer it. I haven't talked to her since she and Nick moved to Houston."

Baylee slides her finger over the screen and angles the phone so we both fit in the little window. "Hey, girl! I'm here with Paige."

"My two favorite people!"

"Hey, roomie! I miss you!" I shout. Abby was briefly my roommate last year. We had so much fun together. I wish I could've stayed with her instead of moving in with Marcus, but if that had happened, she and her boyfriend Nick might not have gotten together.

"How's the NFL treating you and Nick?" Baylee asks. "And how's Hazel?"

Hazel is Nick's adorable five-year-old daughter. Her mom passed away in an accident when she was a baby, and Nick hired Abby to be Hazel's nanny last fall. One thing led to another, and now they're a serious item.

Abby grins. "Nick and Hazelnut are doing great, but it's been a whirlwind—the draft, packing and moving, getting to know the new team. And it's so humid here in Houston. I'm dying, especially now that I'm the size of a beached whale." She shifts the camera, and we get a good look at her baby bump.

"You're perfect, and that baby is just the right size," I say wistfully. All of a sudden, I want a baby so bad. And that's crazy. I just graduated from college. I have lots of time for kids.

Baylee pulls a chair over and sits next to me. "Okay, I need to spill the tea here since Paige obviously isn't going to. Guess who married her high school crush?" She points at me.

Abby's eyes go wide. "You married Rhett? The guy whose calls you never answered?"

I can admit now that was immature, but I wasn't ready to talk to him. "The one and only."

Baylee puts the phone up to her face and whispers, "And now she's having all the sex and pretending like Rhett's not banging her through the headboard every night."

"Baylee Reyes." I elbow her but laugh. "It's true. I'm having all the sex. I've never come so many times in my life."

At that moment, Aunt Syl walks through the back door. She lifts her brow at that statement, then shakes her head. "I'm just gonna pretend I didn't hear that. Morning, girls. Glad you're enjoying your husband, Paige." She disappears into her office.

"Oh, my God," I whisper as I cover my face.

Baylee and Abby howl with laughter before Abby leans close to the phone. "How in the world did this happen?"

I take the cell away from Baylee. "It's a long story. I'll call you when I get home and give you the scoop." I don't think Rhett would care if I told Abby, since she lives in Houston, but I'll run it by him.

"Paige, I'm glad I caught you with Baylee because I need your advice." Abby motions to her belly again. "I don't fit into anything. I'm excited to go to all of Nick's games and events, but I'm not sure what to wear. I don't even fit into the jersey he got me, and I'm not sure I will after the baby comes. You're so good with clothes and fashion. Can you help me again?"

"I'd be happy to. And just to be clear, you look gorgeous pregnant, and Nick is going to love you no matter what you wear."

She smiles. "I know I'm just being self-conscious, but I want him to feel proud when he sees me at his games."

I know the feeling. "Can you send me the jersey? I can tailor it for you or make a jacket or vest you can wear over something more comfortable."

"Really? You'd do that for me?" She starts to sniffle.

"Of course. What are friends for?" In retrospect, I probably should've gone into fashion. I love sewing and clothes, but those skills are probably even more useless in Wild Heart than my communications degree.

"And please don't worry about the weight," Baylee says. "My sister always loses fifteen pounds within days of having her babies."

"That's so good to hear." Abby wipes her eyes. "I love you guys so much. Paige, I'll pay you for your time. I don't want you to think I expect this for free."

I frown. "You don't have to pay me."

Baylee shakes her head. "Abby, don't listen to Paige. Send her money. Whatever you think is fair."

"Baylee!" I turn to my childhood best friend. "I wouldn't charge you, so it's not fair to charge Abby."

"What? Her baby daddy is in the NFL. If my boyfriend was in the NFL, I'd pay you too."

Abby chuckles. "She's right. I'm sending you money no matter what."

Smiling, I hold up my hand. "I can't defend myself against you two."

We chat a few more minutes, and then Abby and I agree to talk later to figure out how she wants me to customize her jersey.

When we hang up, I sigh. "I love her to pieces, and I'm so happy she and Nick found each other."

Baylee puts her phone back on the counter. "They're perfect together." She finishes brushing out my damp hair. "Back to Rhett. I wanna say this one thing, and then I'll shut up. I'm psyched y'all are getting along and he's sexing you up so much that you're walking funny, but..." She whirls my chair around so that I'm facing her. "I don't want you to get your heart crushed. Those Walker brothers don't know what kind of voodoo they wield with their little smirks and tight asses."

She's right, and that makes me sad. "I hear what you're saying, and I'd be lying if I said I wasn't afraid, but I want to give this a real chance."

My best friend's eyes narrow. "Be sure to tell Rhett that I have a shotgun, and I'm not afraid to use it. Does a man really need two kneecaps? One seems sufficient."

I laugh and lean over to hug her. "Thank you."

When I let go, she grabs the hair dye. "Have you had any trouble with the twatwaffle?"

"I've made myself scarce when Amber picks up the boys or drops them off. I'm just not sure how long my luck will last."

The front doorbell rings, and my eyes widen when I see who it is.

Honey McAllister glances around nervously. "Hi. Is it okay that I'm here?"

Wild Heart has invisible lines of loyalty. There are people who are fierce Walker supporters and those who are McAllister ride or die. The whole thing is stupid. It makes nice women like Honey afraid to go to the damn salon.

I wave her in. "Of course."

She points behind her. "I usually go to Darling Divas, but they had a scheduling conflict."

Baylee mumbles, "We are starting shit today. I love it." Then she turns to Honey. "Whatcha need? I might be able to fit you in."

Honey was a year ahead of us in school. We never really spoke, but I liked that she always seemed friendly, unlike her brothers.

She pulls at the end of her hair. "I need a trim. I'm starting my new teaching job, and I want to look the part."

I point at the chair next to me. "Grab a seat."

She gives me a hesitant smile as she sits. "I heard you married Rhett this summer. Congrats."

"Thank you."

Putting a hand over her mouth, she whispers, "Don't tell my brothers, but I had a huge crush on him in high school."

I laugh. "Girl, join the club."

She glances at Baylee. "Are you dating Maverick? I always see y'all together."

"We're not dating." My best friend's lips go flat. "We've *never* dated."

Honey glances between us. "I'm guessing there's a story there, but I don't wanna pry."

"There's no story. We've always just been friends." Baylee turns me around in my chair. "Honey, let me get Paige's color on, and then we can talk about your trim."

An hour and a half later, my hair is done and Baylee's blow-drying Honey when the front door opens again. It's Beau.

"Paige, Rhett's running late—" He freezes when he sees Honey.

She rolls her eyes and mutters something I can't make out.

He stares at her a long minute, tilts his hat to her. "Little Mac." He ignores her scowl and turns to me. "I'm due at the fire station, but if you wanna head home, I can give you a ride right quick."

Beau calls her Little Mac. Oh, my God. That's so cute. Baylee must think so too because she gives me a look.

I gather my things and hug my best friend. Then I wave to

Honey. She's busy giving my brother-in-law a death stare, which morphs into a smile for me.

As my brother-in-law drives me back to the ranch, I can't resist teasing him. "So what's up with you and Honey McAllister?"

It's his turn to scowl. "Not one thing, Miss Nosey."

"If you say so," I sing-song.

There's definitely a story there.

Chapter Twenty-Four
PAIGE

I SHOOT off another text to Abby, who just sent me photos of sweet little Janie.

> Please give her a kiss from her aunt Paige!

She's the most beautiful baby I've ever seen. I'm so excited for her and Nick.

I have to admit this is giving me a vision for my future.

As Rhett and I drive down the bumpy road, I try not to let myself be too happy. With the window down and the fresh scent of cedar in the air, it's hard not to smile, especially when my husband's hand rests possessively on my thigh.

I take him in while trying not to appear like I'm staring. He's wearing a t-shirt that stretches over his broad chest and shoulders, faded jeans, boots, and an old baseball cap that reminds me of what he looked like in high school.

Except now he's sporting a full beard, all those muscles, and those sexy as hell tattoos. My husband is a total smoke show.

"You really don't have to drive me to my PT appointments." He always seems to find an excuse to drive me into town. I can't really take my car because the driveway to the ranch needs to be repaved. I can borrow his truck if I need to, but it's super sweet that he offers.

He shrugs. "Kinda like spending time with you. Besides, your appointments are in the afternoon, which gives me an excuse to avoid going into the office."

He likes spending time with me.

Ugh, I love him so much, but since he refuses to talk about the future, I refuse to say the words. I put myself out there by telling him I wanted more and sleeping with him, but my bravado has limits.

Plus, he hasn't said those three words to me.

Rhett's hand drifts up my thigh, and I grin but put my palm over it to stop him. "You're not allowed to turn me on before PT."

He makes a face. "Why's that?"

I shake my head, a little embarrassed to admit the reason.

Rhett chuckles. "Why're you turning red?"

Fine. I'll tell him the problem. "Because you make me really wet, and I don't have a change of clothes. I refuse to endure an hour of physical therapy with damp panties. It's uncomfortable."

Groaning, he shakes his head. "Fuck. Now I wish I hadn't asked." He reaches down to adjust himself, and I laugh.

"Serves you right. You'd think with all the sex we're having that you'd have it out of your system by now."

Rhett gives me a heated look. "Do you really think two months is all it would take for me to get you 'out of my system?'"

Ignoring his question, I pull up my legs and turn to him. "If we go to bed any earlier, your brothers are going to know we're boning like our lives depend on it."

"Beau and Jace don't care. Hell, they're hardly home at night. And it's good to get Gabriel and Austin to bed early. If they're gonna take over the ranch someday, it's better if they're used to our schedule."

As we pull into town, I motion toward the pharmacy. "Can we pull in here real quick? I need to pick up something."

"Sure thing. I'll wait here." I pop open the lock, but before I open the door, he grabs my hand and tugs me back. "You forgot something."

"What's that?"

"This." He pulls me to him for a kiss.

I run my hand over his beard. "You're a handsome devil, you know that?"

He chuckles. "So I've been told."

Ugh, why doesn't he want to have more children? I swear my body is chanting, *We want babies! We want babies!*

With a smile on my face, I slip out of the truck. I'm back in a few minutes and hand him a package.

"What's this?"

"Just a little something I thought you'd like. Really, I should frame them first, but I can't wait."

He opens the bag and pulls out the packet of photos. He grins as he flips through the pics of him, Jace, and the boys when they went fishing. I made sure Jace took a bunch. "This was really sweet of you. Thank you, honey."

I uploaded them to the pharmacy photo website a while back but kept forgetting to get them. They were such adorable pics, I thought he might want to have printed copies.

Leaning over, he gives me another kiss, but this one is long and sweet, and by the time I pull away, I'm out of breath. "Can we go to my PT appointment before I crawl into your lap?"

He adjusts himself again and nods. "Yes, ma'am." We drive a few more blocks, then turn into a parking lot. "Meet you here in an hour? I need to head to the hardware store. I read that chickens need a perch, so I wanna add a few to their run."

I grin. "When I said I wanted chickens, I thought we'd get a little coop." But Rhett basically built me a mini-barn that houses thirty birds. "I think you're going overboard."

"My wife wants chickens, so we're doing this right."

I love you.

I want to tell him so badly, but instead I kiss him again and then head in for my appointment.

Why does my husband have to be so swoony?

An hour later, I step out into the late afternoon sun. My heart skips a beat when I spot Rhett's truck. I keep waiting for that physical reaction to subside, but every time I see him, especially when he's gone all morning, adrenaline rushes through me and I get giddy.

As I approach, he gets out to open my door. "How'd it go?"

"Great. My ankle is strong enough to do more weight training. My physical therapist said he wants to make sure I'm strong enough before I start tumbling again." I've been jogging in the mornings, but tumbling adds so much more pressure to your joints.

Am I taking rehab slow? Yes. Do I care? Not really.

If I were back at Lone Star State, I would've wrapped this ankle and done my cheer routines regardless of the pain for nationals, but I have to admit it's nice to not kill myself. In fact, I'm enjoying not living at a back-breaking pace. I love life on the Walker Ranch.

And if I'm considering not heading to Boston later this year, well, that's my business for now.

Rhett nods. "Glad to hear it, but, um... He's not getting too friendly, is he? Because I can break one of his hands if he is."

I chuckle. "He's been a total gentleman. Need I remind you that I have therapy in a big room about two feet away from his assistant?" Rhett and I got a tour of the facilities at my first appointment.

"Good. Just making sure."

I get a little thrill knowing Rhett's protective of me.

I'm expecting to head back to the ranch, but instead, he pulls in front of the Prairie Rose Trading Post, which is a country store. "Did you need something here?"

"No, but I figured you do." Me? What do I need? He gets out and comes to my door to help me down. "Now that you're feeling better, I wanted to get you some boots. You used to like horseback riding when you were a kid, and I thought you might enjoy heading out with me some time, but you need boots to do that. Plus, I wanted to get you a graduation gift." He rubs the back of his neck. "Unless there's something else you'd like."

Who knew that gruff Rhett Walker was such a sweetheart?

"I'd love a pair of boots, but I don't want you spending money on me." I've heard the guys talking. If the cattle don't gain enough weight, we won't get the prices we need for them. Or if the prices fall again, we could be in trouble. There are a ridiculous number of variables.

He threads our fingers together. "Darling, I'm really fucking proud of you for getting your degree. Let me get you the boots."

My heart melts. "Okay. I'd love that. If you're sure."

"I'm sure."

We walk into the store hand in hand. Mrs. Nash greets us. "How are my favorite newlyweds doing?"

I haven't seen Mrs. Nash in ages, but she used to give me candy when I was little even though I couldn't afford it. "It's so nice to see you." I let go of Rhett to give her a hug.

"What can I get y'all?"

Rhett wraps his arm around my shoulders. "Wanted to get my wife a pair of boots, a coupla sundresses 'cause she likes those, and maybe some fabric 'cause she loves to sew."

I glare at him. "That's not what we agreed to." And oh, my God, this man has been paying attention. I dated Marcus for ten months and I'm pretty sure he didn't know those things about me.

Rhett chuckles and leans down to kiss me. "It would make me happy to get those things for you."

Damn it. I wave a hand in my face so I don't start crying. "Okay."

Mrs. Nash looks back and forth between us. "Aren't y'all the sweetest! Back in the day, I never would've imagined little Miss Paige would marry you, Rhett, but don't y'all make the cutest couple." She winks at him. "A happy wife makes for a happy life, and obviously Paige is doing something right to put that look on your face."

His ears go red, and I chuckle. I can only imagine what he's thinking right now.

Twenty minutes later, I come out of the dressing room in a burnt orange sundress and a lovely pair of brown boots.

Rhett lets out a wolf whistle. "Damn. You're almost perfect."

"Almost?" I frown.

He puts a cowboy hat on my head and tilts it back. "There ya go."

I catch a glimpse of myself in the full-length mirror. A happy farm girl stares back at me. Her long red hair cascades from her cowboy hat. Her skin is golden brown from the Texas sun, and light freckles dot her rosy cheeks.

Rhett stands right behind me and leans down to whisper, "You're hot as fuck in this outfit." He turns to Mrs. Nash who's behind the register. "We'll take this. Can she wear it home?"

We don't make it back to the ranch because he pulls off the road.

Chapter Twenty-Five
RHETT

"Where are we going?" Paige asks.

"Right here." I pull off onto a narrow road behind the park and turn off my truck. It's dusk, but with all the trees, it's dark back here. I can't wait a minute longer to touch her. "Come here."

I unsnap my seatbelt, then hers, before I tug her over into my lap. She immediately straddles me. "Thank you for my gifts, husband. I love everything." She removes her cowboy hat and lays it on her seat before returning her attention to me.

"You're welcome, beautiful." The country store doesn't carry designer brands, but Paige acted like we were shopping in Beverly Hills. She's so grateful for everything I do for her. I've never been with a woman like her. Amber never appreciated anything.

"You're too good to me." She runs her hands over my beard and into my hair. I reach under her dress and grip her ass and pull her closer.

She grinds against my erection, and I groan. "Been dying to get my hands on you all afternoon."

"And you couldn't wait until tonight?"

"Fucking you in my bed is fine, but out here, where we're alone, you don't have to be quiet." I grip her hair tight the way I know she likes. Then I nip her bottom lip before I kiss her long and deep. "I wanna hear you scream my name when you come on my cock."

Her eyes grow hooded as she grinds against me. I can feel her heat through my jeans.

I reach between us. "Are you wet?"

She nods. "I'm ready."

She tries to unbutton my jeans, but I push her hands away. "Baby, I need to check first." I lower my seat before I snake my hand into her panties. I groan when I feel her hot slickness all over my fingers. I use that to rub her pussy, first around her opening and then around her swollen clit. A minute later, I sink two deep into her. "Work yourself on me."

Paige shivers, and I tug on her sleeve. "Pull down your dress. I wanna see your gorgeous tits." Then she unsnaps her bra, and those luscious beauties are in my face.

I suck on her nipple. I lick her and bite that sweet bud, and she groans.

"Feel good, baby?"

"So good."

Once she's warmed up, I remove my hand and hold the fingers up to her mouth. "Suck. See how good you taste."

Her lips close around my fingers, and when she sucks, my cock swells.

"Take my dick out." Her eager hands reach for my belt. A minute later, I spring up, hard as a baseball bat. "Hold your skirt and get on my cock. Go slow. I wanna watch every second."

I help her up onto her knees. She grips my length and rubs it against her swollen clit several times. "Want you coming on my cock, so you'd better stop." She nods and notches me in her hot pussy. I bunch her dress at her waist as we watch her sink down on me.

Goddamn. How does she feel so fucking good? I keep

thinking our sex can't be as good as I think it is. And then I'm so out of my mind to fuck her, I can't see straight. Or drive.

I lean her back a little and then reach down and pull her pussy lips apart so I can watch. "Baby, your pussy is stretched so tight right now."

With my thumb, I graze her clit, and she shivers. "Rhett."

"That's it, sweetheart. Feel my big cock. Feel how much I want you. You're driving me insane in this sexy little dress and your boots. I wanted to fuck you so bad, I couldn't even wait until we got home."

Her pussy gets wetter, and I rub my finger around where I sink into her body. "Squeeze your tits. Pinch your nipples."

By the time I bottom out, we're both panting.

"Rhett, I need to come."

I reach behind her and grab her ass. "Then let's make that happen. Rub your clit." I bounce her on me, slowly at first as she rubs herself. She starts making those noises I love, and I pick up the pace.

She's a fucking vision. Red hair spilling down her shoulders. High round tits bouncing with every thrust. Her wet pussy a glove on my cock.

I bring her closer and suck on her neck.

All of a sudden, her back goes ramrod straight, her nails dig into my shoulders, and she shrieks my name. I hold out as long as I can, but her hot cunt squeezes me so good that I finally let go with a roar.

I shoot long, hot pulses into her. I keep bouncing her until I feel my cum drip down her thighs.

Mine. This woman is mine.

When we're home, my cum is gonna be dripping out of her sweet cunt. That thought gives me an odd satisfaction.

Sated and pleased I had my caveman moment, I close my eyes, hug her to me, and bury my nose in her hair. I hate to move, but I suppose we should get back to the ranch. I need to get the boys fed.

Something niggles in the back of my mind, like I forgot something.

My eyes fly open. "I forgot to put on a condom. Fuck."

She yawns. "I'm on the pill."

Is that enough? Amber was on birth control when she got pregnant with Gabriel. But I've always wondered how responsible she was about taking that.

Still, I don't want any accidents.

Paige sits up and grabs my face. "Would having another baby really be the end of the world?"

I feel my blood run cold. Amber had severe postpartum depression and refused to get help. It's one of the things that drove us apart. Aside from the cheating, that is. Not only was it torturous to watch her go through the pain of childbirth, she snapped at everyone. My brothers and I walked on eggshells for months.

I can't imagine watching Paige go through that. It would kill me.

When I don't say anything, she looks away. "I see."

She pushes off me, and I reach into the glove compartment to grab some napkins. In the thick silence, we clean ourselves off.

"Wildflower, it's not you. I just can't—"

"It's fine. You don't want kids with me. I get it." She snaps the seatbelt, crosses her arms, and looks out the window.

My heart sinks. I don't know what to say.

Sylvia's words come back to me. I need to do things differently, but how? I've given Paige everything I can.

Chapter Twenty-Six
PAIGE

Sweat drips in my eyes as I jog down the dusty road. I could work out in the barn where the guys have a little gym, but I don't want to see any Walkers right now. I'm still upset about that condom conversation Rhett and I had two days ago. We've been tiptoeing around each other and pretending everything's okay, but I know it's not because he doesn't reach for me at night.

I'm done making the first move. And I'm absolutely done putting myself out there again only to be rejected.

I run so far, I creep up on the McAllister ranch. It hurts to see it. The property is pristine, their machinery state of the art. They have a white picket fence around the perimeter of their huge house. I don't know what the cattle equipment is called, but the chutes are new and not rusted like they are at our place.

Reluctantly, I turn around and start to run back to the Walker Ranch, but a huge black truck comes barreling down the road and slams to a stop right next to me. The tinted window lowers, and I come face to face with Cash McAllister.

His eyes drift down my body. "Look who's all grown up." He whistles. "Paige Lewis, who knew you were gonna grow up to be such a looker. Not sure why you thought you didn't have any prospects and needed to marry Rhett Walker. Think you could've done better."

I scoff. "Like you?"

"I'm not exactly the marrying type, but if you were the tasty treat up for grabs, I'd consider it."

"Cash, I'm happily married."

"That why you're checking out my ranch? Because you're so content living with the Walkers? We both know they're one bad season away from bankruptcy, and when Rhett finally taps out, I'm going to buy all his property."

Shading my face from the sun, I squint at him. "Is that why you've been sabotaging his ranch? So you can get your hands on it?" All this talk about swooping in to buy our ranch makes me think Rhett's right and Cash is behind all of our recent problems.

He laughs. "That's not how I operate. I'm happy to wait until the Walkers implode on their own, and then I'll be there to pick up the pieces."

"What makes you think we aren't doing well?"

He smirks like he has all the answers. "Doesn't take a genius to know that ranch is on its last legs. Old Man Walker never diversified his outfit, and his idiot sons are following in his footsteps."

"What do you mean by diversify?"

"Darlin', just 'cause you're gorgeous doesn't mean I'm gonna cough up all my secrets."

Frustrated, I turn and look at his sprawling property, where I notice little white clouds of cuteness grazing along the pasture. "Do you mean raising sheep?"

He stares at me a long minute. "Sure. That's one way to do it."

Huh. There's so much I don't know about how to run a successful ranch. "Why sheep?"

Cash rubs his chin and glances at his property. "In a nutshell? Because their peaks offset cattle's low prices." He chuckles. "Now don't go saving the Walker Ranch. Those dumbasses probably won't listen to a pretty little thing like you. And when they don't, maybe then you'll consider my offer."

I hold up my middle finger. "You can choke on that offer, Cash McAllister!" I can't believe he's related to Honey. Angry, I take off running.

He laughs, which only makes me fume more. The nerve of that guy. I'm so pissed, I run hard and fast. My ankle is holding up well, though. I have it wrapped. I'm allowed to work out as long as I avoid side-to-side cutting motions and hard landings.

Can we raise sheep? Do we have the pasture to do that? Who can I ask about diversifying?

By the time I reach the Walker Ranch, I'm so hot, I'm queasy. I head for the kitchen and chug some water.

The back door slams shut, and Jace strolls in. He stops short when he sees me. "You don't look so good."

"Just got a little overheated when I was running. I'll be fine." I consider mentioning my run-in with Cash, but figure that's probably a bad idea.

"You were running in this humidity?"

"It wasn't that humid when I started running."

He scratches his cheek. "You can always call one of us if you get in trouble out there."

"I'm far too reliant on you and your brothers as it is."

Jace frowns. "What does that mean? We like helping you."

"I'm done letting you drive me around. I have a car. I should use it."

"These roads are gonna ruin your shocks. I'm sure Rhett explained that to you. That's why we're always offering to take you wherever you need in our trucks."

I don't know why I'm arguing with Jace. I have no problem with him, so I nod. "I know you mean well. Thanks. I'll keep that in mind."

My vision starts to spot for some reason, and I lean against the counter.

Jace stomps closer. "You dizzy?"

I nod and close my eyes.

"Have you eaten today?"

"No. I wanted to get my workout in first."

"Okay, hold tight. Let's get you a snack."

He hands me some potato salad and juice. I eat everything under his watchful eye. "I'm fine. Really. Just got light-headed for a minute. I'm going to take a shower. Thanks for your help."

Jace hugs me. "We love you, Little Lewis. You know that?"

My eyes tear up because Jace isn't who I want to hear those words from. I blink quickly. "Love you too, bro."

He scruffs my head, and I swat at his hand. He sniffs the air. "Get outta here. You stink."

With a chuckle, I shove him away. When I reach my room, I pop my birth control pill with an eye roll. "Are you happy, Rhett?" I mumble to myself.

I asked him if having a baby with me would be the end of the world, and he went stone-cold silent.

Why do I care so much? I feel like I'm fifteen years old all over again. I wish I could flip a switch and be as nonchalant as I said I would be about this whole marriage thing.

When will my life get easier? I just want a family of my own. Is that too much to ask?

Frustrated with myself, I head to the en suite bathroom. I stand under the cool water and replay the conversation I had with him in his truck for the millionth time.

That numbness I haven't felt since I got to the ranch washes over me as I lean against the cold tile.

I let out a sigh.

It's a relief to not feel anything. I used to think being detached was a curse, but maybe it's a blessing. I'd rather not cry over Rhett anymore. Lord knows I spent enough time doing that during my teens.

I'm feeling better… until I puke into the drain.

Gross.

Ugh. I press a hand against my stomach and try to avoid the nastiness at my feet.

After I clean up my mess, I fall into bed and pull the covers over me. I'm supposed to be in the office in a little while, but the room is spinning like I'm drunk. I'm not sure why. I'll just close my eyes for a little while.

I snuggle deeper under the covers and hope Rhett's out on the range all day. I don't have the energy to deal with him right now.

I'm just starting to fall asleep when the rest of my breakfast comes up.

Chapter Twenty-Seven

RHETT

MY PHONE RINGS. It's Jace. I pause unloading a bale of hay. "What's up?" He's talking so fast, I only make out half of what he's saying. "What's wrong with Paige?"

"She's throwing up. She went out for a run and when she returned, she was the color of a tomato. She hadn't eaten, so I made her something and gave her some juice. I thought she was fine, but then she started puking."

"Shit. I'll be back as soon as I can. Keep an eye on her."

"No prob."

I give Beau a quick update, then take off on Apollo. Guilt for being an ass these last two days hits me hard. I got tongue-tied when Paige brought up having kids right after we fucked. Hell, my cock was still lodged deep in her body. She was so standoffish afterward, I didn't want to crowd her. Amber always bit my head off after an argument, so I got used to giving women a wide berth if they were pissed. But now I'm not sure that was the right thing to do.

When I reach the barn, I hand off Apollo to Wayne and then run to the house. I don't bother cleaning off my boots or washing up, just head straight to my bedroom where I find Jace putting a wet towel on Paige, who's flushed and panting.

"Jesus. Are you okay?"

Her eyes flutter open, but she closes them again. "Fine. Just tired."

Jace winces. "I'm thinking she has heat stroke. She had a hard workout, and she's not used to this humidity."

She waves a hand at us, like she's trying to shoo a fly. "I've worked out in humid gyms my whole life."

Her hair is wet. "You took a cool shower?" She nods, but that makes me more alarmed. That should've lowered her body temperature. I kneel next to the bed and place my palm on her forehead. "Darling, you're burning up. Maybe you got dehydrated. It's easy to do, especially on a day like today. Let's take you to the ER."

She groans. "I can't afford that."

"You're on my insurance, remember? I've got you."

"I'm fine. Just let me sleep."

She's not gonna be happy with me, but I don't give a shit. We said "in sickness and in health," and I'll be damned if I let her get worse. I lift her into my arms, and she flails weakly. "Rhett, put me down."

"We're getting you fluids at the ER." I skim her body. "After we get you dressed." She's wearing a tiny tank top and panties. "Jace, if you look at my wife right now, you're a dead man."

He chuckles as he heads for the door. "Call me if you need help."

After I get Paige dressed, I scoop her up again. When I get her out to my truck, I recline the passenger seat and lay her on it before I drag the seatbelt across her chest. "Hang tight, wildflower. We'll get you feeling better soon."

Since I've been bossing her around, I expect more pushback, but all she does is curl up in her seat and close her eyes, which worries me.

I break all the speed limits to get her to the hospital.

When we get there, my truck squeals to a stop. I hop out, and a minute later, I'm carrying her in.

Dr. Joan Bixby, who delivered my boys, is manning the nurses' station. "Whatcha got there, Rhett?"

"My wife got overheated today. I'm worried she got heat stroke and needs fluids."

Joan directs us to a little room where I gently place her on a gurney. "What are Paige's symptoms?"

It doesn't surprise me that Joan knows Paige. I rattle off the reasons I'm concerned as I adjust the pillow behind my wife's head.

Paige's eyes crack open. "I'm just tired."

Joan listens to her heartbeat, checks her pulse and blood pressure, then nods. "Let's get some labs and start an IV to see if that perks her up."

When a nurse jabs her, Paige is so drowsy, she barely flinches. Once the nurse gets the IV going, I pull up a chair next to Paige, who falls asleep again. After a while, her pulse finally slows down and her breathing looks more relaxed, which Joan says is a good sign.

A nurse closes the curtain around us, leaving me and my wife shrouded in a dim light. I thread my fingers through Paige's and brush her hair out of her face. She's so beautiful. Even a little sunburned and exhausted.

I bring her hand to my mouth and kiss it. "Baby, I'm so sorry for the other day. I know I'm an asshole. I'm just overwhelmed. I feel like I can't think beyond getting the ranch's finances figured out." I shake my head. "I want to be more for you. I just don't know how to get there."

Why is it easier to say this to her when she's asleep?

I love you. The thought whispers through my mind.

As much as I wanna tell her, it wouldn't be fair to make that declaration until she's made her decision about whether she wants to stay or go. I don't want to sway her one way or another. I think Danny would approve of me putting her first.

I stroke her soft cheek and smile. This woman strolled right up and stole my heart out of nowhere.

Amber was my first love. We were young and dumb and horny. Had I any sense, I would've thought more with the big head on my shoulders than the little one in my jeans. But I was eager to have a family, to create what was always elusive for me and my brothers. A happy place where my kids didn't have to worry about their father falling down drunk or yelling at us all the time.

Now that I'm older, I'm not as quick to dive off into the deep end of the pool, but I also recognize that Paige and I have the potential to be so much bigger than what I had with my ex.

I kiss the back of Paige's hand again. I might not be able to say the words, but maybe I can show her how I feel.

Once the IV finishes, the machine starts to beep. Paige's eyes flutter open.

"Hey, baby. Are you feeling better?"

"Better. I don't know what happened. Why I got so weak."

Joan and a nurse pop in to turn off the machine and check Paige's vitals. The doctor smiles at Paige. "Missy, I know you're an elite athlete, but the Texas sun and humidity don't play favorites. I've seen triathletes go down in this August heat. Did you work out longer than you expected?"

She nibbles the corner of her lip. "I ran pretty hard on the way home, and I went farther than I planned. I've been rehabbing my ankle all summer, and I guess I'm not in the kind of shape I thought I was."

"On the bright side, being as fit as you are is why you're bouncing back so quickly." She has the nurse remove the IV while she jots notes in Paige's chart. "Just be sure to pace yourself. Before I forget, my daughter is your biggest fan. She and I watched your nationals competition. She wants to fling herself off human pyramids now."

Paige chuckles. "I'm sorry."

Joan pats her shoulder. "Great job snagging those back-to-back championships. And that news interview you did was spectacular. I think that was the year before last? You were so poised. I was really impressed."

I turn to my wife. "You did an interview?"

A flush returns to her cheeks. "It's nothing."

Joan tuts. "Nothing? I beg to differ. Check it out for yourself, Rhett. It's linked on the Broncos' cheerleading website." Then she turns to my wife. "I'm discharging you, but I want you to take it easy and drink plenty of fluids. Come back if you experience any more dizziness."

I start to scoop up Paige, but she growls. "I can walk, Rhett. Jeez."

Joan chuckles. "He just wants to protect you. Looks like you found a good one."

Taking a step back, I offer Paige my hand. "Just in case you need the support, okay?"

She nods, presses her palm in mine, then slides to her feet. As we walk slowly to my truck, I wrap my arm around her slim shoulders. "Was worried about you back there."

"I'm okay."

"How do you feel about ribs? I was thinking of barbecuing when we get home. I can set you up on the couch, you can read that romance book that caught your eye, and I'll fix us something to eat."

She glances at me. "You don't have to baby me."

"But what if I want to?" I ask slowly. We stop to stare at each other. "I like taking care of you, wildflower. Will you let me?"

Her eyes get glassy, and she nods. I open my arms, and she tucks herself against me. Leaning down, I kiss the top of her head.

I don't know what the hell I'm doing, but one thing is certain. I don't wanna fuck this up.

Chapter Twenty-Eight
PAIGE

"Holy shit, Paige." Rhett's attention is glued to the TV where he's watching last year's nationals competition. "You're amazing, but I'm shitting my pants here."

Beau whistles. "Look at you, Little Lewis. Our flying squirrel."

When I do a full front flip off a human pyramid, the guys all hoot and holler.

I chuckle. I'm a little embarrassed to be the center of attention like this. It's been a week since I landed myself in the ER. I'm training again, but I've learned my lesson and will hydrate better before setting off for a long run.

I've been thinking a lot about what Rhett said to me when we were in the hospital, when he thought I was asleep. He said he wants to be more for me but doesn't know how to get there.

I know what he means, feeling like you're giving everything you have. Cheer has been like that for me. I'd plateau and even though I was working my ass off, I couldn't get to that next level. At one point, my friend Roxy had to take me aside to help me find the right mindset.

But relationships aren't that simple. What if Rhett never wants more children? I can't force him to want that with me. Am

I willing to give that up? Are he and the life I'm building at his ranch worth more than hypothetical kids I may or may not have?

What if I never meet anyone who makes me feel like Rhett? He's the only man I've ever loved. That's not something to be squandered.

Even if I'm willing to give up having children, there's a bigger problem. We haven't had sex since the truck a week and a half ago. I figured he'd want to after I recovered from that heat stroke episode, but he only cuddles me at night. I don't know what to do to get beyond the barrier that disagreement created.

Gabriel wedges himself between me and Jace. "Paige, can you show me how to do that stuff there?" He points to the male cheerleaders tumbling across the stage.

"Sure." I look at Rhett. "I mean, if it's okay with your dad."

Rhett frowns. "You're just talking about the cartwheels and flipping around?"

I chuckle at his description. "At first, yes. Tumbling is a form of floor gymnastics. Even if Gabe doesn't want to do cheer, learning those skills will help his balance and coordination and overall athleticism. It's great exercise, and it gives kids an incredible sense of accomplishment. And if he loves it and he's good at it, he could possibly get a gymnastics or cheer scholarship for college like I did."

He considers it a moment. "How can I say no to that?"

Gabriel hops up and down. "Yay!"

Austin crawls up into my lap and wipes his nose with the back of his hand. "I wanna do it too."

After I wipe his face with a napkin, I hug him. "There are a lot of fun activities for boys your age, if your daddy says it's okay."

Rhett's watching me with a softness in his eyes that makes my heart pound. "I know you won't let them do anything too dangerous."

"I'll be right there to spot them."

"That won't hurt your ankle? I thought you had to be careful about cutting side to side."

I love that Rhett pays attention to what I say. "At first, they'll be mostly stretching and doing cartwheels and roundoffs. I can handle that." I turn to the boys. "I was thinking of stopping by my old gym tomorrow. Do you want to come with me? We can do a light session, and I can show you a few moves."

Gabriel flings his arms around me, nearly knocking his brother off my lap. "YES!"

Little Austin squeals in delight, and I laugh.

That night, as I'm snuggled by Rhett's big, warm body, I stare out our bedroom window and wonder how to get him to turn down deserted country roads again to have his way with me.

As much as I love him, as much as I want him, I decide I need to stay firm on my decision to let him make the first move. He has to want this as much as I do.

And if he doesn't? Then maybe we aren't meant to be after all.

Chapter Twenty-Nine
PAIGE

"There you go, just like that!" I high-five Gabriel after he does a beautiful roundoff. "You're learning so fast."

Austin does a wobbly cartwheel, and I cheer just as loudly for him. "That's it, buddy! You got it!"

He stands with a proud smile.

Coach Spencer, who runs the gym, ambles over. "Hey, Paige. Been watching you work with the boys. They're coming along."

"They definitely have their daddy's athleticism." I instruct the kids to take a water break, and they trot off to hydrate.

My old coach retired, which is why I was reluctant to train at All-Star Cheer, but Coach Spencer has been really welcoming. This is our second time visiting the gym this week. Amber was supposed to pick up the boys last weekend, but she told Rhett something came up. The kids seemed bummed, so I thought tumbling might improve their spirits.

Coach Spencer scratches his cheek. "Just wondering what your plans were this fall. I could use some help around here. With all of your experience, you could really elevate our program. I would just need to see you work with a few different age groups first to make sure we're a good fit."

I ask about his classes and camps, and I'm excited to hear that he has advanced high school-aged gymnasts I could train.

"I'd be happy to pop in to work with your kids. I'm just not sure I'm available in the late fall." It pains me to say that. Do I really want to move to Boston? No, but if things don't work out with Rhett, this is the last place I want to live. I'd be bumping into him all the time, and seeing him would rip out my heart. "When would you need an answer? I have another program that has precedence, but honestly, I love that you're close by."

"I'm not surprised you're in demand. Let's play it by ear, and please let me know about your availability."

"You got it."

We make plans for me to help with one of his advanced camps next week. I'm so excited, I'm practically floating.

I've missed this. Being involved with gymnastics and cheer has always made me so happy. It helped me find a place where I belonged when Irma made me feel like a stranger in my own house. It helped me find some peace after my father and Danny died. And it helped me fund college, where I made some of my best friends.

And while I love performing, it's a thrill to help kids achieve these skills and gain confidence.

After our workout, I get the boys buckled into Rhett's truck, and I start the engine. "I need to pop into Thread and Thimble for some sewing supplies, but then I was thinking of stopping at Dunkers. Would y'all like a donut?"

I'm met with cheers of agreement, and I smile. I'm finally starting to feel hopeful again about the future. My ankle is doing better, and I'm well on the road to being able to do high-level floor routines soon. Coaching would be the icing on the cake. Especially if it means I can stay in Wild Heart with Rhett.

And I'm absolutely in love with the tops I'm sewing for Abby. I'm making her a really cute vest and a light jacket, both of which she can wear with comfy t-shirts and jeans. She sent me two extra jerseys, and I'm using one to make a baby quilt for Janie.

We pull onto the main drag and head for the fabric store. I park on the street, get the kids out, and they each grab my hand as we head inside. After I get the thread I need to finish Abby's outfits, we walk to the donut truck, which is around the corner, parked in front of the river. It's a lovely day, and several locals and tourists are enjoying donuts and coffee as they sit at the park benches.

I text Baylee that we're here, and to stop by if she has time. Her salon is just down the street, but she gets really slammed sometimes. As we wait in line, Gabriel tugs on my arm.

He gives me a bashful grin. "Today was fun. I really love tumbling."

Austin nods. "Love it too."

I hop on my toes. "I'm so glad. We're just getting started. There's so much more cool stuff to do."

Misty Reynolds, the sheriff's daughter, waves us forward when it's our turn. "Hey, Paige. Boys, it's good to see you."

"Hi, Misty. It's lovely to see you too." We chitchat about her family for a few minutes. I get the boys their donuts and order a dozen cookies so I can take them to the guys at home, and I grab myself an iced latte.

Misty nods. "It'll be a ten-minute wait on those cookies, but they'll be fresh out of the oven."

"Sounds great. We're not in a rush."

"Wonderful. Hey, are you and the Walker brothers coming to the Moonlight Mixer? My older sister wants to know."

Beau and Jace are popular with the women in this town. Mav is too, but he's in Charming for football training camp. "I'm trying to talk them into going." The Moonlight Mixer is a yearly fundraiser to help local families in need. The highlight of the night is usually when the handsome single men ask the older gals from the nursing home to dance.

"Oh, fantastic. She'll be so excited."

After I get the kids seated with their donuts and cartons of milk, I head back to the donut truck to wait for our order, and I send off another text. I've been added to the super-selective Walker brothers texting group, so I use this opportunity to razz them.

> Me: The ladies of Wild Heart have been inquiring whether the single Walker men will be attending the Moonlight Mixer. What should I tell them? Beau, Jace, will y'all be making an appearance?

> Jace: Isn't that more than a month away?

> Me: It's never too early for the ladies to plan who they want to dance with.

> Beau: Will there be food?

> Jace: Do I have to wear a tie?

> Me: I'm sure there will be food, and you don't need to wear a tie.

> Mav: Am I not invited? I can't go, but I feel left out.

> Me: Of course you're invited, goof.

> Mav: For the record, I still have nightmares about Mrs. Kramer's false teeth!

> Beau: Jesus, I forgot about that. LMFAO.

> Me: Do I want to know what happened?

> Jace: Mrs. Kramer took out her falsies mid-dance with Mav and dropped them into some random person's glass of water.

I cover my mouth. I love my brothers-in-law. They're crazy.

> Me: Sorry I missed that! Hey, before I forget, good luck at your game this weekend, Mav. I'll be cheering for you.

> Mav: Thanks, Paige. Games won't be the same without you on the sidelines.

Graduating is bittersweet. I have an ache in my chest at the thought of not being in attendance at the Broncos' games this fall.

My phone pings again with another text.

> Rhett: Am I required to be in attendance at the Mixer? It's the weekend before the cattle auction. Gonna be a busy time.

My heart sinks. I've been fantasizing about dancing with my husband again. I suppose I can go without him and hang out with Baylee. I decide to be cheeky about it.

> Me: Your wife would love to go. Do with that what you will.

> Beau: Bro, that means yes.

> Jace: Your woman wants to dance.

> Rhett: Guess that means I'm going.

I grin at the screen. I can't wait. Even if we just dance to one or two songs, I'll be happy.

"What the fuck are you smiling about?" a female voice practically shouts.

When I look up, Amber's standing a few feet away, fuming. I glance around, confused why she's yelling. In the last ten minutes, several customers arrived, and there's a line.

"Yes, I'm talking to you, bitch." She glares at me.

She's making a scene that no doubt the whole town will be talking about tomorrow. I whisper, "Lower your voice."

"I'll do no such thing. Look at you, prancing around with *my* children, driving *my* husband's truck, and playing little wife in *my* goddamn house. How does it feel to get sloppy seconds?"

I feel my face go up in flames. Austin starts crying, and I rush over to pick him up. "Come on, boys. Let's get out of here."

"You will *not* drive my boys anywhere. These are my children. You're just a poor stand-in for me. I'm who Rhett really wants. I'm who he's always wanted. There's a saying, have you heard it? 'There's no love like your first love.'"

All of a sudden, Baylee is by my side. "What the fuck is your problem, Amber? Did you get a cactus stuck up your ass this morning?"

Amber ignores Baylee. "Tell me, Paige. How does it feel to sleep in my bed and fuck my husband? Does he ever say my name? Because we both know he's thinking about me and not you."

My eyes sting, but I refuse to let any tears fall. "It's not my fault he figured out you were a cheater."

She gasps like I've slandered her good character. "I did no such thing."

"So you didn't sleep with Kacey Miller or Cash McAllister while you were with Rhett?"

Her eyes bulge, and Baylee tuts. "Amber, close your legs. I mean, your mouth. You're attracting flies."

"You little skank. Shut up."

My best friend chuckles. "Bless your heart, bitch. You think I care what you call me. Isn't that cute?" Then she takes the cookies and my latte from Misty, grabs Gabriel's hand, and nudges me away from the river. Austin clings to my neck and sniffles. Hell, I want to curl up in a ball and cry too.

That psycho follows us to Rhett's truck. "I'm taking my boys home with me. This is my week."

I've had enough of this woman. I hate confrontations and making a scene, but she's pushed me to the brink. I whip around. "Then maybe you should've shown up last weekend when you were supposed to instead of blowing off your boys. Stop pretending to be the maligned party here. You and I both know you were responsible for what happened in your marriage. It's not my fault you kept hopping on other men. Rhett is mine now, and I will cherish him with my whole heart for as long as he'll have me. So you can either get used to that or you can go—" I take a breath, knowing I shouldn't curse in front of the kids. "You can go fly a kite."

"You fucking slut!" she screams as she pulls back her arm to hit me.

Sheriff Reynolds steps in front of her, stopping her at the last minute. "Now, listen here, Amber. I hate arresting women, but if you strike Paige or me, I'll be forced to take you in." Bless Misty. She probably called her father for me.

Seriously, fuck Amber. I get the boys buckled up in the back, hug Baylee, and hop in the driver's seat while the sheriff holds off Rhett's ex. Baylee hands me my coffee and the box of cookies, which I would've forgotten without her help.

As we head home, I glance in the rearview mirror. "Boys, I'm so sorry you had to see that." My voice trembles, and I take a few deep breaths. "I don't mean your mama any harm, I promise. I swear I'm not trying to take her place. I just want to be your friend." My voice is thick with emotion. "And I..." *I love your father.* "I care for your daddy. And I'm so happy to train with you two. But I'll understand if you don't want to do that anymore."

Austin cries quietly, but Gabriel's face is a mask of tension. He stares out the window. His voice comes out a croaky whisper. "I want to keep training."

"Me too!" Austin wails.

Finally, my tears overflow. "I'd love that."

The three of us cry all the way home.

Chapter Thirty
RHETT

My phone keeps pinging with messages. "What the hell is so important right now?" I pat my cow between her big brown eyes. "Want some more pumpkin, sweetheart?" I ask her as I hand her a piece.

Her calf bumps against me, and I chuckle. "You want some too, huh?" I break off a small chunk, which he gobbles out of my hand.

My phone buzzes again, and I grab it out of my back pocket. It's Jace.

> Jace: Is Paige okay?

> Me: Why wouldn't she be?

> Jace: You haven't seen the video yet, huh?
> One sec.

What video? It takes a full five minutes for the damn thing to load. I hold my phone up to try to get another bar, but the signal is weak out here.

Finally, it plays. My stomach drops as I watch my ex tear into my sweet wife. Whoever's recording this follows them back to my truck. I hold my breath as I wait for Paige to start crying because Amber is a viper. And then it's like a switch flips, and Paige yells back. I watch, riveted, as my wife defends herself, but the part that kills me dead is when she yells that I belong to her now. "I will cherish him with my whole heart for as long as he'll have me!"

Fuck, yes, she belongs to me.

I grab my horse's reins, slide my boot into the stirrup, and hoist myself into the saddle. "Let's get home," I tell Apollo.

By the time I open the sliding glass door to the kitchen, my heart is pounding. I have no idea what to expect.

I find Paige and the boys huddled together in front of the TV. Cartoons are playing, but they don't look like they're watching.

"Hey, guys." I kneel in front of them. "Are y'all okay? I heard what happened."

All three of them have bloodshot eyes and red noses. I hold open my arms, and the boys rush into them. Paige's eyes are swollen, and I'm so pissed that Amber hurt her, I wanna howl at the sky like a wild beast.

I can't go another minute without her in my arms. So I sit next to her, scoot Gabriel next to me while I keep my arm around him, put Austin in my lap, and pull Paige to me with my other arm, so that I have all three of them close.

She shoves her face against my chest, and I can feel her shoulders shake as she cries. "Who told you?"

I wince. She's not gonna be excited about this, but I don't wanna lie. "Jace forwarded a video someone took."

Tugging her closer, I rub her back, and she hiccups. "I'm sorry I didn't get the boys out of there quicker."

"Baby, you have nothing to apologize for. I appreciate you not letting her take them." Amber has gone too fucking far.

Paige sits up and wipes her eyes. "I feel bad that Gabe and Austin had to see... had to see that."

I kiss her forehead. "Well, let's do a little family check-in." I look down at my boys. "Today was tough, and I know you two don't understand everything that happened, but the most important thing is that y'all did nothing wrong. And I want you to know I love you both more than I can say. You two are my whole world, and I'll do anything to keep you safe."

Austin starts crying. "I'm sad."

"Aww, buddy, it's okay. I'm sad too that everyone got so upset today."

Gabriel sniffles. "Is Mom gonna take us back this week? 'Cause I don't wanna go."

Austin shakes his head. "Me neither."

"Dad, we wanna stay with you. Mom is always so mean." My tough little dude tears up, and I squeeze him tighter.

"Boys, you don't have to go anywhere you don't want to, okay? I'm gonna talk to my lawyer and see what we can work out." Seeing Amber freak out like that in public makes me wonder. I always assumed she was only like that with me. "Does your mom ever yell like that when you're with her?"

Gabriel finally gives up trying to be strong, and tears stream down his face. "She always yells at us. She hates us. I don't know why she wants us to come over at all. She tells us to shut up and that we're annoying."

Fuck. My throat tightens up, and I pull him in for a hug. "I'm sorry, son. I had no idea. But like I said, you're not going anywhere."

Paige touches my shoulder. "I'm going to give y'all some time to talk."

I grab her hand. "I'm sorry."

"You don't have anything to apologize for." Her eyes get watery, and she points to the kitchen. "I'm going to get dinner started."

I let her go. For now.

After I set Austin down next to me, I wrap my arms around my boys' shoulders. "How was the gym? Did you learn anything?"

Gabriel immediately perks up. "Paige said I did a great roundoff."

"What about you, Austin?"

"I did cartwheels."

"Awesome, boys. Are y'all enjoying that?"

Gabe smiles so wide, I can see all his teeth. "We love it." He leans close like he needs to tell me a secret. "Paige is awesome. Can we keep her?"

Austin nods. "Yeah. Awesome."

I chuckle. "I'm gonna do my best to get her to stay."

Turning, I watch my wife rush around the kitchen, and I realize that if she leaves for Boston, she's gonna take my heart with her.

I don't know who I was fooling with a fake marriage, 'cause my feelings for Paige are as real as it gets.

Chapter Thirty-One
PAIGE

THE FAMILY CHATTERS around me as we eat dinner, but I'm still stuck on that screaming match at Dunkers this afternoon. I knew Amber didn't like me, but I never expected that she'd hate me. For what? She's the one who cheated on Rhett. She gave up on their marriage. I had nothing to do with them falling apart.

"Baby, you gonna eat?" Rhett whispers.

I look down at the slice of pizza I've been nibbling on. "I'm not really hungry. My stomach's been kind of upset." Nothing like public humiliation to make you want to hurl.

Under the table, his hand slides across my thigh. "Can I get you something carbonated to drink? Maybe that will help."

"That would be nice."

Jace shoves half a slice into his mouth. "This pizza is great, Paige."

"It's just a box recipe."

"Tastes homemade to me."

I love cooking for this family. Everyone is so appreciative. Irma always acted like the food I made was barely tolerable. The best part is I get to do the fun stuff, and the guys always clean up afterward.

Rhett returns with a sparkling clear drink, and I take a few sips. "Thanks. That helps."

After dinner, I head for our bedroom. I want to grab a shower and process what happened today. Under the hot stream of water, I wonder if it's always going to be like this. Will Amber freak out every time she sees me in public? I thought that conversation with Rhett in high school was the worst thing that could happen, but I'm not sure I can handle having Amber make a scene any time we're both in the same room. We live in Wild Heart, after all, not a big city where I can avoid her.

Between that and Rhett not wanting more kids, I'm starting to feel like the deck is stacked against me.

It's disheartening to think about.

I drag myself out of the shower and dry off. I throw on a tank top and sleep shorts. It's early, but I'm exhausted. I crawl into bed and pull the covers over me.

In the middle of the night, I wake with Rhett curled around me.

Even though he's right here, I wonder if he'll ever want me again like he did that day in the truck. He hasn't touched me like that since, and I don't know what to do to bridge that divide.

I'm starting to worry it's a hopeless cause.

And then he surprises me.

The next morning, I'm in the office paying bills when Rhett sticks his head in. "Hey, gorgeous." He's wearing his signature jeans and t-shirt that are molded to his strong body. He's sporting brown boots and a baseball hat.

"Hey. What are you doing home?" He usually works out in the fields until later in the day. "Did you need me to do something? I paid those invoices you asked me to."

"As a matter of fact, I do need something," he says as he slides his baseball cap backwards. Damn, he's yummy. "But you need to put on some jeans and wear your boots."

"Okay," I say slowly as I stand. "What's wrong with shorts?"

He chuckles. "Your ass will get sore in the saddle."

My eyes widen. "We're going horseback riding?"

"I need to check out a few things down by the river, and I remembered how much you used to like it down there. So I thought I'd pack us some food, and we could enjoy a picnic."

"That sounds fun. If you're sure I wouldn't be a distraction."

"Darling, you're never a distraction. Plus, I plain like having you around."

I grin. "I just need five minutes to change."

As I walk by him, he grabs me. "I think you forgot something."

Breathless, I stare up at him. "What's that?"

"This." He tilts me over and kisses me until I moan. Then he pats me on the ass. "Go change."

Yes, sir.

My heart races as I run around our bedroom to change. Then I quickly braid my hair down my back and throw on the cowboy hat he got me. I meet him in the living room. When he sees me, he lets out a wolf whistle. "Damn, wife. You look good." He scans my body. "Turn around. Let me see the whole outfit."

I do a little twirl, and when I'm facing away from him, I shake my ass, and he chuckles.

Before we head out, he grabs an insulated bag from the kitchen. "Snacks for our picnic." He winks, and my heart goes into overdrive.

I'm not sure what's gotten into him, but I am on board for this version of my husband.

We head out to the barn where he has two horses saddled up for us. He takes me to a beautiful brown quarter horse. "This is Sunflower. She's a sweet girl. I think you two will get along." The horse nudges him, and he scruffs her behind her ear. "Darling, do you remember how to mount a horse?"

I lift a brow. "I know it's been a few weeks, but I'm pretty sure I didn't have any trouble mounting you."

His cheeks go ruddy, and he lets out a laugh. "Smartass."

He helps me put my boot in the stirrup, and then I pull myself up and over onto Sunflower. Rhett adjusts a few things for me, and then he mounts his horse Apollo. As we head out of the barn, he turns his baseball cap forward. It's so bright outside, every time he looks at me, all I see is the dark shadow under his bill.

We ride across the sloping pasture and over a small ridge until we come to a wooded area and a narrow path. I follow behind him through the dappled sunlight until we reach the river.

"Rhett, I forgot how beautiful it is here. Can we go swimming?" When he doesn't respond, I backtrack. "You know what, never mind. You need to work, right?"

We head to a giant oak where he dismounts and ties the reins of our horses. Then he reaches for me, and I slide off my mount and into his arms. "We can go swimming."

I bite my bottom lip. "I don't have a swimsuit."

His hand cradles my face, and his thumb gently swipes my cheek. "Pretty sure I've already seen you naked, wildflower."

It's my turn to blush. Not sure why he has this effect on me. I'm not usually a shy girl, but he makes me feel vulnerable.

Rhett lets go of me and grabs a blanket that's tied to the back of his saddle, walks over to a shady area, unrolls it, and tosses it down. He clears his throat. "Been wanting to talk to you about something."

A knot immediately forms in the pit of my stomach. Is this about what happened with Amber yesterday? Is he going to tell me to go to Boston? That he's not ready for anything serious right now?

Frozen, I stand rooted in place. "If this is bad news, just spit it out."

He spreads out a few containers of food. "It's not bad, but I think we need to discuss a few things." Rhett sprawls out on the corner of the blanket and pats the spot next to him.

Reluctantly, I join him. "What's going on?" I set my cowboy hat on the grass and brush a few strands of hair out of my face.

"Just had something on my mind."

I brace myself for the sting of rejection.

He hands me a Tupperware of fresh strawberries. I take one and fiddle with the leaves. "Is this about Amber?"

"Not really. Not entirely, I should say." He sighs. "I just want you to know that I have no idea why she got so possessive. There's been nothing between us for years. Even before we split up, we hadn't slept together in a while."

"Can I ask you something? I had the impression your split was mutual. Was it not?"

"No. She screamed and cried it was all a big misunderstanding. Apparently, she wanted to stay married while she fucked my neighbors."

I wince. "I'm so sorry. I wish I had been wrong about her."

"I'm not. Because then I wouldn't be sitting here with you." He takes my hand. "But I am sorry for putting you in the middle of that shit storm. I feel like an asshole 'cause I couldn't protect you from all the nasty things she said."

"I'm okay. I was a little shaken at first because it came out of the blue, but I'll be better prepared for her now that I know she's crazy."

He chuckles. "I really appreciate how you handled things. You tried to deescalate things and... well, I felt like a puffed-up rooster when you said I belonged to you."

I bump his shoulder with mine. "I'm kinda fond of you. Always have been."

He pulls me into his lap. "I know, baby. And here's the truth. I've always been fond of you too. Our relationship is different now than when we were young, obviously, but one thing remains —you are a special woman, and I'm a lucky man. I'm pretty sure I haven't done anything to deserve you."

Shifting, I straddle him and take his handsome face in my

hands. "Don't say that. You deserve all the good things life has to offer. I've always been in awe of how hard you work on this ranch. I know you raised your brothers when you were just a kid yourself." It's obvious in their devotion to him. "I can't imagine how hard that was."

"It's nothing they wouldn't have done for me." Leaning closer, he grazes his lips across mine. "I'm sorry for that argument we had in the truck. I've been kicking myself ever since. Me not wanting more children has everything to do with my baggage and shit that went down with Amber. You're lovely and amazing, and if I could snap my fingers to get over all that, I would. Asking you to not have kids is a major concession on your part, but if you're open to it, then maybe we can still work things out between us long term. Gabriel and Austin love you, and you seem fond of them. Would it be terrible if it was just the four of us moving forward?"

Would it be the end of the world to not have my own children?

The truth is, I'm not sure. But I'm not ready to walk away either.

"Can we wait and see how things go? Play it by ear? I'm not opposed to considering it." It hits me how maybe he doesn't want more kids because he didn't have much of a childhood himself. I've never considered that before.

He gives me a soft smile. "Thank you for sticking around."

"I mean, staying with you will be a challenge. You can be pretty surly when you want to be."

He laughs. "Maybe I need a good woman who can keep me in line."

Nodding, I rest my arms on his shoulders. "I might be available for the job. Are there benefits?"

He gets a naughty little smirk on his face as he grabs my ass and pulls me closer. "There's one big benefit I'm sure you'll enjoy."

I grind against the *benefit* in his jeans. "It's been a while since I've been acquainted with your talents. Maybe I need a refresher before I give my response."

"Like a test drive?"

"Exactly."

He kisses me until I'm out I'm of breath, and then his teeth graze my neck, and I moan. "Are you sure your tight little pussy can handle what I'm offering? We need to make sure you're really wet." Next thing I know, I'm on my back, and Rhett's hovering over me. "Lift your arms." I do as he asks, and he whips my shirt off me. Then he flicks open my bra and palms my breasts.

My thighs clench, and I push my hips up to get relief, but Rhett's so big, there's no moving him.

"Patience, darling. I'm gonna get you off. And out here..." He glances around. "You can scream my name all you want."

My whole body pulses with need. I reach for his shirt and try to yank it off, but I can't get it up his broad chest. Taking the hint, he tosses his baseball hat and shrugs off his shirt. Then he tugs down my boots and socks and unbuttons my jeans. He slides them down my legs until all I'm wearing is some bikini underwear.

His eyes travel possessively over me. "Spread your legs." His gruff, commanding voice makes me shiver, and I immediately comply. Then he shoves his big hand in my panties and groans. "You're soaked. Is this all for me?"

"Y-yes." The truth is I'm always turned on around this man.

He removes his hand and shows me his glistening fingers. I open my mouth because I know what he wants.

I suck myself off him, and his eyes go feral. He practically rips off my underwear before he settles between my legs. Then he returns his wet fingers to my pussy. "Hold yourself open for me, baby."

Reaching down, I do as he asks, and he groans again. He runs a finger along my opening, then lazily circles my clit, and it pulses so hard, I squeeze my eyes shut.

"No. Watch me finger your pretty little cunt."

Jesus, his mouth. He's so dirty. I love it.

I watch him slowly sink one finger, then two into my body. First he just makes shallow thrusts, but then he goes deeper. But what sets me off is when he starts lapping at my clit.

I hold off as long as I can, but then his hand moves faster, deeper as he licks and sucks.

Arching back with a shriek, I pulse around him.

"That's it, baby." He keeps thrusting and hitting this spot deep inside that makes my eyes cross.

Finally, I push him off me. "I can't anymore." I laugh and toss an arm over my face.

He slides up next to me, and I snuggle into his warm body. "Did that feel good?"

"Hmm." After a few minutes of drowsing in the sun, I let my hand wander over his chest and down his stomach. "I still need that test drive."

He chuckles and helps me shove his jeans and boxer briefs down. His huge erection juts out to greet me. I lean over him to take him in my mouth. I lick his tip hungrily and graze my teeth down his length.

"Fuck." He grunts as I suck him like he's a sweet treat. "Love watching this pretty mouth wrapped around my cock." I take him deeper, and he reaches down to untie my hair. He works out the braid and then gathers it in his hand. "Remember, tap my leg if this is too much."

I nod, and his hold tightens. He works me up and down his thick dick until my eyes water and I choke, but I don't tap his leg. His eyes are zeroed in on my mouth, and when I'm sure he's about to come, he yanks me off and pulls me into his lap.

Straddling him, I reach down to notch him in me. "Holy shit." I forgot how much he stretches me. I take my time sinking down.

"There you go. You can take it." He sucks on my neck as he grips my ass. "Good girl."

Inside, I preen at the praise.

Then I remember. "Wait. What about a condom?"

He stills. "You said you're on the pill." When I nod, his gaze searches mine. "I trust you, but if you want a condom, I can get one."

He trusts me. My throat gets tight. He has no idea how much that means to me. "You feel better without one."

His eyes go soft, and he kisses me gently. "You feel fucking amazing without a condom. Come here and let me fuck you."

He helps me move up and down his thick length.

Rhett feels incredible like this, but knowing how much he likes to watch, I lean back and hold onto his thighs. I spread my legs so he has a good view.

We both watch him slide in and out of me. "Fuck, Paige. Can you come again? Wanna feel you squeeze my cock."

I reach between my legs and circle my clit, and he swells inside me. My husband loves to watch himself fuck me. Knowing how turned on he is spurs me on, and I rub harder and faster. My fingers drift to where he's stretching me wide. He pinches my nipple, and I come apart and cry out his name.

Rhett pulls me up to kiss me and holds me tight to him as he finds his release.

With a grunt, he falls backwards, and I lie on top of him, still straddling his dick that kicks again inside me.

Smiling, I close my eyes and fall asleep.

I'm definitely not ready to walk away.

Chapter Thirty-Two
RHETT

My wife and I drowse in the warm afternoon. I kiss the top of her head. Pretty sure she's asleep, but I can't keep it in anymore. "I love you, Paige."

A moment later, she lifts her head. Her wild red hair cascades down her narrow shoulders and covers her breasts. Her eyes go glassy. "I love you too."

I feel like a thief. Like I'm privy to something I'm not supposed to have. For a brief moment, I worry I'm going to wake up and this whole thing will have been a dream. Because she's too good to be true.

This whole thing feels like paradise. Having a picnic in the middle of the day. Fucking her on the bank of the river. Hearing her shout my name when she comes.

My beautiful wife tosses her arms around my shoulders and kisses me. "I need to get up before you bore your way through me."

I chuckle and help her up. My cum drips down her thighs, and the caveman in me beats his chest. I motion to the river. "Let's go wash off."

I take her hand, and we walk down to the water.

All of a sudden, she darts off, then leans down to pick something up from the bank. I get a great look at her perky ass.

When she turns around, she's grinning from ear to ear and I am too because she's fucking gorgeous with her thick red hair hanging down her slender shoulders, her perfect tits playing peek-aboo behind those long strands.

I motion with my finger. "Bend over again."

She chuckles and holds up her hand. "Look what I found." My little river nymph found herself a brilliant white quartz.

"You usually have to break open rocks to find something this pretty. My brothers and I never found anything this nice. Bet this means you'll have good luck for the next seven years."

With that smile locked in place, she trots back to our stuff to drop it off, then runs back to me. I take her hand and turn back for the river. "Careful. Might be slippery."

"That's what she said."

I bark out a laugh and lean over to kiss her.

As we wade in, the cool water makes goosebumps break out all over Paige. Her nipples go tight, and my cock thickens at the sight.

"Come here. Let me clean you." I rub my hands over her soft shoulders and down her perfect tits. I circle her tight nipples. "Gotta get all the dirt off."

She laughs and reaches up to rake her hand through my hair.

We kiss lazily as I reach down to gently wash her pussy. I dip a finger inside her, and she reaches for my dick that's rock hard all over again. We wade deeper into the water, and her legs wrap around my waist. I don't have to tell her what to do. She sticks my cock inside her, and I grip her ass and help her ride me. I move slow and steady so the base of my shaft rubs all the right places.

When she screams my name, I come with a grunt.

"I love you, wife," I whisper as she clings to me.

"Love you more, husband."

As I hold her close, I close my eyes and pray I can be the man she needs me to be.

Today is paradise. I just hope I can make it last.

My alarm goes off way too early the next morning. I hate leaving Paige, but this ranch won't run itself. I slide out from under her, shower, and get breakfast made for the boys and my brothers, who stumble in around five thirty. We make a plan for the day, and I list off everything that needs to be done.

My kids usually go with Pauline, Wayne's wife, while I work, but I wanna spend some time with them. I would've done this yesterday, but one of our border collies was having puppies, and they didn't want to miss that. "Boys, you wanna help me build a mobile run for Paige's chickens? I think they'd like to run around more. Doesn't seem right to make them sit in one spot all the time. Thought we could surprise Paige with it later."

Really, I'm just looking for a project for the three of us to work on. I'm sure that situation with their mother freaked them out, and I wanna reassure them that everything will be okay. I spoke to my attorney yesterday afternoon. I expect I'll be hearing from Amber soon.

Gabriel's eyes widen. "Yeah, Dad. I wanna help."

Austin nods. "Me too."

"All right, guys. Go get dressed, and we'll leave in twenty minutes. Gabe, can you help Austin pick out his clothes?"

They agree and race to their room.

Jace sips his coffee. "Where'd you run off to yesterday afternoon? When you and Paige returned, it looked like y'all had just banged each other's brains out in the river."

I laugh. "Mind your own fucking business."

Beau slaps me on the back. "Glad you're happy, bro. You deserve it."

Jace chuckles. "Must've been a good day if you're building her another chicken run."

"What's some chicken wire and a few two-by-fours? I'm gonna put this one on wheels so every day the little cluckers get a new patch of grass."

My brothers head off as my sweet wife stumbles down the hall. "Y'all already ate?"

Goddamn, she's beautiful. All mussed up and sleepy. I glance at the time. Do I really need to work today? Couldn't I just snatch her in my arms and lock us away in my bedroom? When she gets close, I scoop her into my lap and nuzzle her neck. "We just finished up. Are you hungry? I can make you something."

"Damn it. I was trying to get up early enough to make everyone breakfast."

"Don't worry about that. Been making breakfast for these yahoos my whole life. No need to wake up early on our account."

She snuggles into me. "I know, but I want to do my part."

"You are, sweetheart. You have my office organized, the bills are paid, and you're a delight to wake up to in the morning."

A smile tilts her lips, and her arms come around my shoulders. "Why, thank you. I can't say that's a hardship."

I chuckle. "What are you up to today?"

"I was wondering what you'd like for me to make this weekend. We're all watching Mav's game tomorrow afternoon, right?"

"That's the plan." Beau, Jace, and I never miss our little brother's football games if we can help it.

"Would it be okay if Baylee and her new boyfriend came over? I'm not sure if he can make it, but I thought it would be nice to invite him."

That gets my attention. "Who's she dating?"

"Some guy she met on a dating app." She rests her head on my shoulder. "She can't wait her whole life for Maverick to get a clue."

I have to admit that's solid logic. Still, I hope my brother knows what he's doing and doesn't regret losing his chance with Baylee. They've been best friends forever. I always figured they'd end up together someday. "To answer your question, Baylee and her boyfriend are welcome, and we'll enjoy whatever you feel like making." Maybe this is a good time to tell her. "Babe, don't look at the *Gazette*."

She rolls her eyes. "Georgia wrote about my argument with Amber, didn't she?"

"On the bright side, she didn't use names."

"But everyone knows who she's talking about." She huffs. "Whatever. I licked you, so you're mine, and Amber can go suck a bag of dicks."

I bust out laughing. This woman is too much. "I fucking love you."

"I fucking love you too." She shifts and sucks in a breath.

"What's wrong?" I lower my voice. "Are you sore?"

Paige glances around. "A little."

"I'm sorry. We shouldn't have done it a third time yesterday." When we got home, we took a shower together to wash off the river, and we got a little carried away.

She leans up to kiss me. "We had to make up for lost time."

I thread my fingers through her hair and bite her lower lip. She opens to me, and I—

We jerk apart as someone bangs on the sliding door.

"Who the fuck is that?" I grumble. I stand and slide her off me.

Turning, I see Frank Fletcher. He slams a piece of paper up to the glass. I'm guessing that's the eviction notice. "Stay here. This could get messy."

I unlock the door and slide it open. "What can I do for you, Frank?"

"You're kicking us out? After the back-breaking work I did for your father?"

"It's not like that, and you know it. You've gotten the cabin for a steal for years. Meanwhile, I see all of your toys lined up in the driveway. How many ATVs do you really need?" He took his whole family on a damn cruise last year. I don't remember the last time I went on a fucking vacation.

And it's not like I didn't do the same work I asked him to tackle.

He crumples the paper. "You're gonna regret this."

"Frank, calm down. I gave y'all the option to pay more rent, but you refused. What was I supposed to do? I should've filed for eviction months ago."

He spits on the ground. "Fuck you."

There goes my good mood.

Chapter Thirty-Three
PAIGE

"Aren't you the sweetest thing ever?" I snuggle the border collie puppy to my chest as I pat the mama dog Pearl on her head. She had four babies this week, and they're adorable.

One of the barn cats rubs against my back, and I smile. Reaching behind me, I scratch his head.

"I see that you're in your element," Rhett says, hanging his arms over the stall.

"I don't think I could ever be in a bad mood if I got to play with puppies every day."

"My boys feel the same way. Gabriel and Austin would sleep in the barn if I let them."

"I don't blame them." I kiss the puppy and put him back with the others. Standing, I brush off the hay. "Guess I should get going. People will be here soon for the game."

He opens the stall door for me, then leans down to kiss me. "I think your casserole is ready. Whatever you made smells amazing."

I glance at my phone. "I have five more minutes before I need to take it out of the oven. It's nothing fancy, just a hot chili cheese dip. I thought we could have nachos. I made a bunch of different toppings. Austin said nachos are his favorite."

He tosses his arm around my shoulder. "Sure do appreciate that."

"How, um, how did your conversation go with Amber?"

Rhett sighs. "About how you'd expect. There was a lot of yelling."

"I'm so sorry. I hate that I made her freak out."

"Not your fault, sweetheart. I had no idea she was being so mean to the boys. My attorney's filing an emergency custody order on Monday."

"That's a relief. I can't imagine being that age and having my parent freak out at me like that." I wrap my arms around his waist. "I want to love up on Gabriel and Austin, let them know I'm here for them. I know I'm not their mom, but if they let me, I promise I'll be a great bonus parent."

"My boys are lucky to have you."

I shrug. "I know what it's like to have a terrible stepmother. My one goal with them is to be the opposite of Irma."

Rhett stares down at me. "Have I told you lately how much I love you?"

My heart races at his closeness. "I'm pretty crazy about you too."

Leaning down, he grazes his lips against mine. Within seconds, he has me pinned to a stall.

Suddenly, the alarm on my phone goes off, and I groan. "Unless you want burned chili dip, I have to go."

He lets me slide down his body. Then he adjusts himself. "Guess I'll have to wait for tonight."

"It's a date," I yell as I run out of the barn, smiling.

I make it back to the kitchen and pull out the dip and set it on a potholder. After I taste it, I add it to the other nacho toppings.

The back door opens, and Beau, Jace, and Rhett stroll in with the boys.

Jace yells, "It's game time!"

A few minutes later, the doorbell rings, and I let Baylee in. "Where's Sean?"

"He had a family thing. He invited me, but I'm not going to miss a Bronco game."

I tug her into the kitchen and whisper, "Have you told Mav you're talking to someone?"

"Why would I do that? He has an endless array of women he bangs. It's not like he runs that by me."

"Good point." I hand her a beer. "Get some food before the guys decimate the table."

"I like this plan." She takes a plate and loads up the nachos.

My husband's buddy Brady, who did Rhett's beautiful tattoos, and his wife Kat, join us. As they greet everyone, I smile at the way Brady looks at his wife, like she's his whole world.

Rhett leans close to me and lowers his voice. "You'll like their story. When his brother passed, Brady inherited his baby niece and a lavender farm. He was planning to sell the property and move back to Boston, but then he fell in love with Kat."

"And he couldn't bring himself to leave."

"Pretty much."

I know the feeling. If the cheer camp in Boston offered me a position tomorrow, I'd turn them down in a heartbeat. There's no way anything could entice me to leave Rhett or my life at the ranch.

Bunching my hand in his t-shirt, I pull him down to me and kiss him. "I love you, cowboy."

His eyes twinkle, and he pats my ass. "Love you too, baby."

Feeling like a contented cat in the sun, I call out to our crew. "Food's on. Come and get it. Guests and little men first." I wave over Brady and Kat. "Help yourselves."

Kat grins. "I'm starving, and this looks amazing."

Then I crook my finger to Austin and Gabe. "Come here, you two." I help the boys wash up before I grab paper plates and help them make their nachos.

When my brothers-in-law wander up, I point to the sink. "Kindly wash your hands. I know y'all are filthy."

"In the brain," Jace says with a silly grin as he hugs Baylee. "Hey, troublemaker. Great to have you over."

"Thanks."

"Did I hear you were gonna bring a date?" He lifts an eyebrow. "Not sure how I feel about this. You're like our little sister. He'd better pass muster."

She rolls her eyes, but she's smiling. "He couldn't make it, but you'll like him. He's a good guy."

I hand out napkins. "There's brownie sundaes for dessert and beer in the ice chest next to the TV."

Beau reaches over to give me a noogie. "Have I mentioned how much we love having you? Marrying you is the best thing Rhett ever did."

I grin. "You're just saying that 'cause I feed you."

"Nah, we genuinely love you."

"Aww, thanks, bro."

We all settle around the TV with our food. The screen flashes Florida's logo meshed up against the Lone Star State Bronco, and a familiar pride for my alma mater fills me, reminding me of all the games I cheered at during college.

Those were great times, but this afternoon is special too.

I'm sitting between Rhett and Baylee. Kat and Brady settle on the other side of my husband while Beau and Jace take the short end of the L-shaped couch. The boys sprawl out on the floor in front of us so they can use the coffee table to hold their plates.

I glance at the faces of people I love, and my heart overflows with affection. This week might've been hard because of Amber, but I'm realizing I'll take all the tough times if it means I can have these moments.

During the outro to commercial, the camera pans to the cheerleaders.

Rhett leans close. "Is it hard to give that up?"

"It's bittersweet. There's really not a career path for cheerleaders after graduation, aside from coaching. I miss the squad and being on the field. I mean, look at my team. How could I not be obsessed with the Broncos? I love those guys, and their coach is amazing. He's a hardass, but in a good way."

He nods. "I like Coach Santos. He keeps Mav in line. My brother needs that."

"I'm friends with his daughter Roxy. She's the one who interviewed me for that news segment."

"I still can't believe I only saw that recently," he grouses.

The disgruntled look on his handsome face makes me laugh, and I lean up to kiss him. "Well, I promise if I do any more interviews, you'll be the first to know."

"Damn straight."

Just then, Mav leaps up in the air, pulls down the pass, and bolts for the end zone. Baylee yells at the TV, "You got this, Maverick!"

We all freak out as he races down the field.

When he nabs that touchdown, we high-five each other.

The Broncos win by fourteen points.

That night, when I collapse on my husband with a sated smile, I realize I've never been this happy.

Chapter Thirty-Four
PAIGE

Leaning forward, I finish putting on my lipstick.

"Babe, you ready?" Rhett calls out from the bedroom.

"Yup!" I check myself in the mirror one more time. I'm wearing the dress and boots Rhett bought me, and for once, I took the time to do my makeup.

He comes up behind me and wraps his arms around my shoulders. "Damn, I married a beautiful woman."

I smile at his reflection. "You're looking pretty handsome yourself." He's wearing a button-down light blue shirt, jeans, and boots. His thick beard is trimmed, and it looks like he took the time to comb his hair.

I'm looking forward to messing it up when we get home.

Rhett kisses my neck. "Do we have to go? Because I'd rather sit you on this counter and have my way with you."

"One dance, that's all I'm asking for."

"We can stay longer than that. I'm just teasing. Kinda."

I chuckle. I'm dying to have my way with him too, but we've never been out on the town before, and I'd be lying if I said I didn't want to stake my claim. Amber got Rhett for homecoming and prom and so many firsts I'll never have. So I'll take all of the country dances and fairs and whatever local festivals I can get for the foreseeable future.

In a weird way, I feel like showing up on Rhett's arm tonight proves I wasn't just a sad little wackadoodle in high school.

We hug the boys goodbye. Pauline is babysitting tonight.

I grab a light wraparound sweater in case it gets chilly. Texas in the fall can be so unpredictable. It was sixty last night, but now it's warm and breezy.

I can't believe it's already October. I need to ask the boys what they want to be for Halloween. It'll be fun to sew their costumes.

As Rhett and I drive into town, he's quiet.

"Are you worried about the auction?" It's next weekend, and I've seen his mile-long to-do list.

"Yeah. I'm cutting it a little close 'cause Harlan's loan repayment is due the following Monday, but I wanted to hold off as long as possible to get those steer as heavy as possible."

"Will he be at the Mixer? Should you explain the plan to him so he knows you're on top of everything? You know, to reassure him?"

His hand slips over mine. "That's not a bad idea."

I nibble my bottom lip as I think about what Cash told me over the summer, that we shouldn't put all our eggs in one basket. "Have you ever considered diversifying the ranch so we don't just raise cattle?"

He glances over. "Sure, I've thought about it, but we haven't had the funds to invest in anything else. I'm open to it, though."

"How do you feel about sheep? I've been watching this rancher on YouTube who said she earns four hundred percent more raising sheep than cattle." There's no way I'm going to tell him this was Cash's idea because that might turn him off. But Cash's suggestion made me curious, and I found a lot of info online that supported his assertion about sheep.

Rhett's brows lift. "Four hundred percent?"

"If I send you the link, would you watch a few videos? This rancher has tons of resources on regenerative agriculture. The best part is the return on investment for sheep is nine months versus, what, thirty-three for cattle?"

"I like that turnaround time." He whistles. "Look at my wife, the expert. And yes, I'll watch a few YouTube videos."

A huge smile tilts my lips. And Cash said Rhett wouldn't listen to me. "I just want us to shore ourselves up financially so we can weather the storm if the prices on cattle drop again."

Lifting my hand to his lips, he kisses me. "Sounds good. Thanks for researching that, baby."

I'm grinning the rest of the drive into town.

The Mixer is being held at the grassy square in front of the courthouse, which has a gazebo, benches, and picnic tables. Tonight, it's lit up with twinkle lights that stretch across the oak trees that surround the little park. There's a makeshift dance floor and stage where a country band is playing. Local vendors line the perimeter.

In a few weeks, we'll have a carnival for Halloween and then all of the Christmas festivities. Maybe living in Wild Heart isn't so bad. As I glance around at all of the friendly, familiar faces, a warm feeling settles over me.

Baylee runs up and gives me a hug. "Hello, my spicy burrito. I wanted to introduce you to someone." I give Rhett a look because I've been dying to meet Baylee's new man. She waves forward a handsome guy in a cowboy hat. "This is Sean."

We chitchat a few minutes, and I covertly snap a photo of them smiling at each other and send it to the Walker brothers' chat.

> Check out Baylee's new man. Don't they make a cute couple?

Rhett smirks after he reads it. "I know what you're doing."

"What's that?" I play dumb.

Maverick immediately responds.

> Who the fuck is that?

My husband chuckles when he reads the message. "Houston, we have liftoff."

As I watch Sean twirl Baylee around the dance floor, I whisper, "Mav can shit or get off the pot. I'm just moving things along."

Beau and Jace join us, and Beau waves his phone at me. "Nice play."

I laugh. "I do what I can."

Rhett grabs my hand. "Okay, my little shit-stirrer, we gonna dance or what?"

"I'm all yours."

He swoops me into his arms and twirls me around the dance floor to an old George Straight song. Between the bittersweet notes of the song and the scent of Rhett's heavenly cologne, I'm totally swooning. "I had no idea you could two-step this well."

"I have a few hidden talents."

Glancing around, I realize how many people are watching us. "People are staring. Do you think it's because of Amber?"

He shrugs. "They're just jealous I'm here with the prettiest girl in town."

For a grumpy guy, he can be such a sweet talker. "Is she still pissed at you?"

"Don't care if she is."

Rhett's been granted temporary sole custody, but to make it permanent, the boys have to do a session with a family psychiatrist, who will submit his findings to the court. Since then, he's only communicated with his ex via a parenting app, which he prefers.

Since that showdown with Amber, we've been learning how mean and downright abusive she was to the kids. It's heartbreaking. At the end of the day, I guess it was worth being Amber's punching bag if it means she won't be allowed to emotionally abuse the children anymore.

Over my shoulder, I spot a familiar face. "Harlan's here. Over by the stage." I steel myself for the bomb to drop. Did Marcus tell his uncle we dated or was he too embarrassed to admit I left him and got hitched to someone else a week later?

Once the song is over, Rhett and I go over to say hi.

"If it isn't my favorite newlyweds. How's married life treating you?" Harlan asks.

Relieved he isn't calling me out for fraud, I grin up at my husband. "Great. Rhett built me a chicken coop, and now we have farm-fresh eggs every day."

Rhett winks at me. "Someone once told me, 'Happy wife, happy life.' Can't say they're wrong."

Harlan nods. "That's the secret." He shakes out his wrist and glances at his huge gold watch. "Where's Mary Sue? That woman said she'd only be gone ten minutes. She's coordinating the winter food drive at the church."

I hold up my phone. "Please tell her to call me if she needs volunteers. I'd love to help."

"Why, thank you, darling. That's mighty nice."

A distinguished-looking gentleman joins us. Harlan pats the man's back. "Paige, have you met my brother Prescott? He oversees the bank here in town."

Prescott holds up his beer to Harlan. "And don't you forget it."

Harlan chuckles. From what Rhett has explained, Harlan is the president of the company, but his younger brother is the local branch manager.

Prescott motions to Harlan. "Have you seen Tiffany? She's supposed to meet me here." He rolls his eyes playfully when he turns to us. "My wife means well, but she's late for everything."

Another guy walks up to our group, and Harlan mumbles something to him I can't make out before he introduces him.

"This here is my son Jimmy. Took some hard work, but he finally got the Gibson ranch up and running."

Jimmy's tall and lanky, and he doesn't smile. Just nods at us.

After a minute, Harlan turns the conversation to business. "How are things on the ranch? You gearing up for the auction?"

My husband nods. "Yes, sir. We'll be ready."

"No trouble fattening up your herd?"

"No. They're looking good."

Stepping back, I motion behind me. "I'm going to say hi to some friends and let you chat."

I say a little prayer my husband has all the right words to inspire Harlan's confidence. We're so close to our goal, and I don't want anything to go wrong.

Chapter Thirty-Five
RHETT

THE MOMENT my wife walks away, Harlan's eyes go hard. He turns to me and lowers his voice. "Can we speak privately for a moment?"

Unease settles over me as I follow him a few feet away from Prescott and Jimmy, off to the side of the stage. "Is something wrong?"

"I need to ask you a question." After I nod, he reaches into his pocket and pulls out a cigar. It's illegal to smoke in the downtown area, but no one's gonna tell Harlan his business. "How long have you known Paige?"

Shit. This can't be good. "For years. I was best friends with her brother, Danny, before he passed away. Why?"

He cants his head as he studies me. "Son, don't take this the wrong way, but I have it on good authority she was dating someone else until recently. Until just before you two got married." He pulls out a trimmer and clips off the head of his cigar.

So that little dickhead Marcus finally spilled the beans? I try to look unaffected by Harlan's words. I shrug like I don't give a damn because I don't, but I have to tread carefully since Marcus is his nephew. "She told me about her ex. As I understand it, things were over for a while before they officially broke up. The truth is I've always been fond of Paige. Sure, we moved a little fast, but when you know, you know. I dated my first wife for years, and I did everything by the book, but we were miserable from the start. I thought I'd do things differently this time."

He chuckles as he stares across the dance floor where my wife is talking to Frannie Tate. "Can't say I blame you for locking her down. She's a pretty little thing."

I fight like hell not to bristle. I don't really care for any man checking out my wife, but I try not to take offense. "I've never been happier." And that's the God's honest truth.

Harlan pats me on the back. "I'm glad to hear that. Since your father is gone, rest his soul, I felt like someone should be looking out for you and your brothers. I'd be remiss not to mention it."

"I appreciate your concern, sir, but you don't need to worry. My wife is the best thing to happen to me. She supports the ranch and loves my kids. She even organized my office."

"God bless her. If your office is anything like mine at home..." he chuckles as he pulls out a gold lighter engraved with his initials. "Would you care for a cigar? I always carry an extra one. It's from my personal collection I import from Cuba. Nobody smokes them right anymore. You need a soft flame to light them. This lighter here has a split flame valve to accommodate the width of the cigar."

"I'd better not. You enjoy it." Itching for this conversation to be over, I hold out my hand. "Thank you for the talk. It's nice to know you have my back."

We shake, and he tilts his head. "So I'll see you in, what, nine days?"

"It's circled red on my calendar." I can't fucking wait to repay this loan. I hate lying to Harlan. Granted, Paige and I are working out, but I don't like being dishonest.

Nodding, he leans forward. "Good because I don't give extensions. I have another project I'm looking to invest in, but I'd like to have your loan repaid first. Our bank is different because I always make sure we have plenty of capital on hand. Call me old fashioned, but my grandfather started this bank and weathered the Great Depression by not taking on too much risk."

"Harlan, I appreciate you taking a chance on me. I won't let you down."

And I mean it.

Chapter Thirty-Six
PAIGE

"I'm thrilled you and Rhett are doing well," Judge Tate says as she wraps me in a hug. "Call me next week so I can add you to our quilting group."

"I've only made a baby quilt, and it wasn't fancy," I admit.

She waves her hand. "Sylvia Reyes says you're a fantastic seamstress. You'll learn advanced techniques in no time." Leaning in, she whispers, "We call it the Sewers and Sippers Society because we like our margaritas."

I laugh. "Sounds like fun."

After I jot her number in my cell, I go in search of fried dough. The festival is getting crowded, and as I weave around a large group, I run into Irma and Ty. My stomach tightens, and I force a smile. "Hi. How are y'all?"

Ty gives me a genuine grin. "Great. I just finished selling off the rest of our puppies. I'm making bank."

I hate that he's running a puppy mill. "What about the mama dogs? How much time do you give them between litters?"

Irma rolls her eyes. "They're just dogs."

"Mom, don't talk like that." Ty shakes his head. "This is my last batch. I'm getting tired of cleaning up crap all the time. I'm gonna invest the money and do something else."

I'm relieved he's not continuing with his original plan. "I'm so glad to hear that." It's great to see my brother. I know we're not full siblings, but he's the only blood relative I have left. "Ty, we should grab lunch sometime."

He nods. "I'd like that."

We make plans to hang out later this week. Irma doesn't look happy, but that's too bad.

Baylee waves me over, and I join her by the churro truck. "Sean is a hottie."

We watch him dance with one of the nursing home gals, and Baylee nods. "He's great. I really like him." She points to the caramel corn. "Want to share an order with me?"

I sniff the air, and my stomach turns. "I was going to eat some fried dough, but the smell is grossing me out."

"How about a brownie? My mom is manning the Fudge Delight table, and she made a few batches of her Better than Sex brownies."

I chuckle. "I can't believe she calls them that."

As we wait in Aunt Sylvia's line, I watch everyone dance. I sigh happily when Rhett asks Mrs. Campbell for a spin. She has to be ninety years old, but she eagerly hops out of her wheelchair when he holds out his hand.

Tonight feels perfect. Amber isn't here to ruin it, and talking to Ty made me feel like I can really set down roots here again. And I'm ridiculously excited about the quilting group. The icing on the cake is knowing Rhett's going to get a great price for his cattle next week, so we can build a life together.

Baylee loops her arm through mine. "Did you say the Fletchers finally moved out?"

"Yeah. I hope that's the end of the problems we were having with our fences getting cut. The sheriff never figured out who was behind it, but Frank was so pissed about the rent increase that I have to wonder if it was him all along. They trashed the cabin on the way out."

"That sucks. What dicks."

"At least he's gone. We'll fix it up and either Beau can live there or we'll rent it. The extra income wouldn't hurt."

Now that I'm helping Rhett with the books and I see how much overhead we have, I understand why he's always stressed out about the ranch. The payroll, vet bills, mortgage, maintaining our vehicles and tractors—it all costs a small fortune.

"Oh, shit," Baylee mumbles.

"What?"

She folds her lips and blinks slowly, like she's searching for the right thing to say. "Did Rhett ever talk to his friend with benefits?"

"That Darlene girl? I don't know. He said he'd let her know he couldn't meet up anymore, but we've been so busy, I forgot to ask about her. Why?"

"Because she's here."

My head jerks. "Where?"

Baylee makes a face. "Headed straight for your husband. That brunette."

I follow where she's looking, and my heart sinks because Darlene is drop-dead gorgeous. Like, this woman should be a model. She's tall and elegant with long brown hair and perfect skin. I know I'm no troll, but I'm also self-aware enough to know I'm no model.

Based on Darlene's expression, she's pissed. "You got married?" she shouts at Rhett. "We were together for a year and a half, and you didn't have the decency to tell me you had a side chick?"

Oh, God. She thinks he cheated on her?

The minute those words are out of her mouth, the whole town turns to look at me.

I've never wanted a hole to open up beneath me and swallow me this badly before. At least I don't see Harlan in the crowd. I'd be mortified if he saw this.

Rhett squints at her and lowers his voice, but I'm still close enough to hear. "You and I were never together. And Paige isn't a side chick. Look, it's complicated." He helps Mrs. Campbell back to her wheelchair.

Darlene follows him. "Complicated? Would it have killed you to give me a heads-up that you were getting married? Or to answer my calls?"

Baylee tugs on my arm. "Let's get out of here."

"No." I need to hear Rhett's response.

But he doesn't say anything, just takes Darlene's elbow and ushers her to a dark corner of the park under a great oak where he talks to her in hushed tones.

I stalk closer until I can hear him. "Darlene, I called you at least three times to let you know what was going on."

"You never left any messages." The hurt in her voice kills me a little. That's so Rhett. I roll my eyes.

He glances around, probably wondering where I am, but I'm standing behind him, so he doesn't see me. His voice gets quiet, but the band is taking a break, so I can hear every word. "We agreed from the very beginning that we were friends with benefits. You had to know we weren't serious. We fucked in my truck in bar parking lots, for Pete's sake. What part of that says committed relationship?"

They had sex in his truck.

Regularly.

My stomach drops. Here I was thinking that when we did it in his truck after he bought me this outfit, it was special. That *I* was special. That he was so into me, he couldn't wait until we got home to have me. In reality, that's just a typical Friday night for him.

He was treating me like his hookup.

My eyes sting, and I blink furiously.

That's when Cash and Trig McAllister walk up, and Trig yells, "Damn, Walker. Were you keeping your friend with bennies on standby in case your marriage didn't work out?"

My eyes widen.

Rhett whips around, and when he sees me, his face goes blank. What does that mean? Is Trig right?

What the hell? Did Rhett deliberately not end things with Darlene in case he and I went south?

Cash elbows his brother. "Don't listen to him, Paige. Trig's just being an asshole."

But it's too late. I heard it. So did the rest of the town. The Amber meltdown was bad enough, but now the gossips will be talking about this for months.

I turn on my heel and race through the crowd. Baylee follows me, and when we reach the parking lot, she hugs me.

Over her shoulder, I see a woman giving some guy a blow job. Headlights flash across the man's face and recognition hits me. He's older now, but still familiar. *Kacey Miller's still a player.* Some things never change.

Behind me, someone calls my name, but I'm not ready to talk to anyone, much less Rhett. Baylee takes my hand and pulls me to her car, and I jump in.

"Take me home."

"Are you sure you don't want to come to my place?"

It's tempting. Because right now, I want to hide under a rock for the next ten years until the humiliation of tonight wears off. I have a feeling it's going to take that long to get over this.

Except I know I can't do that.

Even though I'm hurting, if I want this marriage to have a shot, I can't run away when times get tough.

When I get back to the ranch, it's dark and quiet. The boys are asleep. I thank Pauline for babysitting, and she heads home.

Truthfully, I have no idea what I'll say to Rhett. When I reach our bedroom, I'm too upset to crawl into our bed, so I grab my pillow and some blankets and curl up on the couch. I'm exhausted. If I fall asleep, I suppose we can talk in the morning.

I try to wait up for Rhett, but sleep overpowers me.

And in the morning, he's already gone.

Chapter Thirty-Seven
PAIGE

Wordlessly, I flip pancakes on the griddle.

"Is it okay that we're having pancakes for lunch?" Gabriel asks.

"Of course." Frankly, I don't give a fuck if Rhett has a problem with it. That asshole left for work this morning without a word. It's past time for lunch, and he still hasn't returned. Neither have his brothers.

In fact, now that I think about it, their text message group has been strangely silent.

It makes me wonder if they cut me out of it. Or if they started a new one without me.

My throat closes up, and I take several deep breaths so I don't lose it.

When I finish making lunch, I serve the boys, and the three of us sit down to eat. I force myself to smile and chat. It's not their fault their father is a dickhead.

I could call him, but damn. He's the one who made a scene with his former hookup in front of the whole town. Why isn't *he* calling *me*?

I clear my throat. "Boys, did you see your father this morning?"

Gabriel nods as he shovels a huge bite into his mouth. "He was mad because of the cows."

"What's going on with the cows?"

He shrugs. "Dunno."

That's helpful. "I know I said we could go to the gym this afternoon, but I'm feeling really run-down." I hope I'm not coming down with something. "Want to watch a movie when we're done? You two can pick it."

After lunch, we curl up in front of the TV, but they can't decide on what they want to watch.

I hand Gabriel the remote, and he starts clicking through the channels and stops on a show about sharks. "I love Shark Week," he says. "It's a whole week about sharks. How they attack. Where they swim. What they eat."

Shark Week. As I nod, something bothers me. Like I forgot to turn off the stove. I check the range, but I turned everything off after I finished cooking.

Shark Week!

Dread spreads through my chest.

When was the last time I got my period?

"Boys, I need to go to the bathroom. Be right back." I grab my phone and rush to the bedroom. The screen lights up with another notification from the *Gazette*, which I swipe away.

I wanted something to take my mind off Darlene. Well, I found it.

Frantic, I scroll through my digital calendar. I got my period after the truck sex. It was super light, but I didn't note anything last month.

Hoping I'm misremembering, I riffle through the cabinet in the bathroom and grab my box of tampons, which is almost full.

I close my eyes.

I'm not misremembering anything. I definitely didn't get it last month.

I speed-dial the only person I trust to help me figure this out. When Baylee answers, I blurt out, "I think I'm pregnant."

"Whoa. Whoa. No. Really? Shut up."

I start to hyperventilate. "I still haven't spoken to Rhett about Darlene. I slept on the couch, and he was gone this morning. It's Sunday. He usually doesn't take off at the ass crack of dawn on Sundays, but he did today."

"Motherfucker. I'm going to string that man up by his balls."

"What do I do?" I try to suck in a deep breath.

"Look, let's not rush things. You've been under a lot of stress. Let's start with a pregnancy test. I'll pick you up, and we'll go grab one."

"I have the boys with me."

"They don't need to know what you're getting at the pharmacy."

True. Okay.

I lean against the vanity. "I'm scared."

"Everything's gonna be fine. I promise. If you're pregnant, it's not the end of the world. Rhett would be lucky to have a kid with you."

My heart sinks.

But I can't bring myself to tell my best friend that my husband doesn't want more children.

After I get off the phone, I splash my face with cold water and try to calm my ass down. I hear talking out in the living room and run out there hoping it's Rhett, but it's Beau talking to the boys.

"Paige. Hey." He's filthy. There's thick mud on his boots, dirt on his jeans, and hay sticking out of his hair.

"Where's your brother?"

"Out on the north field. We have a situation."

I laugh humorously. "That's not the only one."

He winces. "He feels bad about last night."

"Sure seems like it." I wave my hand at him. "Rhett always seems to send you when he doesn't want to deal with me."

"It's not like that. I swear."

Baylee honks, and I grab my purse. "I have to run some errands. Do you want me to take the boys or do you want them to stay with you?"

"Can you keep them? I need to head back out."

I don't bother responding because I'm afraid of what I'll say to my brother-in-law. "Gabriel. Austin. Put your shoes on. Baylee is taking us for a drive."

As we head out the door, Beau calls out, "When will y'all be back?"

I glare at him. He wants to be nebulous about shit? I can dish that out too. "Later."

Chapter Thirty-Eight
RHETT

SON OF A BITCH.

"He's got a fever." The bull stomps his hoof as I remove the thermometer from his ass. "Sorry, man. I hate doing this too."

Jace shakes his head. "How did this happen? They've been healthy all season."

"I don't fucking know." This is the fifth steer we've had to isolate. "When did the vet say he'd get here?"

"Hopefully by three. Thank God the cow-calf pairs are in that far back pasture."

"This is probably bluetongue, which isn't contagious animal-to-animal, but I wanna play it safe just in case."

Because if this is serious, it could get bad, fast.

We've been out here since the break of dawn checking each and every animal. I got a call early this morning that one of the bulls was drooling and had blisters on his lower lip. That sent us all into action. Isolating the sick animals is our top priority right now. We have too much on the line to take any chances.

Something viral could take down my whole herd.

Which means we'd default on our loan.

Fuck.

I shuck off the glove and toss it in the large trash bin.

Jace wipes the sweat off his face. "Should we get some lunch? I'm starving."

"There's no time to eat. Go grab something if you need to, but we have to make sure this shit is contained and that we get the sick ones fluids and soft feed."

Beau's truck pulls up alongside the animal chute. "Brought y'all some sandwiches."

Wayne taps my shoulder. "Boss, we got a problem." Not what I wanna hear right now. He motions to the animal in front of me. "This is the steer that went missing this summer."

That makes no sense.

I hang my hands on my hips. "Did we miss him somehow? Was he with the herd the whole time?"

"No, we count the herd every time we move them to a new field. Plus, he's not in the vet's reports we did last week. I just double-checked."

I pinch the bridge of my nose. "So how did he get *back* in the herd? We haven't had any cut fences lately, right?"

He shakes his head. "Checked that this morning. Everything looked good."

When he walks away, I motion to Jace. "Can you walk the perimeter of the field where these guys were grazing?"

"Sure thing. What am I looking for?"

It takes me a minute to consider. "Repairs. Fences that were cut but then fixed."

My brother chuckles. "Someone returned our steer and repaired the fence afterward? Who would do that?"

A sense of dread washes over me. "Someone trying to sabotage our operation."

Like the fucking McAllisters.

We get the sick steer into a holding pen and resume checking the others. As Beau is checking the animal's mouth, I motion to the house. "Are Paige and the kids okay? Did you tell them we'll be working late tonight?"

"She, um, she's still pretty pissed about last night."

Shit. "Did you tell her we have sick animals? That this might affect whether or not we can repay Harlan's loan? That our whole fucking operation revolves around these animals not being contagious?" I scrub my face. "I get that she's upset, but she was dead asleep when I got home, and even though I tried to wake her, she didn't budge. What was I supposed to do? Douse her with cold water?"

I tried to follow her home, but I had a flat tire, and it took me a while to change it in the dark. Then I found her sleeping on the couch.

As I think about it, my heart sinks. The woman must be livid. I don't blame her, but it's not like I planned to hash out shit with Darlene in the middle of a goddamn festival.

When that fuckhead Trig said I was keeping Darlene on standby, I could've killed him. But seeing the devastation on Paige's face after he said that caught me off guard.

Does she really believe I could do that to her? Play her like she's a chess piece I could discard?

Beau shoots me a look. "Don't get mad at me. She really didn't give me a chance to explain. Just said she needed to run some errands with Baylee and took the boys with her. Talk to her when you get home."

"Yeah, I'm really looking forward to that after inspecting the mouth and asses of a hundred cattle today."

He laughs. "You mean this ain't fun for you?"

"Ha ha, asshole. I'm having a blast."

I'm not much of a church-going man, but I can't lie. I say a little prayer that we've found all the sick animals and that we'll make it through this.

Because the entire future of my family—my wife, the boys, my brothers, and all my employees—depends on it.

Chapter Thirty-Nine

PAIGE

My heart is in my throat as I walk down the contraception aisle at the pharmacy. I look over my shoulder to make sure the boys are still in the front of the store with Baylee. She gives me a thumbs-up, and I stop in front of the pregnancy tests.

I start to panic as I scan all the boxes.

Who knew there were so many? I've never missed a period in my life, so I've never had a reason to get a test before. Some have alarms, some give you a pink cross if it's positive, another one gives you a double line.

I can't stop thinking about that day at the river when Rhett told me he trusted me. Will he think I did this on purpose? That I'm trying to baby-trap him? I don't want him to think I'm irresponsible. I've never missed taking a birth control pill. Not once. I don't know how this happened.

I grab a test and scan the back, wondering if I should go with a name brand or something generic.

The pharmacist comes up behind me. "Can I help you find something?"

Flinching, I drop the box. I pick it up and nearly fumble it again. "No, I'm all set."

I knew we should've gone two towns over to buy this, but I didn't want to keep the boys out that long. As upset as I am with Rhett, I want to talk to him about last night.

The older man glances at the pregnancy test and gives me a kind smile. Lowering his voice, he points to the one with the plus. "I'm told this is the easiest to figure out."

"Th-thank you." I look at the boxes. Maybe I need more than one? Because they're not always correct, or so my friends have told me. So I grab a three-pack and tuck it beneath the bag of Doritos I'm buying to camouflage the real reason I'm here.

On our way home, I can't stop bouncing my leg.

Baylee glances at the boys in the rearview mirror before whispering, "It'll be okay. Whatever the results. Rhett loves you."

But does he love me enough to have a baby when he said he didn't want any more?

When we get back to the ranch, I let out a sigh of relief that the guys are still out. My car is the only one parked next to the house.

I don't want to have to lie about anything, and it'll be easier to find out the results first and have a little time to process that before I share it with anyone.

Maybe I missed my period because of stress.

Please, God, let it be stress.

Baylee and I get the boys out of the backseat. I'm wrestling with Austin's car seat when I lose my grip and my purse slides off my shoulder, dumping its contents onto the driveway.

Gabriel picks up the three-pack of pregnancy tests. "What's this?"

Shit.

Fortunately, Baylee comes to my rescue again and grabs it. "Just girlie stuff." She shoves it into my purse.

We get the boys settled in the living room with their giant set of Legos before Baylee and I lock ourselves in the powder room with a pregnancy test.

She leans against the door as I sit on the toilet. After a second, I start to laugh. "Don't watch me pee. I can't handle the pressure."

Baylee snickers. "Remember when we were in first grade, and Mrs. Jenkins wouldn't let me use the bathroom, and I peed my pants? I never forgave that bitch."

"Don't be too hard on her. Remember when you almost stepped in dog crap in eighth grade, and I tried to yank you to safety, but I accidentally ripped your shirt open? I'll never forget the way all those buttons went flying. You didn't talk to me for a week."

She gives me a droll look. "I flashed our entire class of boys. I should've disowned you then and there as my best friend."

I finish up my test, set it down on a paper towel, and wash my hands. "I kept you from stepping on dog shit, dude. That's a good friend right there. So the boys saw your bra. Was that really traumatic?"

Talking about all the dumb stuff we've done over the years relaxes me.

In the living room, a door slams, and male voices fill the house. My eyes widen as I look at the pregnancy test.

My stomach drops.

It's freaking positive.

My eyes sting, and Baylee immediately hugs me. "You might not want to hear this right now, but I'm really excited about being an aunt. You can trust that my mom will throw you the biggest baby shower in Texas."

I nod and wipe my eyes. She lets me go, and I look around. "I left my purse in the other room. What do I do with the test?"

"Toss it in the trash and put a bunch of toilet paper over it like we did when my mom almost caught us drinking that time."

"Solid plan." After I toss everything, she and I ball up the toilet paper until it covers the evidence.

Because I'm not ready to tell Rhett yet.

Chapter Forty
PAIGE

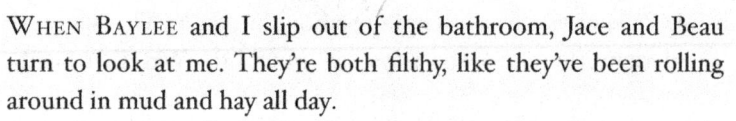

WHEN BAYLEE and I slip out of the bathroom, Jace and Beau turn to look at me. They're both filthy, like they've been rolling around in mud and hay all day.

Jace chuckles. "I know girls like to go to the bathroom at the same time, but isn't the powder room kinda small for y'all to be whizzing together?"

Baylee motions to her back. "Actually, I have a rash that I wanted to show Paige." A rash? I give her a look, and she shrugs, like, *What was I supposed to tell him?* "Sean was helping me break in my new hammock, and we fell out."

I choke on a laugh, and Jace shakes his head. "Hopefully, that's all he broke in."

"Jace!" I yell.

He holds up his hands. "What? Can I help that I want Baylee to be my sister-in-law?" Jace turns to my best friend. "You're dating the wrong man."

Her jaw tightens. "Maybe if Maverick wasn't screwing all of South Texas, we could entertain that sister-in-law situation. But since he's the biggest manwhore I've ever met next to you, that's obviously not going to happen. So what if I want Sean to break my back? I don't owe Mav anything."

Gabriel trots in and tugs on Jace's arm. "What's 'breaking my back' mean?"

I slap a hand over my mouth and try not to laugh as Jace struggles to answer. Beau finally pipes up. "Little man, Baylee was talking about a horse she was thinking about getting, but he needs to be broken in." He motions back to the living room. "Go play."

"Nice save," Jace mumbles.

"On that note, I gotta go." Baylee hugs me. "Call me later."

I nod and almost tear up again when she leaves. Sniffling, I turn to grab a glass of water. "Where's Rhett? Is he on his way home?" Jace and Beau give each other a look. "What?"

Jace motions to the kitchen table. "Why don't we sit?"

My eyes narrow. "What's going on? Why were y'all gone all day? You didn't even come home for lunch." He ushers me over to a chair, and I plunk down, confused.

Jace sits next to me at the head of the table. "We have a situation."

"You're scaring me."

"Some of the steers are sick."

"Okay? And?"

"They're really sick. Rhett's talking to the vet right now, but it's not looking good." The easy-going expression he was sporting a few minutes ago has vanished.

The door opens, and the three of us whip around to see Rhett walk in looking grimmer than I've ever seen him.

Gabriel and Austin leap off the couch and run to him. "Hi, Dad. Look at the dinosaur we made." Gabe points to a block of Legos that looks like an octopus.

Rhett forces a smile. "Looks good, son." He squats down to hug them, and in that moment, I realize that whatever he's dealing with right now is bad. I catch a glimpse of his face, and it's a slab of granite.

They scale him, and he picks them both up and carries them to the couch, where he sits like he's too tired to walk a few more steps to the kitchen.

I want to run to him and sit in his lap too, but he hasn't spoken a word to me since last night.

My throat closes up. I love this man with my whole heart and soul, but right now, I feel shut out. *His whole life is wrapped up in those cattle, Paige. This is his livelihood. Get a grip. There will be time to discuss what happened last night.*

Beau leans over to me. "Just give him a few minutes to get his bearings. It's been a bad day."

I've had a bad day too, I want to tell him. Pressure builds in my chest and the back of my throat when I think of that positive pregnancy test. Blinking quickly to keep the tears at bay, I nod, but the more time stretches out, the worse I feel.

Jace finally wanders into the living room and sits on the coffee table to face his older brother. "What did the vet say?"

Rhett shakes his head. "He's worried it's serious. The Hollybrook farm had an outbreak of vesicular stomatitis, and he says he needs to notify the state in case that's what this is."

"Son of a bitch." Jace rakes his hands through his hair. "But I thought we isolated all the cattle who had a fever."

"He says there's a chance the rest of them are still within the incubation period and could start showing symptoms."

I turn to Beau. "What does that mean?" I whisper. "Will they get better in a few days?"

"Hopefully, but until we get their test results back, it's hard to tell if this is a minor respiratory thing or something more serious, like vesicular stomatitis, which is viral and super contagious. I'm hoping we're just jumping the gun. Except…"

"Except what?"

"We won't get the vet clearance in time for the auction. Especially if a state agency gets involved. Which means…"

"That we'll default on the loan." I cover my mouth.

He nods.

I push away from the kitchen table and run over to Rhett. "Go talk to Harlan. Ask for an extension. A week or two. He'll give it to you. I'm sure we can sort everything out by then."

My husband's expression goes flat. "The man just told me last night that he couldn't extend the terms."

"But he doesn't know what we're dealing with."

"He said he needs the money to invest in another project and can't put it off."

"But maybe he'll change his mind if we explain. Your families go way back together, and I'm sure—"

"Paige, he said no. How many ways do I need to explain that to you?" he barks.

I flinch, and my eyes flood. Embarrassed, I shuffle backwards. "You're right. What do I know?" I run to our bedroom and lock myself in the bathroom.

All of a sudden, I'm fifteen years old again, wishing I had a window I could escape through.

A few minutes later, a knock at the door makes me jump.

"I'm sorry, Paige." Rhett's gruff voice is muffled. "I didn't mean to yell at you."

I force a lightness into my voice I don't feel. "No problem. I'm just going to take a shower."

He starts to say something, but I flip on the water. I'm not ready to hear what he has to say.

I strip out of my clothes and stand under the hot water, where I cry until there aren't any tears left.

My life here—my marriage, this ranch, my future—everything feels like it's crumbling.

And I have no idea how to save it.

Chapter Forty-One
PAIGE

I don't know why I expect to see Rhett in the morning. Of course he's gone.

From the couch, I stare at the empty bed. Rhett's side is perfectly made. I don't know if that means he slept in the living room last night or made it before he left.

More concerning is why I'm still exhausted after sleeping twelve hours. I've never slept that long before.

After I get dressed for the day, I drag myself into the office, where I find a vet bill that makes my eyes bulge.

We've waited as long as we could for the auction, but that also means our funds are getting low. I cut the check and stare at it with a stone in my stomach.

I turn to the wall calendar, where this Friday and Saturday are circled in bright red Sharpie. Will we be able to sell any of our animals this weekend? Will the farm be ruined if we don't?

I can't believe that Harlan would pull the rug out from under us. Is he that heartless? Rhett must know him better than I do, but I don't think we should give up.

My phone rings. It's Abby.

When I answer, her happy voice makes me smile. "How's the baby?"

"Janie's doing great. She's such a happy girl. Nick says she's perfect."

"Of course she is." That knot I'm getting familiar with tightens my throat. "I'm so happy for you. Send me photos when you get a chance." I might be in misery, but I love Abby and Nick and want the best for them.

"I wore your vest to Saturday's game. I got so many compliments. I hope you don't mind, but I gave your info to a few of the other wives and girlfriends."

I tilt my head. "You mean *NFL players'* wives and girlfriends?"

She chuckles. "Yes."

"That's... wow. That's cool."

"Think you could make me something else if I send you more jerseys? I want to get in the queue in case you get busy."

This is the perfect project to get my mind off everything. I grab a piece of paper to take notes. "What did you have in mind?"

When I get off the phone, I'm feeling more hopeful. I decide that Rhett needs me to be optimistic. We can figure our way out of this situation if we put our heads together.

I'll deal with him and the Darlene situation later. There's a reckoning coming for sure, but first we have to make sure we don't go bankrupt. Then I'll chew out his ass.

I get into the kitchen and start making lunch. I'm sure the guys are going to have another long day. The least I can do is get them something to eat. Eventually, Pauline brings the boys in, and I feed them a pasta salad and some grilled ham and cheese sandwiches with pickles.

After an hour, though, I start to worry that the guys aren't going to make it home again, when I hear a truck door slam.

Beau and Rhett are back. They look exhausted.

"Hey, guys." I force some cheer into my voice because they

look like they could use it. Rhett and I might not be in a good place right now, but I know he's going through a lot. So I put the Darlene drama and my pregnancy and the fact that he's being distant aside. "I'm making lunch. Are you hungry?"

Beau gives me a small smile. "Food would be great."

Rhett barely looks at me. "Sure."

Sure? When we get done with this crisis, I'm going to throttle him for being an asshole. In the meanwhile, I practice deep breathing.

I return to the stove, where I grill their sandwiches. On the counter, my phone lights up with a message. I don't recognize the number. I pull it up and press speaker so I can finish cooking.

"Hi, Paige. This is Lauren Wilcox from Elite Cheer in Florida. I got your number from your former coach, who said you might be available this fall. I need a full-time coach to work with my advanced high school-aged kids. Are you interested? Give me a call so we can chat. Here's the thing, though. I would need to know as soon as possible."

Holy shit. I grin, excited that they thought of me. Obviously, I can't run off to Florida now, but I'm so honored they thought of me.

Looking up, I find Rhett watching me. "That's the sister program to the one in Austin."

"Are you gonna go?" he asks.

I frown. "They're in Florida."

He shrugs. "So? They're a good program, right? Isn't that what you wanted?"

Is he for real right now? Why is he acting like this? "Rhett, I'm not sure why—"

Someone rings the doorbell, and he pushes out of his chair to answer it.

Beau gives me a sympathetic smile. "That's probably the guy from the Texas Livestock Commission, Eugene Dods. We've been waiting to hear from him."

Rhett steps outside, and Beau joins him.

I run to the front window and see them talking to a slender man with glasses and a bushy black mustache. The guy is jotting notes on a clipboard and shaking his head.

I can't hear what they're saying, but Rhett looks pissed. I crack open the front door.

"But the test results aren't in yet," my husband argues. "How the hell can you quarantine my entire herd? Only five have gotten sick, and we don't know if it's viral yet."

The guy adjusts his glasses. "Sir, I'm just doing my job, and that means containing this outbreak." He must be from that state agency.

"It's not an outbreak. How can you call it that when we don't have confirmation yet? What if the rest are fine? You're going to lock down my healthy cattle too when I have an auction I need to get to this weekend? They got a clean bill of health two weeks ago."

Dods tears off a sheet of paper and hands it to Rhett. "Here are my findings. I'm sorry, but you can't transport any animals from this property until I clear you."

"And when might that be?"

"Hard to say. A few weeks. Maybe a month."

"A month?" Rhett bellows. "Are you insane?"

Beau wraps his arm around his brother's shoulders and tugs him back a few steps. The agency guy scuttles off to his truck like he's afraid Rhett might beat his ass.

As his taillights disappear in the distance, I realize our best shot of turning around this situation is speeding down our potholed driveway like the devil is on his tail.

My heart hurts as I watch my husband.

I've never seen that kind of devastation in his eyes before. I want to throw my arms around him. I want to scream and cry at the injustice of this situation.

But more than anything, I want my husband to come to me. I

want him to let me soothe his pain and be the rock he needs. I want us to be the partners he said we'd be.

Instead, he stalks off toward the barn.

Chapter Forty-Two
RHETT

Sitting on Apollo, I watch the sky shift from pink to purple to black, my mood darkening with each minute that passes.

Exhaustion pulls at my eyes, but I can't stop wrestling with the very real possibility that I'm going to default on Harlan's loan.

If that happens, he'll take our trucks, horses, and equipment.

Which means there'll be no way to run our ranch, and I'll be forced to sell it.

Could I sell some land and use that to stay afloat? Is there time to do that before I have to repay Harlan next week?

Even if I could unload a parcel of land, I'm not sure I'd find a buyer and get the sale done in a matter of days.

The bottom line is that we need every acre we have to support our cattle. Our whole operation is a careful symbiosis. Slicing up our property means we'd have to downsize the number of cattle too. With fewer animals, if the price of steer dips any more, we won't make enough to cover our expenses.

The moon creeps out briefly from behind the clouds, and I can make out the hills that stretch past the horizon. I know every sinkhole, gully, and outcropping for miles. This is my family heritage. Our legacy. My legacy.

And I'm going to lose it.

I'm the dumbfuck who let it happen. Sure, my father's second mortgage didn't help, but I compounded the problem with Harlan's bridge loan.

Shame and humiliation crawl over me like fire ants.

I've never been much of a drinker. Watching my father become an alcoholic made me steer clear of booze, but I admit I need a drink tonight.

Pulling on the reins, I turn Apollo and head back to the house. With each stride of my horse, my heart sinks. Paige and I have some shit to work through, but the memory of her smiling when she got that job offer makes something in my chest ache.

Without the ranch, what kind of life can I give her? What kind of future can we build? I won't even have a fucking truck after next week, and it won't be long before we lose the roof over our heads. If I have to put down my whole herd...

I just can't fathom that.

Never in the history of this ranch have we experienced anything this catastrophic.

Tilting up my head, I search for stars as though they might offer me a glimmer of hope, but the clouds hang thick above me like a bad omen.

Maybe the writing is on the wall. My ship is going down.

But Paige can still live her dream. If she takes that job, she can go do what she set out to accomplish when she agreed to marry me. She's recovered from her injury, she's saved some money, and now she can take that life raft. She'll eventually settle down and marry someone who can give her the family she wants, the family she deserves.

I suck in a breath. Goddamn, I don't know when that woman burrowed in deep, but I'm afraid I'm never gonna get over her.

I'm sorry, Danny. I fucked everything up. But I'm gonna make this right. I'm gonna do right by your sister.

I had no business messing with Paige's life.
I won't ruin it.
I love her enough to let her go.

Chapter Forty-Three
PAIGE

I WAKE with a start and scramble to look at the clock. It's after midnight.

Rhett's bed is empty, but maybe he's home.

My hand presses to my belly. *I'm having Rhett's baby.*

My lips tilt up. I know that's not the news he wants right now, but I want this child more than I've ever wanted anything in my life. Don't people always say that all you need is love? That love conquers all? I'm going to hold onto that right now and believe that we'll get through this. We'll figure out a way to keep the ranch and, sometime next year, we'll welcome our sweet little peanut.

Isn't that what marriage is about? In good times and in bad? It can't get much worse than this. And when you hit rock bottom, life can only get better.

As much as I want to tell Rhett about my pregnancy, I decide to hold off a few more days. Until we can figure out what we're doing with the ranch. He doesn't need the added stress of a baby on top of everything.

Nodding to myself, I wrap a blanket around my shoulders and

tiptoe into the hallway. There's a light coming from his father's office, which no one ever uses.

Peeking in, I see Rhett sitting at his father's old oak desk with a bottle of Jim Beam and a shot glass. A small desk lamp is on, which throws just enough light to see the hollowness in my husband's stare. The room smells musty, like dust and Old Spice. It smells like Rhett's dad.

"Hey. Are you okay?" I move closer.

His eyes shift to me, but there's no emotion behind them, and a chill rushes through me. "Have a seat." He motions to the chair across from him.

I still.

Why do I feel like I'm about to be fired?

That has to be in my head.

I perch at the edge of the chair and lean toward the desk. "I know you had a terrible day. I just want you to know that we'll fight this. We'll figure out a way to—"

"You should take that job." He downs the whiskey.

"What job?"

"The one in Florida."

Pain flares hot and bright in my heart. "You want me to go?"

"Why not? It's what you wanted, right? The whole reason you married me? Well, you've recovered. You can do your backflips and whatever. Now you can get that dream job."

"Rhett, it's on the other side of the country."

He reaches for the half-empty bottle and pours another shot. Was it full when he started? "I'll send you the divorce papers. I'll need some time, but I'll take care of everything."

My eyes sting. "You'll get rid of me just like that? Like I don't matter to you at all?" Trig's words about Darlene ring loud and clear in my head. Maybe Rhett never thought we were going to work out. Maybe he just sold me on this marriage so I'd play the part.

His jaw tightens, and he takes another shot. "I'll always care for you, Paige," he slurs. "How could I not? But don't you understand? There's nothing here for you. Besides, you and I want different things. You want kids and a husband who can provide. That's not me. Obviously." He laughs harshly, and I flinch.

"Don't do this. Don't push me away." Angrily, I wipe tears with the back of my arm. "You said you loved me. Were you bullshitting me this whole time?" I search his face, but it goes expressionless the way it did at the Moonlight Mixer when Trig asked him if he was keeping Darlene as a backup.

He clears his throat. "Do you need money? I have a little cash."

My husband doesn't love me. He never did.

I push out of my chair, and it screeches across the hardwood floor. "Fuck you, Rhett Walker. I don't want your damn money. You can shove it right up your ass."

For just a moment, his bloodshot eyes look so desolate, but I must have imagined it because he blinks, and his stoic mask is back. "Wildflower, if it means anything, I'm sorry for dragging you into this."

My vision goes blurry with tears. "Not as sorry as I am."

Turning on my heel, I run out of the office and back to his room where I pack my shit as fast as I can. I'm sure I'm forgetting things, but I can't stand to be here another minute. I text Baylee that I'm coming over and then I'm out the door.

My car turns over several times because I haven't driven it in so long, but thankfully, it finally starts. I fling it into reverse and take off down the driveway. The potholes are merciless. They jar my car so hard, my teeth clank.

By the time I make it to the main drag, I realize where I need to go.

Not to Baylee's.

To the cemetery.

Twenty minutes later, I have a serious sense of déjà vu.

Shivering against my brother's headstone, I tuck my legs

under my t-shirt. "I'm so mad at him, Danny. Why couldn't he love me the way I love him? The way I've always loved him?" I stare out at the dark cemetery, dejected. "I guess I need to take that job now."

Because there is no way on God's green earth I'm staying in this town. That will mean running into Rhett when he starts up with Darlene again, and my heart can't handle that.

"I'll wait until I'm settled in Florida before I tell him about the baby. I don't want him to have a crisis of conscience and take me back because I'm pregnant." Rhett might be a huge asshole, but he's a good man deep down, and he would never kick me out if he knew I was pregnant.

In fact, it would piss him the hell off to know I was at the cemetery in the middle of the night, which means I have every intention of staying right in this spot until morning.

"My new employer is going to love that I'll need maternity leave soon." I rub my temple, where a headache blooms.

I get a hoodie out of my gym bag and toss it over my legs before I yank my backpack closer and rest my head on it.

I'm exhausted and hungry and cold, but somehow manage to fall asleep.

Because I know that here, next to my brother, I'm safe.

Besides, who would come to a cemetery in the middle of the night?

Chapter Forty-Four
RHETT

My eyes fly open.

"Son of a bitch."

The throbbing in my temple isn't one I'm used to. I never drink more than a beer or two, but last night, I had a wild hair up my ass and thought several shots of whiskey would help me make sense of my financial troubles.

It didn't.

Groaning as I sit up on my father's worn couch that I don't really fit on, I squint into the early morning light.

I probably slept more last night than I have in several days put together, but the whiskey didn't do me any favors.

Then I see it in my head. That conversation with Paige comes back to me like a flickering old movie.

I see the pain in her eyes.

The pain I put there.

The rejection.

The devastation.

Did I really tell her to go to Florida?

Shutting my eyes, I try to remember our conversation last night. I cringe as I replay it in my head.

She asked if I loved her, and I asked her if she needed cash?

I pinch the bridge of my nose.

Fuck, I'm an idiot.

Truth be told, I've been an asshole since that damn festival downtown. Why do I always shut down when there's trouble? Why didn't I come home that night, scoop Paige off my fucking couch, and tuck her into bed with me? Why didn't I return for lunch the next day? Even with sick cows, even with the financial pit I'm dealing with, I owe my wife that respect.

Why did I let distance grow between us?

Since the moment I heard she got that job, I've been steeling myself for her announcement that she's changed her mind and is leaving. That she thinks I'm too hard to live with, too demanding, too difficult to love. That living out on this ranch isn't as easy as she thought it would be. That I'm about to be broke and homeless, and that's not what she signed up for.

But that's shit Amber would've spouted at me.

Those are the arguments my mother had with my father.

Those are the ghosts that linger in this house.

Not something my sweet Paige has said.

My ex-wife yanked me around more times than I can count. One day she hated me, the next she never wanted to leave. When I filed for divorce, she wailed and screamed in my face that she loved me even though she'd fucked Cash and Kacey and God knows who else.

I stagger to my feet. I need to apologize. I need to find Paige, fall on my knees, and beg for her forgiveness. If she wants to go, it will grind up what's left of my heart, but I'll understand and support her.

Except I have to tell her that's not what I want. I have to tell her that I love her with every fiber of my being, and if she'll stay, I'll do everything in my power to make her happy.

With a new resolve, I stagger down the hall and fling open the bedroom door. It looks like a tornado swept through here.

"Paige?" I peek in the bathroom. It's empty.

Really empty.

Where the hell are all her toiletries? Her lotions and makeup? That soft band of fabric she uses to hold her hair back when she washes her face?

A panic starts to take root in my gut, and I look in the closet. Her half is mostly empty. A few things still sit on hangers, but her shoes are gone. Her dresser drawer is open, and it almost looks like she stuck in a hand, grabbed a few things, and hightailed it out of here.

Because I made her feel like shit.

I made her feel like I didn't care whether she stayed or left.

How could I have said those things to her?

I make a slow circle, my eyes falling on her scattered clothes. A sock here. A t-shirt there. Would she have left so many things behind if she was gone for good?

Then my attention lands on her sewing machine on the small table in the corner that I set up for her projects.

That gives me a glimmer of hope.

Maybe she just went to Baylee's.

Paige couldn't have caught a flight overnight, could she? That would require her to drive to Austin.

There wasn't time for all that.

I don't think.

Fuck.

I rush to the living room, where my brothers look as grim as I do. It's late for us, and the fact that we're all loitering in the house at sunrise tells me they're just as fucked up about our financial situation as I am.

The only difference is they didn't just douse their marriage in kerosene and light a match.

From the couch in the living room, Gabriel hops up. "Hi, Dad."

"Hi, buddy." I spot Austin with him, playing Legos. "Did y'all eat breakfast?"

He bounces a ball on the ground, and it lands with a thud that makes my temple throb. "Uncle Beau fed us."

"Good." I turn back to my brothers and lower my voice. "Have y'all seen Paige this morning?"

Beau shakes his head. "Been waiting for you to wake up. Figured you needed a good night's rest for once so we can make a plan."

"A plan?"

I've never seen defeat in my brother's eyes, but it's there now. "Yeah. To liquidate."

Liquidate. He means sell our ranch.

Because we can't fucking afford it.

My throat is thick, and I struggle to suck in a breath. I wander to the front window where I see the empty spot where my wife's car is always parked.

Nice job, asshole. You ran her off.

The boys start throwing the ball back and forth to each other, but Austin can't catch that well, and it goes flying against the corner of the living room. I've been a big enough dick this week, so I don't bark that they shouldn't play ball in the house.

I rub the back of my neck. Everything hangs in the balance. My house, the ranch, our livestock. My relationship with Paige.

And as much as I've bled for this ranch, if Paige leaves, she's taking my heart and soul with her.

I return to my brothers at the kitchen table. "The cattle aren't the priority right now," I say for the first time in my life. Because the ranch has always been the most important thing.

Beau and Jace give each other a wary look, and Jace scrubs his stubbled face. "I don't know how much you drank last night, bro, but the state inspector shut us down indefinitely. Until we can get his damn stamp of approval."

"I'll deal with that later. Where's my phone?"

Just then, it buzzes on the counter by the coffee pot. It's Baylee.

I don't get a chance to even say her name before she shouts, "Where's Paige?"

"I'm not sure. I just realized she wasn't here."

"She texted me after midnight that she was coming over, but I was asleep and didn't see it until just now. I tried calling, but no one answered."

Fear like I've never known spreads like ice through my veins.

All the worries I've been carrying around with me for months melt away as it becomes imperative that I find Paige.

Because she's what matters here. Not this land. Not the wood and brick of this house. Not my family's stupid legacy.

My wife.

"I'll find her." I put her on speakerphone. "Do you think she could've driven back to Charming?"

"She would've told me she was doing that." Baylee whimpers. "I'm worried, Rhett."

That ball goes thudding across the kitchen, and my boys trail after it, laughing like they don't know my whole world is coming apart at the seams.

I glance at my brothers. "We'll go look for her." They immediately nod, concern etched on their faces. "Any idea where she might've gone?"

That's when the ball goes sailing across the room and clatters around in the bathroom. Gabriel streaks in there. "Uh-oh."

Beau rolls his eyes and pushes out of his chair to wrangle my kids.

Baylee and I agree to check in within an hour. I hang up and shove the phone in my back pocket. "We need to split up and drive around town. Maybe she got a flat tire." It's easy enough to do on our country roads.

Beau ushers Gabriel out of the powder room, but he has a box in his hand. "Um. Rhett."

"Where are my keys?" Jesus, I'm a mess.

"Brother." The seriousness in his voice makes me freeze.

He holds up a box. I squint until the words come into focus.

It's a pregnancy test.

There's only one woman in this house.

"Where'd you find that?"

Beau motions behind him. "The boys knocked over the trash, and it fell out."

I practically trip over myself to grab that box and shake it. "Where's the actual test?" I rush into the bathroom and turn over the trash can. Balled-up tissue falls out.

And then the small plastic wand clatters to the ground.

With my heart in my throat, I grab the damn thing.

It's positive.

The realization that I kicked out my pregnant wife is almost too much to bear. Needing support, I lean against the counter. As I think about all the ugly things I said last night, grief like I've never known spears me, making it difficult to breathe.

Paige didn't tell me that she was pregnant. She could have.

Instead, she asked me if I loved her.

And like a royal ass, I all but offered to buy her a ticket to Florida.

I have to find her. I have to track her down and beg for forgiveness.

My wife is pregnant.
With my child.

For a second, fear of repeating all the mistakes in my first marriage slams into me, but I give myself an internal shake. This is Paige we're talking about, not Amber. Paige, who's a natural mom with my boys. Paige, who loves the ranch and my kids and my stupid ass. Paige, who's never wavered in her commitment to me.

Like clouds parting in my dumb, thick skull, I realize I want this baby. More than my next breath.

But first I need my wife, safe and sound, back in my arms.

For as long as she'll have me.

"Get your keys," I shout. "We need to find Paige."

Chapter Forty-Five

PAIGE

I WAKE to the sound of low murmurs. It's pretty early, judging by the early morning light.

The cemetery doesn't open until nine. Maybe those voices belong to gravediggers. I'd better go before they catch me.

Yawning, I sit up. Every muscle in my body aches from sleeping on the ground. I slide my arms through my hoodie.

"That's not the amount we agreed on," a male voice says.

I peer over the headstone and see two men talking next to a car parked along the back alley behind a row of trees.

"The job's not done yet," a second man says. He waves his arm, and something gold catches the sun. It seems oddly familiar. "You'll get the rest when it's done."

I know that voice.

"Harlan, with all due respect..." *Harlan?* As in our banker? "I can't jeopardize my job anymore."

I squint to see better. That's definitely Harlan Calhoun.

What's he doing at the cemetery at this hour?

On reflex, I grab my phone, focus on the men talking, and hit record. If I had done this all those years ago when I spotted

Amber talking to Kacey, if Rhett could've seen what I saw, maybe he would've believed that she was cheating and not married her.

Harlan shifts, and I get a clear view of the other person. The man has a bushy black mustache.

It's the state agency guy who shut down the ranch, Mr. Dods.

Are they exchanging money? An eerie feeling settles over me, and goosebumps break out along my arms.

"It's just one last time, Eugene," Harlan says. "The Walkers are going to default, and I'll get the ranch for a song. Rhett will be begging me to buy it. Just keep those cattle out of commission until I tell you."

Blood drains from my face, and I brace myself against my brother's headstone.

"I need more money. I'm the one taking all the risks."

"Bullshit. My son's the one cutting fences in the middle of the night and moving sick cattle from his ranch to theirs."

What. The. Fuck.

Harlan was the one sabotaging the ranch this whole time. How did I not know? We invited this nice old man into our home for our wedding, and he's the asshole trying to destroy us?

Suddenly, my phone blares, and I fumble to turn it off. Shit. I look up and realize they're staring in my direction.

"Goddamn it," Harlan yells. "Get her, and shove her in the trunk. Bring her to my place when you catch her."

Shit! With my heart in my throat, I run in the opposite direction. I hurdle over tombstones and memorials and floral arrangements. *I'm sorry for running over your graves, dead people! I'll bring you all fresh flowers if I make it out of here alive.*

I nearly trip over a tree root, and my phone goes flying into a bush. I'm too afraid to slow down to grab it.

Footsteps behind me make me sprint faster, and a male voice shouts, "Stop now or this will be worse when I catch you!"

They plan to put me in a trunk. How much worse can it get? I have a feeling if I end up there, I'm not coming out. I don't recognize that voice, but I don't bother turning around to see who it is.

"No one's gonna find your body when I'm done with you, bitch!" he shouts, closer now.

Terror grips me, and I pick up speed. As I cut through the cemetery, I worry my ankle won't hold up, but it stays strong, and I pump my arms faster.

A million thoughts rush through my mind. Why didn't I tell Rhett that I loved him last night? That we could get through the hard times together if he let me? That I didn't care if he had a ranch or a straw roof over his head?

And now I might never get the chance.

Beyond this side of the cemetery is a forested area.

I sprint toward it like my life depends on it.

Because it does.

Chapter Forty-Six
RHETT

I CURSE under my breath as my truck skids across the gravel road.

Jace braces himself against his door. "Bro, don't kill us. I have a big gig coming up."

He's trying to lighten the mood, but I don't laugh. I can barely fucking breathe. "What if something happened to her?" I'll never forgive myself for upsetting Paige like that.

"She's probably sleeping in her car again. Calm your ass down. The park is just a few more blocks."

Something's wrong with that assumption, but I can't put my finger on it. As I turn down the road that will take us to the park, I remember her telling me about Danny's funeral.

She slept at the cemetery that night.

I yank the steering wheel and make a U-turn.

"Whoa." Jace slaps the dash. "The park's that way."

"She's not there." I can't explain why I know this. It's just a gut feeling.

A sense of dread gnaws at my chest. *Please let her be okay.*

About a mile down the road, I spot her car. My heart thunders as we pull up to it.

I unsnap my seatbelt and lean over my brother, who shakes his head. "She's not here."

"She's at the cemetery. It's only a block away." I throw my truck into drive and gun it.

"Why would she go there?"

"I'll tell you later." We pull up to the locked gates, and I screech to a halt in the driveway. "Come on."

I slide between two pillars, and my brother follows. Then I sprint for my best friend's plot.

I'm sorry, Danny. I said I'd take care of her, and then I fucked up royally.

As we crest a small hill, my heart sinks because I can tell she's not here.

But then my eyes snag on a backpack.

I pick it up. "This is hers." Frantic, I scan the area.

A shrill scream cuts through the silence.

Jace and I look at each other, and then we're both in a dead sprint toward the forested area that butts up to one end of the cemetery.

"Paige!" I shout. "Paige!"

"Help!" she screams.

There's a small path that winds through the trees and shrubs, and we follow that as I call out to her. "Baby, where are you?"

"Over here."

I spot the body first and nearly have a heart attack until I realize it's not my wife. Paige is huddled a few feet away.

I kneel in front of her and cradle her face, which has cuts and scrapes. "Are you hurt?"

"N-no." With a sob, she leaps into my arms.

"It's okay, baby. I got you." I look over at my brother, who's checking out the body. "Don't touch anything. If I have to bury this guy, I don't want you involved."

Paige sniffles and leans back to look at me. "You'd bury a body for me?"

"This asshole here who obviously tried to hurt you? Fuck, yes, I would."

She grabs my face. "I love you. I'm sorry we argued."

I don't bother responding. Just press my mouth to hers. "I love you, Paige. I'm so fucking sorry I was an asshole last night. Please forgive me. I don't want you to move to Florida. I know that's your dream, to coach at that camp. If you give me some time to figure out things here, maybe I can move there with you."

She hiccups. "You'd... you'd do that?"

"To be with you? Yeah." With my thumbs, I gently wipe her tears. "I'd do anything for you and our baby."

Her smile fades. "You know."

"That you're pregnant? Yes."

A frown mars her beautiful face. "Is that why you want to stay together? Because I don't want to—"

"No. I was gonna beg for your forgiveness before I realized you were pregnant."

"How did you find out? Did Baylee tell you?"

I explain how the boys knocked over the trash.

Her voice cracks. "You're not upset about the baby? I know that's not what you want. I think it happened the day I went to the ER because I threw up after I took my birth control. I'm so sorry."

I kiss her again. "Don't apologize. I was a dumbass. Of course I want this baby, if you'll do me the honor of having a family with me. A bigger one, that is." I have no fucking idea where we'll live since I'm probably going to lose the ranch, but I have a feeling that with Paige by my side, I can weather any storm. I stroke her hair. "I'm just glad you're okay. That's all that matters right now."

Her bottom lip quivers. "Because of the physical therapy you got me, I was able to outrun this asshole. Look at the path." She points behind us. "I never would've been able to run that a few months ago, much less at full speed. My ankle held up."

Turning, I take stock of the terrain and realize she's right. It's rocky and full of tree roots and rocks. Fuck. What if she hadn't fully rehabbed her ankle? What if she hadn't been an elite cheerleader and in amazing shape? "Jesus. Wildflower, I can't imagine—"

Before I can say anything else, she throws her arms around my neck and kisses me. I let out a groan and pull her closer.

Jace coughs dramatically. "I hate to break up this happy reunion, but we have a situation over here."

The guy moans, and I smirk. "Look at that. He's not dead. Guess I don't need my shovel." I look at my wife. "Who is this guy? What did he do to you? Because I can still break both his legs."

Paige bites her bottom lip. "Call the sheriff. It's bad."

A growl rumbles through me. "If this son of a bitch touched one hair on your head…"

She shakes her head. "I'm fine. This isn't about me. It's about the ranch."

I let out a sigh of relief and reach for my cell. With my other arm, I hold her close and kiss her forehead. I don't let her go as I call the sheriff.

In fact, I'm never letting her go.

Chapter Forty-Seven
PAIGE

Shivers rack my body by the time the sheriff's cruiser arrives. Rhett waves him over to the path that leads to my attacker, who's being guarded by Jace.

Rhett hasn't let go of me since he found me, and I lean into his side.

As Sheriff Reynolds strides toward us, my heart beats harder.

That fear I had when I was in high school, the worry Rhett won't believe what I saw this morning, makes my stomach hurt. I haven't told him what happened yet. I've spent the last few minutes trying to gather my thoughts.

But then I glance up at my husband, and the look he gives me makes all that negativity melt away. Leaning down, he presses a kiss to my forehead, and I hug him closer, his sturdy presence centering me.

"What do we got here?" the sheriff asks.

Rhett motions behind us. "Some asshole attacked Paige this morning. Chased her into the damn forest."

"Who is it?"

I shake my head. "I never got a good look at him."

And since the guy's face is kinda smashed from where I took

him out with a thick branch, Rhett couldn't figure out who he was.

We head down the trail to where Jace is leaning against a tree. At his feet, my attacker is moaning and holding his face.

The sheriff frowns when he sees him. "Jimmy Calhoun? That you? Or did you steal Jimmy's belt buckle?"

That's when I notice the gaudy JC belt he's sporting.

Harlan's son.

Jimmy moans. "That bitch hit me."

Rhett growls, and I grab his arm.

Sheriff Reynolds turns to me. "Can you explain what happened?"

I rush to get out the important stuff. "He's the one sabotaging the ranch. He and Harlan. They've been stealing our cattle, making them sick, and returning them to infect the others." If I understood them correctly. "He was paying off the state livestock guy, someone named Dods, to quarantine our herd so that we'd miss the auction this weekend, default on our loan, and be forced to sell him our ranch dirt cheap. I overheard them talking this morning behind the cemetery. They saw me, and then Jimmy chased me."

My husband curses under his breath, and that anxiety resurges. I'm making claims against his long-time family friend. What if Rhett doesn't believe me? Nauseous, I cross my arms.

The sheriff lifts a brow. "Those are mighty big accusations."

Rhett's nostrils flare. "You calling my wife a liar? Do you think she ran out into the forest and attacked a man for shits and giggles? If Paige says that's what happened, that's what fucking happened."

I blink, needing a moment to replay what he just said.

He believes me.

Rhett's on my side. Relief hits me so hard, I almost stagger.

Reynolds holds up his hands. "Cool your jets, Walker. I'm just saying, that's a lot to swallow." He turns to me. "You got any proof?"

"I recorded them talking, but when Jimmy started chasing me, I dropped my phone in the cemetery. I'm not sure what I got on video." It's possible the footage is grainy or it didn't capture much audio.

The sheriff calls an ambulance while Rhett and I look for my cell, which we find under a bushy hedge.

Nervously, I thumb through my phone until I get to the video.

Rhett's hand comes over mine. "You don't need to be anxious, wildflower. Whether you caught something on video or not, I got your back."

My eyes well, and I sniffle. "Thank you. You don't know how much that means to me."

He gently cradles my face. "I have a feeling I do. And I want you to know I'll never doubt you again."

I push up on my tiptoes and kiss him. "I haven't forgiven you for touching Darlene's elbow at the Moonlight Mixer and one or two other things, but we'll talk about that later."

"Darlene who? As far as I'm concerned, there's only been you."

I grin and shake my head. "You smooth talker."

The sound of an ambulance makes us turn. Jace joins us, and we watch paramedics rush into the forest.

Taking a deep breath, I play the video.

It's wobbly and a little grainy.

Harlan's voice is clear as day. Rhett stands next to me vibrating with anger, but when he hears Harlan bark to *"get her and shove her in the trunk,"* my husband loses it.

"That motherfucker."

My video kept recording after I dropped it, and you can hear me screaming in the distance as I try to outrun that asshole Jimmy.

"Jesus Christ." Rhett closes his eyes. When he opens them,

there's so much fear and grief in them. He opens his arms, and I press myself to his chest and cry because hearing that video makes me realize how close I came to losing everything. Rhett's soothing voice coos in my ear. "You're okay, baby. Take a deep breath." I do as he says while he runs his hand up and down my back. "You're so strong and courageous. You got through it. You beat these assholes at their own game."

When the sheriff sees the video, he shakes his head and unclips his CB radio. Bringing it to his mouth, he says, "I'm headed to the old Gibson farm and will need backup in fifteen minutes. Put an APB out for Harlan Calhoun."

"Sorry, Chief. Did you say Harlan Calhoun?" a male voice on the other end asks.

"Yeah."

Silence.

"Sir, are you sure? Harlan just donated to the new gym at the high school."

The sheriff rolls his eyes. "I'm not debating this." Then he turns to us. "I want the paramedics to check you out, Paige, and then y'all go home. I'll come by later this afternoon with an update."

Rhett scowls. "I want to go with you to the Gibson farm."

"Do you want this guy put away behind bars? Or do you wanna do something dumb that could get your case thrown out of court?"

I tug on my husband's arm. "Let's go home. I'm starving." I don't know if it was the running or crying, but I'm ready to eat.

His eyes soften and his hand goes to my belly. "Are you sure you're okay?"

I'm having Rhett's baby. The reminder makes the residual fear from this morning recede. This pregnancy is inconvenient and a huge shock, but I couldn't be happier about it. I put my hand over his. "I think so. I just got scraped up when I was running in the forest."

Jace jumps on his brother. "Guess we're having another little Walker to add to our collection of wildings." He hugs me. "Congrats, sister."

"Thank you." I look over at Danny's headstone. "Can I get a minute?"

Rhett immediately understands. "We'll wait over here, sweetheart."

I nod and walk over to my mom and brother's headstones. Kneeling down, I put my hand on Danny's grave. "I just wanted to let you know that I'll be okay. Rhett's got me, and so do his brothers. You don't need to worry about me anymore."

Just then, the clouds part, and the sun shines through the cemetery, and in my heart, I know Danny heard me.

Chapter Forty-Eight

PAIGE

Rhett has his rough palm resting protectively on my thigh as he drives. "Tacos?" he asks. "Or do you feel like something else?"

"That's fine." I yawn, exhausted.

It's just us now. Beau swung by to pick up Jace, and they're driving over to the police station to give their statements about the sick cattle and Mr. Dods.

"Are you sure you don't need to go with your brothers?"

"They can handle it. You're my priority right now. I can give my statement after I've fed you." He smacks the steering wheel. "I still can't believe Harlan was behind this. He had the nerve to pull me aside at the Moonlight Mixer to ask if I knew you had a boyfriend until recently."

"Are you serious?"

"He was acting like some kind of father figure who was looking out for me." Rhett shakes his head. "And the whole time, he was plotting our demise."

"At least we figured it out in time to do something about it."

Glancing over, he reaches for my hand and kisses the back of it. "*You* figured it out. I'm hoping the bank will give me an extension given the circumstances."

"You going to talk to them on Monday?"

"Yup." He squeezes my hand. "Want to come with me? I'll ask the sheriff for a copy of his report to take with us. Maybe if they hear what you saw, they'll give me a few weeks to untangle this mess."

I'm so relieved he's fighting for the ranch again. "I'd be happy to help however I can."

He pulls up to the Guac 'N' Roll food truck and orders us breakfast.

On our way home, I motion to a golden field full of wildflowers. "Can we eat over here? It's so pretty." I'm also hoping to have some privacy so we can talk about what happened at the Moonlight Mixer.

He pulls over and parks. I start to open the paper bag with our food, but Rhett motions to the bed of the truck. "C'mon. Let's have a picnic."

Coming around my side, he helps me hop out, then lowers the tailgate, picks me up, and sets me on the back of his truck. With our food between us, we stare out at the horizon.

I take a few bites of my taco as I try to gather my thoughts. The more I think about that night at the Mixer, the more upset I get.

The old me would shove down the hurt and avoid this conversation altogether, but if I want this marriage to work, I can't be afraid to say what I need to. No more sneaking out of the ranch in the middle of the night.

"You okay?" he asks.

"Yeah. Just... I want to clear the air before we head back to the ranch."

With a frown, he sets down his food. "I know I've been an asshole this week. I'm sorry."

"You're grumpy. You've always been grumpy. I don't have a problem with that."

"But I shouldn't have yelled at you when you told me to talk to Harlan. You were just trying to help."

"My feelings were really hurt, but I know you were going through a lot."

He reaches for my hand and kisses my palm. "That's no excuse."

"When you told me to go to Florida, I wanted to crawl under a rock."

"Baby." He tries to tug me close, but I pull my hand back. For a moment, he squeezes his eyes shut. When he opens them, I see a fresh wave of regret behind them. "I thought my ship was sinking, that I was about to lose the ranch and had nothing to offer you, but I figured you still had a chance to achieve your dream. You could take that coaching position and do what you set out to do when we agreed to get married."

That makes sense, actually. "You were really drunk last night."

"Which was stupid. I don't want to travel down that road. It messed up my father and his marriage to my mother. I won't turn to booze again."

I nod. That's good to know.

There's still one more thing that's really bothering me. I take a deep breath. "I was pretty humiliated when you had that discussion with Darlene at the festival. Everyone heard her freaking out and accusing you of cheating on her with me."

"Sweetheart, you know it wasn't like that. She and I were clear from the beginning that we were just hooking up."

It's scary to be this vulnerable, but I think it's important to get everything on the table. "When you said y'all screwed in your truck, I felt like our one time when we did that wasn't special anymore. Like it was just a typical Friday evening for you."

"Shit. Wildflower, I'm sorry." He groans and scrubs his face. "You have to know you and Darlene mean completely different things to me. Having sex with her there was about convenience. I pulled over that day with you because I can't keep my hands off you. Because I can't get enough of you. Because I'm going a little crazy with how much I want you. Every single time I hop in my truck now, I think about that afternoon with you."

"Really?"

"Swear to God."

The sincerity in his gaze smooths over my ruffled feathers a little.

I bite my bottom lip. "Why didn't you talk to her and let her know you and I were together?"

"She always called at the worst possible time. When I was working or with the kids." He shrugs. "It just didn't seem like a priority. When I returned her calls, I'd get voice mail, and I just felt like an asshole trying to leave a message."

I chuckle. I shouldn't laugh, but he looks adorable with that frown on his face. "For the record, I don't care how dumb you feel, I want you to leave messages on my voice mail when we need to talk."

He nods. "I know this. And I promise I'll try to be better about that."

"Thank you." I swallow past the nervousness, needing to know more. "So you weren't keeping Darlene on the back burner in case you and I didn't work out?"

His head jerks back. "No, of course not. Fucking Trig McAllister. I should kick his ass for saying that." He sets our food aside and pulls me into his lap. "Paige, get this into your pretty head. I haven't thought about another woman since I yanked you out of your car and threw you over my shoulder. You've consumed all my thoughts. And I might have wavered about my ability to be married again, but that had everything to do with my baggage, not with you. You're fucking perfect. Let me be clear—I'm all in here. You, me, our kids, our marriage? That's everything to me."

I wrap my arms around his broad shoulders. "You swear you don't regret marrying me?"

His hand cradles my face, and his thumb grazes my cheek.

"How could I regret the best thing to ever happen to me?" He kisses me softly. "While we're clearing the air, can I ask a few favors?"

"Sure."

"One of the reasons I've been against having more children is because Amber had severe postpartum depression and refused to get help."

His ex has always seemed temperamental. I can only imagine how much worse that got with PPD. "I had no idea."

"It would kill me to watch you go through something similar. Once we have the baby, I want you to let me know if you're not feeling right. I swear I'll be there for midnight feedings and diaper changes and every doctor appointment. But please communicate if you're feeling off or overwhelmed, so I can get you more rest or vitamins or medicine—whatever you need. I don't want you to be afraid to share what's going on with you, the good, the bad, and the ugly. I'm here for all of it."

My eyes sting, and I blink to clear them. His reluctance to have more kids makes so much sense now. "I can do that."

He takes a relieved breath, and his lips tilt up in a crooked smile. "Thank you."

It's so easy to make him happy. I cradle his handsome face in my palm. "Was there something else you wanted to talk about?"

"Just one more thing. Can you promise me you won't have any more solo sleepovers in the cemetery? If you want, I'll go with you, and if you're pissed off at me for some reason, I'll sleep several feet away. But it's not safe for you to do that by yourself, and it would fucking kill me if anything happened to you."

"I promise. I meant to go to Baylee's, but I was upset and talking to Danny last night seemed like a good idea at the time."

"That's my fault. I might've been dealing with sick cattle, but that's no excuse. This whole thing with us got bad because we needed to talk after the festival. I should've made that a priority. I promise I won't let the ranch take precedence over our relationship again. I see now that's my way to avoid shit, and it ends here."

Shifting, I straddle him. "You know how you said that cheer job was my dream? You have to know that's not really true. Being your wife, making a life on the ranch, us having kids—that's my dream. It's always been my dream, if I'm being honest. If I can coach on the side and maybe do some custom sewing projects for my friends, I'll have everything I ever wanted."

"I love you, Paige, and I have no fucking idea what I've done to deserve you, but I'm not letting go."

"Promise?" I kiss him.

He pulls me closer. "Cross my heart." Then he pats my ass. "Now eat that taco so I can take you home and enjoy *your* taco."

I bust out laughing, and he smiles, a devilish grin on his face.

"I'm going to hold you to that promise."

Chapter Forty-Nine
PAIGE

An hour later, I groan as Rhett washes my hair. "You have magical hands, husband."

"It's my pleasure, wife." His mouth grazes my neck as he presses against my back, and he sucks on my pulse, sending little bolts of pleasure shooting through my body. "I've never washed a woman's hair before, but I think we should add this to our daily routine. I love getting you soapy."

His giant hand grips my breast, and I stretch up to rake my fingers through his hair and push my ass back against his erection. "I'm at your beck and call."

"Let's finish your hair before I bend you over and fuck you." His gruff voice in my ear makes me shiver.

"That's a problem why?" My core pulses at the thought.

"I'm trying to do a good job here."

Closing my eyes, I smile. He rinses my hair, conditions it, then sprays me off, taking extra time to wash off my boobs. Then he snakes a hand between my legs and groans. "Fuck, you're so wet."

I turn to face him and run my hands over the swells of my breasts while he groans again. "Are you going to do something about that?"

Gripping himself, he shuttles his hand over his swollen cock. "I had every intention of letting you take a nap first. I wanted to make love to you in a bed. Show you I could be gentle and prove I'm not a caveman."

Tossing my arms over his shoulders, I push up on my toes to kiss him. "Maybe I like that caveman." I hike my leg over his hip, and he takes the hint and pulls me up to his waist.

I scramble for purchase on his body, and he pulls me closer and whispers, "I got you."

He does, doesn't he? He knew I was at the cemetery this morning. No one told him that. He and I are a work in progress, but there's a part of him that understands me in a way no one else ever will.

The joy I didn't let myself feel when we got married filters through me, like the sun breaking through the clouds.

Rhett is mine. He will always be mine. And I'm his.

Turning, he leans me against the tile, and I nip his bottom lip. "Please fuck me, husband."

"I'm yours to command, wife." He holds me by my ass and lines himself up to my opening. Our eyes meet as he slowly slides into me. I see love shining back at me. Love and so much affection.

My breath catches as he works his way into me.

The stretch, the feel of him, is drugging. He's almost too much. Almost too big. But he doesn't rush. He takes his time until he bottoms out, and we both moan.

This connection is magical. It's not just the sex. It's not just how our bodies fit together or the places he touches me. It's not the physical that makes our bond so incredible.

It's the soul-deep connection I've never had with anyone else.

He squeezes me tight. "You're everything to me, Paige. I love you."

"I love you too."

He kisses me long and slow as he moves in and out of my

body. We come together beneath the steamy water with quiet moans until we shatter.

Shaking in his arms, I press my face into his shoulder, and he kisses my temple. "You know, if I hadn't already put a baby in you, I'd be wanting to now."

Leaning back, I grin. "I love a goal-oriented man. Looks like you hit your target without even trying."

He winks. "I love hitting your target."

Drowsy, I yawn and reach for Rhett, but his side of the bed is empty. A minute later, the bedroom door opens, and he pokes his head in.

"Hey, baby. You get a good nap?"

"Yes." I sit up. "When did you get up?"

"About two hours ago. Talked to the sheriff. He said to call him because he has a few questions." He sits on the edge of the bed. "They arrested Harlan and his son, and they issued an arrest warrant for Dods."

"Oh, my God. That's great news."

He wraps his arm around my shoulders. "Because of what you recorded on your phone, I have another shot at saving this ranch. I had Jace inspect the fence again, and he found where Jimmy must've mended it after sneaking sick steer back onto our property last week."

"It's crazy how far they went to screw with us." I nuzzle against him. "I'm so happy everything is working out."

Rhett kisses the top of my head. "Brought you some coffee. Sorry it's decaf. You can't have full-caf, right?"

"Damn. That's right," I say as he hands me the mug. "This smells good though."

"We need to make an OBGYN appointment, don't we?"

I nod. "Would you... would you like to go with me? I mean, you don't have to come. I know you're busy."

"I'm never too busy for you. I know I've had the wrong priorities, but I aim to change that." He kisses me again. "I swear, I'll never miss a chance to see our baby on an ultrasound."

Our baby. I'm having Rhett's baby. I'm ridiculously happy about that.

"Do the boys know yet?"

He shakes his head. "They might've been the ones to uncover the pregnancy test, but they were too busy playing to take notice."

"Will they be okay when they hear the news? I know this might be hard for them."

"They'll be fine. Now that they're not going back and forth to their mother's place, they seem a lot more settled. But we can hold off on telling them for a bit."

"I hope we can be one big, happy family. I want Austin and Gabriel to know they're just as important as any new additions."

He smiles. "Thanks, wildflower. That means a lot to me."

"Will Amber freak out when she hears we're having a baby?"

"Probably, but it's high time she gets a grip on her life. She has to learn she can't keep throwing tantrums. She used to get me all twisted up and upset, and now I realize it was her way of getting what she wanted. Well, I'm over it. She can either act like an adult or fuck off."

I'm relieved to know that her hold on him is broken.

Needing to wake up, I take a sip of coffee, and my stomach rumbles. "How am I hungry again? Didn't we just have breakfast?"

"It's been a while since you ate." He gives me a naughty grin. "Plus, maybe you worked up an appetite in the shower."

My eyes go a little hazy with the memory. "That's true." I check out my husband, who's sporting his usual attire—a t-shirt, jeans, and boots, plus that sexy backwards baseball cap.

"Wife, if you keep looking at me like that, we're never gonna leave the bedroom today."

"Why is this a problem?" It must be the pregnancy hormones because I'm ready to pounce on him again.

"Because half the town is in our living room right now, wanting to see you."

"What? Why?"

He brushes a strand of hair out of my eyes. "People heard what happened, that you were attacked, and now we have a table full of casseroles and baked goods. Sylvia and Baylee have been here for a while. They wanted to see you with their own eyes. Apparently, me saying you're fine isn't enough."

I chuckle. "Well, let's not worry them. Give me five minutes to get dressed."

His brow lifts. "Can I watch?"

Playfully, I shove him. "Not if you want me to greet our guests."

"Fine," he grumbles.

Once I get changed, I head out to join him in the living room. My eyes widen when I see so many people. I thought he was joking when he said I had a lot of visitors. Judge Tate is here, Ty, Mabel from the ice cream shop, Mrs. Nash from the trading post, several of my high school teachers, and of course Baylee and Aunt Syl.

But before I get a chance to greet anyone, Gabriel and Austin tackle me in hugs. "Are you okay?" Gabe asks.

I lean down to squeeze them both. "I'm just a little scratched up. That's all."

"We were worried," he says quietly while Austin nods.

"Aww, boys. I'm fine. I promise." How sweet are these two? As I have them both in my arms, my eyes meet Rhett's, and he winks.

Gabriel scratches the back of his head. "Can we still tumble this week?"

"I might need a few days to rest up, but then I should be good to go."

The grin he gives me makes my heart so happy. When the boys run off, Baylee and Aunt Syl wrap me up in hugs.

"*Mija*, I'm so glad you weren't hurt," Aunt Syl says. "*Gracias a Dios.* I've never liked Harlan Calhoun. I can't believe that man." Then she lets out a string of curses in Spanish that makes Baylee laugh.

My best friend shakes me. "You scared me to death this morning. When I saw your message from last night and realized you never came over, I nearly had a heart attack."

"I'm sorry. I never meant to worry you."

Sylvia squints at me. "I'm assuming by the beard burn on your neck that you and your husband made up."

I slap my hand on my neck. "Aunt Syl!" I chuckle. "Yes, we're in a good place now."

She lowers her voice. "And did I hear we'll have a stork visit soon?"

"Yes, but we haven't told anyone yet. Rhett's brothers and you guys are the only ones who know."

"This is so exciting! My lips are sealed." She zips her hand across her mouth.

I glance around the living room. "I'm surprised so many people came out today."

Baylee snorts. "I'm not. Everyone loves you."

Syl nods and takes my hand. "This town has missed you."

My eyes get watery. "When people showed up for our wedding, I thought they only came because they were nosy. But seeing everyone today, I think I was wrong." And for the last few days, I've been worried everyone judged me because of what Darlene said at the Moonlight Mixer, but based on the relieved looks on people's faces when they see me, they don't care about the gossip.

"We're a little nosy," Sylvia admits with a grin. "But mostly, we care about you. I know you went through a lot in high school, and I think that distorted your perception of Wild Heart. It's a good town with good people. And it's a great place to raise a family, which you'll soon learn."

Rhett comes up behind me and wraps his arm around my shoulders. "Can I have my wife back now?"

Sylvia smacks him. "Oh, hush."

He chuckles. "Glad you two could make it today."

She glances between me and Rhett. "In case I haven't said it, y'all make an adorable couple. And Rhett?"

"Yes, ma'am?"

"I'm glad you pulled your head out of your ass."

My eyes widen, and Rhett chuckles again. "Never said I was perfect, but I'm trying."

Sylvia nods. "I can see that. And I'm happy for y'all. Now stop hogging Paige, and let her talk to the rest of your guests."

My husband's chest shakes with laughter. "Yes, ma'am."

As I chat with our neighbors and friends, my heart is full. I'm really grateful to have so much support.

Now I just need to get through Monday when we meet with the bank. I say a little prayer that we'll be able to get the extension Rhett needs to untangle this mess that Harlan made.

Chapter Fifty

RHETT

The ride to Cornerstone Bank & Trust is quiet. Paige's leg keeps shaking, and I reach over and put my hand on it.

"It'll be okay." It has to be okay. Given the fact that Harlan tried to rip me off, the bank has to have some flexibility, don't they?

She nods. "It'll be okay."

Fuck, she's scared this won't work out either.

We pull up to Cornerstone, and I turn off my truck. After I help Paige out, I take her hand. "Whatever happens, I want you to know that we're in this together. If I default on this loan, maybe they'll fine me or something but still give me time to pay it back."

"I'm on board with that, but I'm not going down without a fight."

I grin at my beautiful, feisty woman. "You make a damn good rancher's wife."

That gets me a beaming smile. "I got your back, babe."

Leaning down, I kiss her. "Thank you, darling."

Inside, Paige and I take a seat on that bench in front of

Harlan's old office. Someone's in there, but he's facing the back windows. When he swivels his chair around, I let out a curse.

Paige turns to me. "What's wrong?" I motion to the douchebag behind the desk, and her eyes widen. "Are you serious? We have to deal with Kacey Miller? This is bullshit."

She looks so incensed, I almost laugh, but the fact that I now have to argue my case with my ex-wife's former lover is sobering.

I'm adjusting my tie for the tenth time when Paige whispers, "Do you feel bad for accusing the McAllisters of trying to sabotage our ranch?"

"Hell, no. Cash would take my ranch in a heartbeat if he could." As I think back about the last few months, I admit it was dumb to charge over there like an angry bull. My wife was right to make me stand down and let the sheriff investigate.

I lean over and kiss her temple. Paige is level-headed. I need that in my life.

"Is Isaiah really coming home for Christmas?" she asks. "I don't think I've seen him since I was a kid."

"I'm shocked too, but he swears he'll be here." I figure there's a fifty-fifty chance my elusive brother actually returns.

Kacey's assistant finally tells us we can go in, and I take my wife's hand in mine. She squeezes it hard. "You got this, Rhett. Don't let this little weasel win."

A smarmy grin stretches across Kacey's mouth. "Howdy, Rhett. How's it going? I hear you've had some trouble with your loan."

"I've had trouble with the president of your bank trying to sabotage my ranch."

He tilts his head. "Well, now that's hearsay until he's tried in court, isn't it?"

That's how he wants to play it? "Harlan, his son, and the Texas Livestock Commission investigator all got arrested last week. I have copies of the arrest warrants from the sheriff, and my wife has a video of Harlan basically admitting to his crimes. Would you like to watch it?"

He waves it off. "That doesn't have any bearing on your ability to repay that bridge loan our bank extended to you."

"It does when Harlan stole my cattle, got them sick, and then paid off someone at the state to shut down my ranch so I couldn't sell them at auction."

Kacey shrugs. "That's not really my problem. You either repay that loan today as you agreed to do or you default and we seize all of the assets you listed on the loan application."

I have a sudden fantasy of leaping over the desk and strangling this little piece of shit.

My wife growls, and I place my hand over her leg to reassure her. "Kacey," she says with a strange nonchalance in her voice. "Did you have a nice time at the Moonlight Mixer?"

His brows furrow. "I guess. Why?"

"I saw a funny thing out in the parking lot that night."

He stills. "What are you talking about?"

"You mean you don't remember getting a blow job from Prescott's wife?"

What the hell is she talking about?

The douchebag straightens his tie. "I think you have me mistaken for someone else."

"Really? So if I strolled upstairs to your boss's office and mentioned this, do you think he's going to be confused too? Do you think he'll care that his wife was sucking your dick that night?" His eyes widen, and then Paige taps her chin. "Better yet, what if I called Georgia Hightower at the *Gazette* and mentioned this to her? You know how much she loves a good story. That way, we can get the whole town in on this juicy situation."

Kacey starts coughing. "I'm sure I have no idea what you're talking about, but I've reconsidered your loan situation. Maybe we can work something out. What if I gave you a three-week extension, Rhett? Would that be long enough to take your cattle to auction? I don't want to be unreasonable, and you made a good point about Harlan causing your troubles to begin with."

I give him a shit-eating grin. "Three weeks should work."

Paige taps on his desk. "We'd like the extension in writing. Today. Before we leave."

Kacey tugs at his tie. "That shouldn't be a problem."

When we walk out of the bank an hour later, I press her against my truck and kiss her. "How'd you know Kacey was fucking Tiffany Calhoun?"

"I saw it with my own two eyes. Only I wasn't sure who he was messing around with. Fortunately, my best friend hears everything at the salon, and Baylee filled me in on the scuttlebutt when she drove me home that night."

My wife is a fucking genius.

I'm gonna build her a bigger chicken coop.

EPILOGUE
PAIGE

Did I say I wanted to have lots of babies? Holy shit, contractions hurt like a bitch. One might be enough. At least we got our driveway regraded, so when Rhett races down the road, my guts don't fall out.

I shut my eyes and grit my way through another contraction. "How much longer?"

Rhett hums. "Might be a few minutes. Don't worry. I'll get you there in time."

He's remarkably calm. It's hard to believe this is the same man who didn't want more children. In the last few months, he cleared out his father's office, painted it, set up the crib, and even had his friend Brady paint a field of wildflowers across one wall.

Thanks to that video I took of Harlan, we were able to get the Texas Livestock Commission out again to give our cattle a bill of clean health two weeks after he was arrested. We got them to auction and repaid our loan.

Harlan, his son Jimmy, and Eugene Dods are awaiting trial for conspiring to defraud several ranchers out of their property, which they planned to lease for mining rights.

Apparently, we have a huge high-quality quartz reserve on our ranch, which the Calhouns discovered when they were scouting the Gibson property two years ago. These kinds of gems are in demand for manufacturing semiconductors.

But Harlan definitely played the long game, offering Rhett's father the second mortgage through an affiliate bank and then making sure the statements went to the nursing home. While we're not totally sure what Gus did with those funds, we suspect he blew them gambling online.

I try not to dwell on what happened because it still upsets me. The lengths the Calhouns went to acquire our property are jaw-dropping. Jimmy even messed with our trailer last spring so Rhett couldn't take any animals to auction.

Because Jimmy didn't want to go down for attempted murder when he chased me, presumably to throw me in a damn trunk, he spilled the beans on all the dastardly things his father was doing. Including why Harlan offered Rhett the bridge loan when he already had the Walkers in so much debt. Harlan thought the second mortgage might be contested since Gus was in a nursing home when he signed off on that paperwork, but getting Rhett wrapped up in financial trouble would close that final loophole.

However, the investigation cleared Prescott of any wrongdoing. As far as I know, Marcus wasn't involved either.

On a side note, the younger Calhoun brother recently fired Kacey after he received an anonymous tip that his employee was banging his wife Tiffany. Cough, cough.

Once the dust settled from Harlan's maniacal attempt to steal our ranch, Rhett and I settled into married life. We've been doing a better job communicating, especially when we're stressed or worried. I found a few marriage podcasts that we listen to that have been helpful, and we always make sure to discuss anything that's been bothering us before bed so it doesn't fester.

Between coaching at All-Star Cheer and sewing custom outfits for the NFL wives that Abby introduced me to, I've been pretty busy. I've saved up quite the nest egg from all those custom jobs.

I'm so happy to not be that penniless girl I was a year ago. I can buy all the chickens I want.

Or, in this case, sheep.

Rhett agreed investing in sheep is a fantastic way to weather downturns in cattle prices. Since I have the funds, I'm buying the flock. In return, I'm becoming an official co-owner of the Walker Ranch with my husband and his brothers.

We crawl to a standstill, and I growl. We're stuck in traffic. There's never traffic in Wild Heart, but there is today. "Don't tell me today's the cowboy parade."

He squeezes my hand. "Okay, I won't tell you."

"Rhett."

My husband chuckles, then lifts my hand to his mouth and presses a kiss to my palm. "It'll be okay. I promise. Do you know how many calves I've delivered over the years? It's gotta be hundreds."

My expression goes flat. "Am I the cow in this analogy?"

He laughs. "Sweetheart, I would never say such a thing. Swear to God, you're all baby. Well, and tits. You've got really big tits now."

He makes a face to show me how excited he is about my boobs, and I chuckle. "Don't make me laugh. My guts feel like they're going to explode."

His eyes grow serious. "If I could take that pain away from you, I would do it in a heartbeat. But since I can't, let's focus on the moment we meet our daughter. She'll have your beautiful eyes and cute little nose. All your sweetness and sass. She'll have her brothers and uncles wrapped around her pinky. I'll probably have to threaten the boys who come sniffing around her with bodily harm if they touch her."

He's so sweet. I love my husband. I'm about to tell him that when a contraction tries to split my body in two, and I cry out.

He curses under his breath. Then he rolls down the window

and yells, "Hey, y'all! Paige needs to get to the hospital. The baby's coming!"

A cheer rises up from the sidewalk, and I peer out to see our neighbors and friends waving at me. They pause the cowboy parade so we can cross the street.

Panting, I wipe my sweaty forehead. "I don't know whether I should be embarrassed or impressed."

He smirks. "Impressed, definitely."

Once we reach the other side of the street, he guns it, and we barrel through town.

I glance at my phone where I'm tracking my contractions. "Um. So this is weird."

He glances at me as he takes a turn. "What's weird?"

"My contractions were coming every five minutes, but now they're a minute apart."

He growls. "I knew we should've left sooner."

"I thought it was false labor again." He's already rushed me to the hospital three other times. "I need to push."

"Hang on."

"No," I groan. "I can't fucking hang on. Our baby is tunneling her way through my vagina *right now*."

"We're almost there, Paige. One more minute."

I don't think I have a minute. Tears stream down my face as I prepare myself to deliver this kid in my husband's truck.

But then he stops the vehicle, hops out, and starts yelling. My door opens and he scoops me up.

I wave at my body. "She's here. I feel her head."

His eyes widen, but he somehow manages to keep his cool. He sets me down. "Hang on to the truck." After he closes the door, I grip the handle.

"Can I pull down your shorts?"

"Do it." I glance around. The parking lot is pretty empty, and my t-shirt is on the long side, but I'm in too much pain to care.

He pushes down my shorts and undies as I curse myself for not leaving for the hospital sooner.

A nurse runs toward us with a wheelchair, but she's too late. I squat and push because my baby is coming right the fuck now. I screech, "She's here!"

My husband reaches between my legs with one hand, holds onto me with the other, and looks in my eyes. "I got you. And I've got her. Do your thing, sweetheart. Breathe through it, like we learned in Lamaze class."

He mimics the breaths, and I breathe with him. My husband did every class with me and read all the baby books even though this is his third child. The confidence radiating from him calms me down immediately.

I can do this.

I push again.

My legs shake with the pressure and pain. I blink, and a second later, there she is, our sweet, precious baby, who lets out an angry howl.

"Oh, my God. She's beautiful." A sob escapes me, and Rhett presses a kiss to my sweaty forehead.

"You did great, Paige. She's perfect." My husband whips off his shirt, wipes her little face, and then wraps it around her. The nurse takes a minute to check on the baby and then helps me into the wheelchair.

"Why do you look like that"—I wave a hand around my thirst trap of a husband—"and I look like this?" A limp strand of hair hangs in my face, and I blow it away.

Rhett gives me a crooked grin. "You're gorgeous and so fucking strong. I'm so proud of you." He kisses me.

The nurse covers my lap with a blanket and wheels me inside while my husband carries our daughter.

After the doctors check me and the baby, we get admitted and moved to a room so we can be observed for two days.

Rhett's perched on the bed next to me as we watch our little sweetheart. I kiss her fuzzy head. "Welcome to the world, Daniella."

I glance up at my husband, who beams a proud smile. "You did good, Mama. She's incredible. Just like you."

An hour later, my best friend blows through our door. She's carrying a tower of balloons, a basket of mommy gifts, and an armful of flowers. The moment she sees Ella, she bursts into tears.

"I can't believe you had a baby. I love her already." She leans over to hug me and kiss the top of Ella's head.

When Rhett ducks into the hallway to make a phone call, she whispers, "I have a secret."

"He proposed!"

"Sadly, no." She sighs.

I take her hand in mine. "Give it time. Y'all just moved in together."

Baylee nods slowly. "It's just... I don't have that much time... before the baby arrives."

My eyes widen. "You're pregnant?"

"Shh!" She glances at the door. "I haven't told anyone. You're the only person who knows."

I tilt my head. "Except Sean, right?"

Her eyes go squinty. "I haven't gotten the nerve to tell him yet."

"Baylee Reyes. Since when have you ever wussed out on a confrontation?"

Her shoulders slump. "Once or twice, I'm afraid."

She looks so dejected, it breaks my heart. I pull her into a hug. "Don't squish the baby."

My best friend chuckles. "I would never squish our princess." She coos at Daniella. "On the bright side, we always said we wanted to have kids at the same time."

A knot forms in my throat. "Our children will grow up together."

We both make a silly squeal just as Rhett pops back into the room. He lifts a brow. "I'm afraid to ask."

"Don't ask," I agree. "I'm sworn to secrecy."

Baylee nods. "We've got the sisterhood of silence over here."

He chuckles. "I would never do anything to infringe upon the sisterhood."

Leaning over, he kisses me, and I swoon. "You did good today, husband."

He kisses me again. "You kicked ass today, wife."

Baylee rolls her eyes. "Y'all are kinda disgusting. No wonder you got preggers weeks after your wedding. Now give me this baby so she can get to know her auntie Bay."

An hour after Baylee's visit, Ty busts through the door. "Where's my beautiful niece?" His whole face lights up when he sees her. "She's gorgeous, Paige. You did good."

In the last few months, Ty and I have spent more time together, grabbing lunch and hanging out. Rhett's invited him over several times for dinner, and we're finally at a place where Ty feels like family should. It helps that he never brings Irma around.

No sooner does Ty leave than Rhett's brothers stream in one at a time, carrying flowers and stuffed animals and chocolate. I make grabby hands for the sweet treats as they pass my daughter around.

"She's a beauty," Beau says as he runs his finger over her crown of auburn hair.

Gabriel, who's sitting on the hospital bed with me, tugs on my gown. "Can I hold her?"

"Sure." I hug him. "I'm sure she'd love to be held by her big brothers."

Austin jumps up and down. "I wanna hold her too."

I pat the bed. "Come sit with me, and I'll show you how to do it. You always have to hold her head."

His brows furrow adorably. "Why? Does it come off?"

I snort. "No, but she's delicate."

Gabriel's shoulders slump. "So we can't take her fishing yet?"

"Not yet, but soon." I glance at my husband, who's giving me that look, the one that makes babies grow in my belly. "Soon, she'll be chasing after y'all and wanting to do all the things that you and your friends do." I remember the long days of running after Danny and Rhett. How they never made me feel unwelcome. How Rhett used to make me crowns of wildflowers.

The thought makes my eyes burn.

My husband lifts Austin and the two of them sit on the other side of me. He wraps me with his strong arm and kisses the top of my head. Then he whispers, "I have a feeling Danny is really happy today."

I swallow past the knot in my throat and lean into his strong chest. "Thank you. I needed to hear that."

Later, when it's just me, Ella, and Rhett, he stretches out next to me as I feed the baby.

"She's a hungry little thing," he says as she grips his finger.

"The nurse says she has a great appetite."

When she's done eating, he places her on his shoulder and burps her like a pro. After she lets out a sleepy yawn, he wraps her like a burrito and tucks her in the bassinet next to my bed.

"Nice job, Daddy. You're a natural."

His eyes go hot. "Daddy, huh?"

I chuckle. "We're gonna have to hold off on some of our shenanigans for a while so my lady parts can heal, but I do love oral TLC."

He laces our hands together. "As much as I would love to take you up on that, doesn't seem fair that I should be getting some while you have to recuperate."

"But if I offer, that's my way of telling you I'm happy to do it. And personally, I think if your wife wants to go down on you, you should let her."

He chuckles. "How about I keep track of all the head you give me so I can reciprocate when you're up for it?"

My laughter joins his. "I'm sure we can work something out."

Content, I lean against him and close my eyes. But then he clears his throat, and I turn to look at him.

"I have something for you. I've been waiting for everyone to leave."

There's a seriousness in his tone that has me worried. "What's wrong?"

"Nothing's wrong." He brushes the hair out of my face. "I just want you to know how much I love you. How building this family with you makes me happy in a way I didn't know was possible."

Cue the tears. "I'm really happy too."

"Oh, baby, don't cry." He pulls me closer. "I told myself I was gonna do this right, so you gotta stop crying."

I sniffle. "Okay. I'm good."

Gently, he wipes my tears. Then he gets up out of the bed, reaches into his back pocket, and pulls out a little black box.

When he goes down on one knee, my mouth drops open.

"Paige, I know we're already married, but I don't feel right about how we did things. You're the mother of my children, and you've opened your heart to Austin and Gabriel and my idiot brothers." I chuckle, and he smiles and grabs my hand and kisses it. "You've always been important to me, but in the last year, you've become my entire world. You helped me save the ranch and my family's legacy. You brought me back to life when I didn't know I wasn't really living. You're the bravest, sweetest, and most caring woman I've ever known, and I'm so fucking honored you're mine." He clears his throat. "I bought you an engagement ring because we didn't get to do that the first time around."

He takes it out and slides it up my finger, where it sits against my wedding band. "It's beautiful." I'm choked up, but somehow manage to keep it together. "I love it, but you didn't need to do this. I'm already yours."

"I wanted to give you something to know that I'm all in on this with you. Every step of the way. I was hoping we could renew our vows. Maybe at our one-year anniversary this summer. Not for the town or our neighbors or the gossip column, but something for you and me. Something the boys can be a part of because they love you. Something just for us and our closest friends."

A tear slips down my cheek, and I tug on his arm. He slides up next to me on the bed. "You've been stealing my heart at every turn since I was a girl. It's always belonged to you." I sniffle. "I'd be honored to marry you again."

He smiles and kisses me. "Good. 'Cause you're stuck with me now."

BONUS SCENE ONE

Three Years Later

RHETT

"Dad?" Austin asks as he shovels a fistful of popcorn in his mouth.

"Don't talk until you chew all that. Don't want you to choke."

He nods and chews. While I wait for him to gulp that down, I take a bite of my nachos as we sit in the stands at the high school football game.

On my other side, Ella jumps up and down on her chair. "Hi, Mommy!" Down on the field, my gorgeous wife waves at us, and my daughter lifts her pom-poms in the air.

My daughter is decked out in a mini-cheer outfit just like the girls on the field. My wife hand-stitched the costume, and Ella is obsessed with it.

"Honey, sit down. I don't want you to fall."

She holds out her hand, and I help her sit. "Thank you."

"You're welcome, princess."

Austin tugs on my shirt. "When I get bigger, can I tumble at the games like Gabe?"

"Sure thing." Because Paige coaches the cheerleading squad at the high school now, she also pulls in the different cohorts from

All-Star Cheer to do halftime exhibitions. "Think you still might want to tumble if Gabe decides to do football next year?"

Austin thinks about that as he steals one of my chips. "Maybe."

"There's no rush to figure it out. Do what you love. I'll support you either way."

He gives me a big grin that's dripping in nacho cheese, and I chuckle.

Because it's alumni night, the stands are packed with people I went to high school with. My ex-wife is here too, sitting in another section. When we make eye contact, we both nod politely.

"Austin, your mom's here. Wanna go say hi?"

He shrugs. "I don't wanna miss Mommy's thing."

Amber is Mom, and Paige is Mommy. That was Austin's decision. Gabriel calls my ex by her first name, and Paige is Mom. Again, his decision.

Things were rough for a while with Amber after I filed for sole custody. She eventually agreed to get therapy and confessed she had a drug problem. I'll admit she's worked hard to get sober. She stops over sometimes to see the boys, but they're still reluctant to spend time with her. I won't force them. Maybe over time they'll build a relationship if she keeps making an effort.

In order to get into my house, she had to apologize to Paige for how she treated her and promise to keep things civil. She agreed, and since then, we haven't had any problems. My wife, being the sweetheart that she is, even invited Amber over for Christmas last year so she could spend the holidays with the boys, but Amber declined.

The principal takes the mic. "Welcome to Alumni Night! We're so excited to have so many familiar faces here this evening. We're kicking off our halftime show with one of our favorite alums, Coach Walker! Paige is a Lone Star State graduate and a two-time national cheer champion."

Paige is wearing her usual coaching gear—jeans and a fitted t-shirt. She waves at the crowd, and a second later, she runs down the track and launches into a series of backflips. Over and over she goes, her lithe body tossing through the air effortlessly. Or at least, it looks effortless. I know how hard she works to stay in shape like that.

The crowd stands and cheers when she lands on the other side of the track with her arms raised triumphantly.

"All right, baby!" I yell. Damn, my little cheerleader is hot.

"Yay, Mommy!" Austin and Ella shout.

Ella's up on her seat again, and I hold her hand so she doesn't topple over.

The principal takes the mic again. "Great job, Coach! Next up are our junior tumblers from All-Star Cheer. Let's hear it for the Storm Squad!"

Gabe and his friends run out onto the track. When the music blasts through the sound system, they launch into their tumbling routine. I shout and cheer with the crowd. I have to admit my son is really talented. I'm not sure if he'll want to give this up for football.

When they're done, he runs up to Paige and hugs her, and my heart swells with love for this woman. My sons adore my wife, and it's obvious how much she loves them in every cookie she bakes for them, every bedtime story she reads to them, and every tumbling routine she patiently teaches them.

I couldn't have asked for a more amazing wife.

After the game, I wait for Paige by the gym. When she spots me leaning against my truck, her whole face lights up. She jogs to me, and I pick her up and kiss her. "You killed it out there."

She laughs. "That's the easiest routine I ever had to do."

"Well, no one knows that." I set her down.

Smiling, she glances around. "Where are the kids?"

"I ran into Sylvia, and she asked if the kids wanted to stay with her tonight so they could make s'mores in her backyard."

Her brows lift. "You mean it's just us tonight?"

I sweep her into my arms again. "Yup. I was thinking we could go for some ice cream and then maybe take the long way home."

She nibbles on her bottom lip coyly. "Husband, are you trying to have your way with me?"

"Only if you're not too tired. Otherwise, we can go home, and I'll draw you a bath and wash your hair."

Her eyes go hooded, and I chuckle. "Can we do both?"

I pat her ass. "Your wish is my command, wildflower."

BONUS SCENE TWO

TWO YEARS LATER

PAIGE

A truck door slams out front, and a minute later, my children bound into the house.

I'm about to ask if they're hungry when I see their faces. "What in heaven's name happened to you?" Ella, Austin, and Gabe are covered in grease.

Ella grins. "We helped Daddy change his tire."

Just then, Rhett walks in behind them. "Got a flat at the tractor supply store. Figured it was a good time to show the kids how to deal with it."

Gabe holds up his fist. "I love power tools!"

I chuckle. "Okay, my little grease monkeys. Go get cleaned up so we can have lunch. Please wash your hands and faces." They race down the hallway, jostling for position. "Don't knock each other over!" I yell.

I used to worry the boys were too rough for Ella, but that kid can hold her own.

Rhett leans down to kiss me. "You having a good day?" he asks as he rubs my swollen belly. "How's our little girl?"

I place my hand over his. "She's doing well, and I took a nap, so I feel rested."

"Great. I'm gonna run out back real quick. Wanna check on something."

"Be back in ten so we can eat."

"Yes, ma'am."

By the time I get the kids seated around the kitchen table, he hasn't returned yet.

"Where's Daddy?" Ella asks.

"Probably snuggling Clover." That's our mini-donkey we rescued last year, who's obsessed with Rhett. He's black with a white clover-like marking on his forehead.

Just then, my husband knocks on the sliding glass door with the little donkey in his arms. Laughing, I open it for him, and he gives me an exasperated look. "I can't get any work done. This dude just follows me everywhere and cries when I leave him behind."

I give Clover a scratch behind the ears, and I swear the donkey smiles. "Aren't you too sweet for words?"

Rhett grumbles, "I thought *I* was too sweet for words when I agreed to adopt a damn donkey, and those rabbits, and let's not forget about the ducklings."

I lean up to kiss him. "Thank you, darling. You are a true prince. Rescuer of small animals and damsels in distress."

He cracks a smile as he sets down Clover.

Our daughter slaps the counter. "Daddy, you said damn. That's a dollar."

We all look at the jar that's overflowing with cash, thanks to Rhett and his brothers.

My husband lets out a long sigh and removes his cowboy hat to wipe his forehead. "Do you take credit? Don't have any cash on me."

Ella runs and grabs a piece of paper. "You can write an IOU."

He gives me a look that says he's excited I taught her what an

IOU means. I chuckle as he writes on the strip of paper. He tucks it into the jar. "Are you happy now?"

Ella nods. "Yes. Thank you, Daddy."

"You're welcome, princess."

After he washes up, Rhett joins us at the table, and I pass around a giant platter of pancakes and sausage. "I hope having breakfast for lunch is okay with everyone. I had a craving."

The boys are already stuffing bites in their mouths while they nod. Gabe gives me a thumbs-up. "It's good."

My family is always happy with whatever I make. Fortunately, my kids are not picky eaters.

When we're done, I open up the wet wipes. "Can y'all wipe your hands, please?" Otherwise, I'll have sticky handprints all over the house. "How do you guys feel about homemade pizzas? I want to use some of the herbs and tomatoes from our garden. We could make them tomorrow night and watch a movie."

Austin shouts, "Pizza!"

Ella holds up her hand like she just learned in preschool. "Can we watch a movie about a princess?"

The boys groan. "Again?" they say almost simultaneously.

I lean over to brush hair out of Ella's face. "Sweetheart, I think it's your brothers' turn to pick a movie."

A fuzzy face bumps me, and I reach back to scratch Clover between his eyes. "Gabe, can you take Clover out? I don't want him to have an accident."

He and Austin head out with our donkey, and Ella traipses behind them.

A duck waddles past us, and I laugh. "Take Quackers with you!" I have no idea who let our feathered friend in the house. Gabe runs back and picks up Quackers, who nuzzles him. "Thank you. I'll be out in a bit."

Our kids and our little zoo make me so happy.

I lean my head against my husband. "Did I say I felt rested? I'm tired again."

Rhett kisses my temple. "Take it easy, wildflower. You're growing a human."

After a few minutes, our kids charge back inside, the donkey on their heels, and Gabe yells, "Dad! Mom! We caught a rattlesnake. It almost bit one of the dogs, but then Uncle Beau came to the rescue."

Rhett holds up his hand. "Calm down. Let's go take a look. Hopefully, there aren't any nests."

My eyes widen. "Kids, stay with me." They groan, but I give them my no-nonsense face. "You can stay on the back patio, but that's it. We don't mess around with rattlesnakes."

Gabe laughs and makes wiggly fingers in my face. "Are you afraid of a little ol' snake? Dad always says they're more afraid of us than we're afraid of them."

"Doubtful." That's the only downside to living in the country.

The children race out to the back patio, and Rhett wraps his arm around me and whispers, "You weren't afraid of my big ol' snake last night."

I playfully pinch him. "Stop." He starts to leave, but I tug him back. "Promise me you'll be careful."

He places a hand over my stomach and kisses me. "Cross my heart."

Clover trots after Rhett and makes a sad honking sound when it's obvious my husband isn't taking the donkey with him. I run after him and grab his halter. "It's okay, buddy. Daddy will be back soon." My husband gives me a look, and I chuckle. And because I love torturing the man, I add, "Guess what I found this morning? My cheer outfit. I was thinking I should try it on later." It might be a stretch over my stomach since I wasn't four months pregnant the last time I wore it, but I don't think Rhett cares.

His expression goes flat, and he marches to me and whispers, "Haven't we talked about not giving me boners when I have to work?"

"You'll need to punish me later."

His eyes go hot, and he growls. I jump back with a laugh when he tries to catch me.

Honk! Clover leaps between us and nuzzles Rhett.

Rhett scratches behind Clover's ear and turns to me. "I'd better go. Take it easy this afternoon, baby. Call me if you need anything."

Leaning over our donkey, he kisses me, and I smile. "Love you, honey."

He winks. "Love you more."

Not even possible.

Clover and I head out to the back patio to watch the children play on the enormous swing set their father and uncles built them.

Smiling, I turn my face to the sun.

Life has never been better.

WHAT TO READ NEXT

Thanks for reading! If you enjoyed Stealing Hearts, I hope you'll consider leaving a review. I try to read each one.

To stay up-to-date with my new releases, be sure to subscribe to my newsletter, which you can find on my website, www.lexmartinwrites.com.

If Brady and Kat's story piqued your interest, keep flipping to read the synopsis of SHAMELESS, which is a USA Today bestseller and one of my most popular books! If you love the idea of a Harley-riding tattoo artist who inherits his baby niece and a lavender farm, this book is for you! It's free in Kindle Unlimited.

Next up is FALLING STARS, Baylee and Maverick's book! If you're looking for major swoon and spice and all the drama, you won't want to miss their story.

SHAMELESS SYNOPSIS
A USA Today bestseller

Brady...

What do I know about raising a baby? Nothing. Not a damn thing.

Yet here I am, the sole guardian of my niece. I'd be lost if it weren't for Katherine, the beautiful girl who seems to have all the answers. Katherine, who's slowly finding her way into my cynical heart.

I keep reminding myself that I can't fall for someone when we don't have a future. But telling myself this lie and believing it are two different things.

Katherine...

When Brady shows up on a Harley, looking like an avenging angel—six feet, three inches of chiseled muscle, eyes the color of wild sage, and sun-kissed skin emblazoned with tattoos—I'm not sure if I should fall at his feet or run like hell. Because if I tell him what happened the night his family died, he might hate me.

What I don't count on are the nights we spend together trying to forget the heartache that brought us here. I promise him it won't mean anything, that I won't fall in love.

I shouldn't make promises I can't keep.

ACKNOWLEDGMENTS

I always have to start my acknowledgments by thanking my husband because he's the best. I'm so grateful to Matt and my daughters for all of their amazing support.

Thanks also to my lovely parents for always believing in me. I recently lost my mom, and she called me a writer long before I realized that was a skill I possessed. Rest in peace, sweet angel. You're my original wildflower.

I have an incredible team of people who help me reach the finish line: my agent Kimberly Brower, editor RJ Locksley, proofreader Julia Griffis, photographer Lindee Robinson, cover designer Najla Qamber, Jen DeJong and Olivia Rose with Grey's Promotions, and Shauna Casey and Becca Smith with The Author Agency.

My PA and dear friend Serena McDonald does a million things for me, and I'm so grateful for her friendship.

In addition to Serena, I have some amazing beta readers who are super generous with their time. Leslie McAdam, Victoria Denault, Christine Yates, Riley Kelm, Jess Hodge, Jan Corona, Jerrica MacMillan, and Kenna Rae—thank you for kicking the tires on my stories and helping me craft the best books possible!

Lastly, a huge thanks to my readers in Wildcats, my ARC team, author friends, fans, bloggers, and influencers who've spread the word about my books. You have my deepest appreciation. Thanks for picking up my books!

Rhett and Paige were such a joy to write. I hope they captured your heart like they captured mine. Next up is Baylee and Maverick's story. Falling Stars will be a single mother, friends to lovers romance with lots of angst and steam. Stay tuned because I can't wait to show you what else is in store for my cowboys of Wild Heart, Texas!

ALSO BY LEX MARTIN

Wild at Heart:
Stealing Hearts (Paige & Rhett)
Falling Stars (Baylee & Maverick)

Varsity Dads:
The Varsity Dad Dilemma (Gabby & Rider)
Tight Ends & Tiaras (Sienna & Ben)
The Baby Blitz (Magnolia & Olly)
Second Down Darling (Charlotte & Jake)
Heartbreaker Handoff (Roxy & Billy)
Blindside Beauty (Abigail & Nick)

Texas Nights:
Shameless (Kat & Brady)
Reckless (Tori & Ethan)
Breathless (Joey & Logan)

The Dearest Series:
Dearest Clementine (Clementine & Gavin)
Finding Dandelion (Dani & Jax)
Kissing Madeline (Maddie & Daren)

Cowritten with Leslie McAdam
All About the D (Evie & Josh)
Surprise, Baby! (Kendall & Drew)

ABOUT THE AUTHOR

Lex Martin is the *USA Today* bestselling author of Varsity Dads, Texas Nights, and the Dearest series, books she hopes readers love but her parents avoid. A former high school English teacher and freelance journalist, she resides in Texas with her husband, twin daughters, a bunny, and their rambunctious Shih Tzu.

To stay up-to-date with her releases, stop by her website and **subscribe to her newsletter,** or join her Facebook group, **Lex Martin's Wildcats.**

www.lexmartinwrites.com

Made in United States
Orlando, FL
15 February 2025